¡BAN c/s THIS!

THE BSP ANTHOLOGY OF XICAN@ LITERATURE

Edited by Santino J. Rivera

Other Books Available from

BROKEN SWORD PUBLICATIONS

Alcohol Soaked & Nicotine Stained (2002)

Demon in the Mirror (2007)

Amerikkkan Stories (2011)

BROKEN SWORD PUBLICATIONS

BROKEN SWORD PUBLICATIONS

¡Ban This! The BSP Anthology of Xican@ Literature
©2012 Broken Sword Publications
First Printing
Published in the United States of America by Broken Sword Publications, LLC
Saint Augustine, Florida.
Broken Sword Publications, LLC and the Broken Sword Publications, LLC logo are registered trademarks of Broken Sword Publications, LLC.

Book cover design and book layout by **Josh Divine**, a contemporary artist and vinyl aficionado from Longmont, Colorado. For more of his remarkable work please visit www.joshdivine.com
ISBN 978-0-615-60730-6
Broken Sword Publications, LLC
Murder Capital of Florida, USA
Web: www.brokenswordpublications.com
E-Mail: mail@brokenswordpublications.com
Twitter: @sjrivera @brokenswordpub

¡BAN c/s THIS!

THE BSP ANTHOLOGY OF XICAN@ LITERATURE

Edited by Santino J. Rivera

¡Ban This!

For anyone who has ever sought a book that either did not exist or was taken away from them.

CONTENTS

◊ Sheriff Joe: Sex Crime

◊ Rush: Speedo

◊ Rush: Whore

◊ Colombia

◊ McCain, the Racist Bear

◊ Heil Sherriff Joe

◊   September 16: Morning

ACKNOWLEDGEMENTS

Choosing and representing a body of work like this does not happen overnight and certainly not single-handedly. I cannot thank those who have contributed their work to this effort enough. To all of the universities, the educators, the students, the activists, the artists, the writers, the workers, the bloggers, the librarians, the tweeters, and to the people – I want to express my gratitude.

I want to thank David Cid and also the National Association for Chicana and Chicano Studies for helping to get the word out regarding submissions and for generating a strong interest in this work.

I want to thank Luis Alberto Urrea for his inspiration, his wisdom and his words regarding this book.

I would also like to thank the Los Angeles Public Library, Art Meza and Alice Rodriguez for their help in promoting not only Chicano and Chicana literacy but literacy for all in their respective communities.

My immense gratitude goes out to all of those involved with the Aztlán Reads movement and the Librotraficante movement for their continued efforts in fighting for education and against censorship.

INTRODUCTION

The Paradox Endures

What is a Xican@? Allow me to count the ways…truly, it depends whom you ask but if you ever want to start an argument among a group of Chicanos regarding self-identity, just try to define terms. It's funny because here we are all these years later and we are still bickering about self-identity. Irene I. Blea once said that 'to be Xicana is to be political' - I happen to agree. But that's not what this book is about, at least not entirely.

I imagine people not hep to the X's and @'s of Chicanismo will stare at this book and wonder: A.) how to pronounce it and B.) what it is about. C.) why there is an "@" symbol in the title. These are not bad things. The answers to all three of these questions are in this book…and not in a dictionary definition kind of way.

It is my hope that this book goes beyond the scope of Chicanos and Chicanas. I would hope that *everyone* will give this book a chance. It is time. These are our stories – American stories - and they deserve to be heard.

This is a new day and though the same old problems persist, the revolution continues. The scent of a new Chicano renaissance wafts through the air like that of so many potent carne asada tacos at your favorite restaurant or taco cart. Believe it or not, this is the new dawn - the age of life on the hyphen between Mexican and American. Aquarius can take a seat because though times are tight, we are on the rise. Right this moment, when everyone else is ready to punch their ticket and check out via false prophesies of doom (see: any commercial sensationalizing the Mayan calendar), many Chicanos/as are gearing up for Neo Aztlán. But I am getting ahead of myself.

This book started out as a dream – one that I've had for as long as I can remember. Over the course of my lifetime I have often set out in search of books like this very one and just as often come up empty-handed. I sought to change that.

This book has been in the works for some time – probably since I was searching the shelves of my modest high school library for anything even remotely close to the material in this book.

I am not a scholar, I'm barely an academic; if you look up the definition of what a professional editor of literature is supposed to look like, you are most certainly not going to find my picture there. But that's all part of what drove me to publish this book. Does everything happen for a reason? I don't know but what I do know that this book came together the way it did with a little bit of magic behind it.

To put this in a manner that everyone can understand: anthologies of Xican@ literature simply do not fall of off trees (if at all depending on where you are). If you're lucky enough to be in the areas that cater to Chicanos you may find some gems but if you are anywhere else you'd be lucky to find a phonebook with a Spanish surname in it. That said, independent publishing and the internet are changing all of that. As we enter the future, it is evident that social media networks are a new way for organizing movements. This is creating a new Xican@ paradigm that insists on redefining what it means to be Xican@.

Through the marvel of modern technology and communication, I have been able to make some amazing connections – the result is this book that you hold in your hands, mind and hopefully heart. This book is sure to incense some people and elate others. It is by no means a perfect book but I am immensely proud of it. This is in no way to claim that this book is the be all, end all of Xican@ lit, because it's not...but it's a start.

Over the course of the last year, this book transformed into an act of defiance - activism in pulp/digital format. Again, to be Xican@ is to be political, remember?

Activism you say? Yes.

I am not a resident of Arizona but part of my family's history has been there (as well as in New Mexico and Colorado), since long before lines in the sand were drawn. What happens there reverberates across the country now as we are all tied to the same web of information.

When I heard about the Tucson Unified School District banning books and banning Mexican-American Studies I knew I had to do *something*. This book is that something.

When people ban books – when they strip words and language and history – how do you begin to respond to that? In literature and on the silver screen such acts are deemed villainous but the hero always seems to right the wrongs...somehow. In the real world, in the land of legislation, lies and lobbying - in this labyrinth of propaganda and media frenzy, the answer is much more complicated.

¡Ban This!

It seems inconceivable to have the same exact thought everyday but here I am: each day seems more ridiculous than the last. How is that possible? And this is where we go beyond Arizona – this is where our experiences across these so-called United States are tied together. In Lak'ech …

A young woman quipped to me online that she did not want to bring children into this cruel world. My response was that the world has always been cruel yet, how does it *seem* more cruel now?

As I write this, lawmakers in Arizona are setting their sights on Chicano studies at the University level next. Will they succeed? I honestly don't know. I don't know what to expect any more. I would have never thought they would have banned an entire academic program much less world renowned literature but here we are. That's the problem with this brave new world – anything is possible, no matter how ridiculous or inconceivable.

What I do know for a fact is how we respond matters. *This* matters. What we do now will affect future generations and beyond. Wholesale book banning and the demonization of the study of history should scare the hell out of people…yet many simply move on to the next headline.

This book is a small step but one I hope will have a big impact. They might be able to ban books in a school district in Tucson. They might be able to distort the facts on the news. They might be able to *try* and suppress the voice of reason, of logic and of justice but in that effort they will fail…if only we keep moving forward and onward, carrying with us the spirit of the Crusade for Justice. Let them try and ban this! They will not succeed for we are one. Let this book be a message to Aztlán and to the world: We shall endure!

¡Ban This!

FRANK MUNDO

Frank Mundo has been a writer, poet and book reviewer in Los Angeles for the last 20 years. Author of The Brubury Tales and Gary, the Four-Eyed Fairy and Other Stories, his work has appeared in numerous literary journals and anthologies. Frank lives in Los Angeles with his wife Nancy.

HOW I BECAME A MEXICAN

When I was eleven years old, I became a Mexican. I didn't plan on it or anything. And it wasn't by choice either. It just kind of happened. I went to bed one night and, when I woke up, I was a Mexican.

Back then, I was a lot of things, so the new title didn't really surprise me too much. I was a son and a brother. I was an artist and a comic book writer. I loved riding bikes, collecting baseball cards, and I was a huge Washington Redskins fan. I was also one of the best athletes in my school and, in my mind, probably one of the best basketball players in the world! I didn't know what a Mexican was just yet, but that didn't matter. Whatever it was, I was going to be the best at that, too. I guess I was a little arrogant back then as well.

It happened so fast. I really didn't have much time to think about it. It was during recess on a new basketball court at a new school in a new state, and it was go-time, baby. Time to show these California fools how it was done, son – Maryland style. I may have been the "new kid" for now, but I was about to introduce myself, to put on a show they'd never forget. I was about to take these chumps to school.

In Maryland, we shot free throws to decide team captains, who would then pick their teams. This was a fair and democratic process, and no one ever questioned it. And why would they? It was strictly about skills, and that's all that mattered on the basketball court in Maryland.

In California, however, they had their own system which seemed far more efficient. A variation on the old shirts-and-skins theme, they called it Whites versus Mexicans, and it was pretty simple. Everyone with brown skin was on one team, and everyone with white skin was on the other. And while it seemed like an odd way to divide into teams at the time, I was very impressed. Recess was pretty short, which meant there was little time to waste shooting free throws and picking teams. And I wanted as much time as possible to play, to show them what a wizard I was on a basketball court.

And it didn't take very long.

I looked over at my team: seven brown-skinned kids like me all huddled-up on the other side of the court. They knew the drill. I, however, was still standing near the top of the key on the White team's side, not sure what happened next.

"Shoot for ball," one of the white kids filled me in, challenging me with a wicked bounce pass I clearly wasn't supposed to handle. But I short-hopped it like a pro and, in one slick move, bounced the ball back between my legs in front of me where I held it with both hands.

"Our ball," I declared, before even shooting it, a promise soundly fulfilled with the metallic echo of the chain net as the ball sailed through the hole like money in the bank – cha-ching!

I walked back to our side, the Mexicans' side, with a new swagger, clearly the team's captain.

"Who wants to sub?" I asked, and three of the Mexicans quickly volunteered to sit out and sub in later.

"Let's do this," I said to the rest of them, and the game began.

Needless to say, the Mexicans prevailed. I don't remember all of the details, but I do remember playing better than I even imagined, and that we'd won handily by the time the bell announced that recess was over and it was time to head back to class.

Two hours before that triumph, I stood awkwardly in front of that same classroom as our teacher introduced me to her students – the new kid. Actually she sort of interviewed me, because I wasn't saying much of anything on my own – and no one had said a word to me since I'd walked into class, a few minutes late and not sure yet where I was supposed to sit or put my things.

Nervous and extremely uncomfortable, I remember feeling everyone's eyes on me as I did everything I could to avoid their stares and their judgments. It probably didn't help much that I dropped my pencil at least three times during the interview, forcing me to bend over and pick it up, feeling like an idiot each time. If nothing else, I was sure that my classmates thought

I was clumsy and awkward and not much of a conversationalist.

But now, only a couple hours later, everyone was impressed with me and thoroughly interested in what I had to say – the Mexicans and the Whites. I made friends fast, like eleven year-olds do. Real friends. Good friends. Friends for life. My friends for the last 27 years, in fact. Over the years we've probably played hundreds, maybe thousands, of games of Mexicans versus Whites basketball.

But more about that later.

Because, friends or not, I wasn't a Mexican for long – at least not to the girls. That title was quickly stripped from me by a few of the girls that year and replaced often by other young Mexican girls and Mexican women for many years to come.

In elementary school, I became a "pocho" when it was revealed that my Spanish wasn't very good. In junior high, the girls downgraded me to "creído" when my Spanish didn't improve and neither did my effort to improve it. And, in high school, I became simply a "gringo" or "guero" once it became clear to them that I was hopeless and would never learn to speak their language -- a language they were utterly convinced, in those beautiful almond-shaped eyes, should've been my language as well.

I don't blame them really. They must've been as confused about me as I was back then when we first moved to California and I became a Mexican. Especially about my race. It's something everyone else around me has struggled with my entire life. I say "everyone else" because it never really bothered me all that much, because I've never really identified with a single race. It might sound weird, but the subject of race simply didn't come up until I was eleven years old and we moved to California.

In Maryland, no one told me I was different than my white family members and friends. Even my black friends never said a thing about it. I mean, sure, I was brown and my last name was Mundo, but all I knew for sure was that Mundo meant "world" in Spanish and that Spanish was some language people spoke in Spain, which is probably as much as my friends knew about it, too. Sometimes people did ask me if I was adopted, but I always told them what my mother had always told me: I was brown and dark-haired because I looked like my father, and my brother was white and blonde-haired because he looked like my mother. My father went to prison and my parents got divorced, and I lived with my mother who didn't speak Spanish. That information usually stopped them in their tracks and almost always ended the adoption conversations right there.

There were only two occasions I remember when my mother's explanation wasn't enough to satisfy the curiosities of some especially nosy kids. Both times my older and much whiter brother stepped in and ended it his way – with a mean one-two punch to the face of the offenders. Afterwards he'd apologize to me and carefully assured me that I was his real brother and that anyone who said otherwise needed to talk to him about it. I didn't know it back then, but my brother had a much harder time than I ever did of squaring his relationships with our father, our family, and our race.

That's because I was an infant when my father went to prison, and I was just learning to speak (apparently English and Spanish) when my parents' marriage officially ended. My mother married twice after that, both to white men, before we moved to California, and I was just the "brown" white kid of an interracial marriage gone bad who was NOT adopted. We never really talked about it. Not even on Halloween when my mother got creative with her mismatched sons, and our skin colors became props to her themed-based costume creations. One year my brother was a Cowboy and I was the Indian. Another year we were an Angel and a Devil. We were Ponch and John from the TV show "Chips" one year, and even Hall and Oates once in the early 80's when their music was extremely popular.

But all this changed when we moved to Los Angeles. In Los Angeles, my brownness could no longer be ignored or easily explained away, and my last name was like a Scarlett Letter "M". In Los Angeles, I was marked on the very first day of school -- and for the rest of my life. And not just by the white people or Mexican girls. By everyone - even the State.

You see, I wasn't the only person who became a Mexican that day. There were at least three other brown-skinned ballers on the Mexican team who were not Mexican or even Latino for that matter. The most blatant violation was committed against my friend Mike Farzan. Mike was Iranian, and his family had given up almost everything they owned to come to the US to escape the Shah. Another of my teammates was Danny Gonzales, who we called "Speedy" because he was fast, he was Mexican, and because we thought we were super clever. It turned out, however, that his family actually hailed from Italy and later moved to the US by way of Portugal. There was another kid named Tim, who had a Hispanic last name I can't remember right now, but was actually Dominican I believe. And, while I can't say for sure, I would bet my life that at least one of the Mexicans on our winning team was actually from El Salvador or Guatemala or Peru or any number of countries in Central or South America. But, in Los Angeles, that didn't matter. In Los Angeles, they were Mexicans, and so was I. It was written all over our skin.

I always wondered what I would be considered by other people if I grew up in New York or maybe Oregon or Georgia or Wyoming – or even if we ended up staying in Maryland. Would I be called Cuban or Puerto Rican? I don't think it would have really mattered though what state I was in. It's not like I even had a choice what to call myself. There was no way, in any kind of good faith, I could check the box denoting my race as White, and neither could my parents.

After all, it wasn't just my new white teammates and those suspicious Mexican girls with the beautiful almond-shaped eyes who were confused about my race. Even the government seemed uncertain. I was officially "Hispanic or Latino" according to my school records, the Census Bureau, the DMV and other government departments – not to mention every job and college application I'd ever fill out over the years, or basically any official form or document that inquired about race. Hispanic or Latino! As if the government wasn't quite sure which was which.

I think there must've been some kind of protest over the years about this because, by the time I graduated from college, I did start noticing a strange option showing up on some official forms that was never there before. A new box that read: OTHER. And, while I must admit that the idea of OTHER as a race became awfully intriguing to me for a little while, I ultimately rejected it. I just wasn't the kind of person to protest or take a stand on something that seemed so trivial. Besides, I kind of like the fact that the government can't quite nail down my race. It's funny to me. And it really sums up a major portion of my life.

It was in college that I realized just how humorous it was. I was taking a literature course and one of the subjects we discussed was "liminal" characters, which were these mystical sort of beings or creatures (or monsters even), both good and evil, that lived simultaneously "in the threshold" between two distinct realms or realities. Ambiguous, they eluded classification and, while visible were, at the same time, invisible.

I was fascinated by this concept and so excited about its implications! For the first time in my life, there was a being I recognized and an existence that mirrored my own – that was me. I was a liminal character in a threshold between races, between worlds. I was a white Latino, a Mexican gringo who could play on either basketball team or even both teams at the same time.

I learned a lot in that class, not just about myself, but why everyone around me always worried more about my race than I ever did. It's because I am a monster. A "liminal" creature, I ruin culture, I kill tradition and I devour race. I'm the mucky residue on the rim of the melting pot, and my very existence is repulsive and horrifying because I represent the future. I represent change: a necessarily ambiguous mixed-raced American human, void of classification, stereotypes and, by extension, pride. I am what, one day in the future, everyone will be: EQUAL.

Which finally brings us back to the great friends I made on my first day of elementary school. I say great friends, not just because we've been friends ever since, but because over the years we realized the mistakes we made about each other and the colors of our skin -- and we fixed them. We changed. We grew up and saw each other through our own eyes, and with our own perceptions -- and we're still great friends.

I say great friends because there are no other people in Los Angeles or in the whole world who know me and accept me for who I really am with all of my labels. White people may see me as Mexican and Mexican girls may think of me as white. The government will almost certainly continue to identify me as Hispanic or Latino or even OTHER. But I don't care. I'm a lot of things, and my true friends know that these titles don't matter because I'm so much more.

I'm a son, a brother, and a husband now, too. I'm a poet and a short story writer. I love travelling, collecting first-edition books, and I'm a huge Washington Redskins fan. But, most importantly, when my friends and I get together for a game of Whites versus Mexicans basketball, I'm a Mexican and a White. The team captain, in fact. And my team always wins.

FRANCISCO X. ALARCÓN

Francisco X. Alarcón, Chicano poet and educator, is author of twelve volumes of poetry, including, From the Other Side of Night: New and Selected Poems (University of Arizona Press 2002), Snake Poems: An Aztec Invocation (Chronicle Books 1992). His latest books are Ce•Uno•One: Poems for the New Sun (Swan Scythe Press 2010), and for children, Animal Poems of the Iguazú (Children's Book Press 2008). He created the Facebook page "Poets Responding to SB 1070." He teaches at the UC Davis.

BANNED AND BOXED-UP POEM

this poem has

indigenous features

and a brown skin

like Mother Earth

always will be under

"reasonable suspicion"

this poem roams

the open desert before

any barbed wire

it runs tumultuous

like a creek after

a monsoon rain

POEMA PROHIBIDO Y ENCAJONADO

este poema tiene

rasgos indígenas

y una piel color café

como la Madre Tierra

siempre causa será

de "sospecha razonable"

este poema recorre

el desierto abierto antes

cualquier alambre de púas

corre tumultuoso

como un arroyo tras

a una lluvia tormentosa

this poem breathes

the air free of charge

like a cloud in the sky

it has no need

for any legal papers

because it's borderless

this poem doesn't

believe in any imposed

mythical melting pot

it dreams the dreams

of the Native American

and Chicano/a authors

whose books were taken

away from classrooms

and boxed up in Tucson

this poem is breaking

away from these boxes

and joining in walkouts -

este poema respira

el aire libre de cargos

como nube en el cielo

no tiene necesidad

de papeles legales

pues no tiene fronteras

este poema no cree

en ningún cresol

mítico impuesto

sueña los sueños

de los autores nativos

y los autores chicanos

cuyos libros fueron

sacados de clases y

encajonados en Tucson

este poema se escapa

de estas cajas para unirse

a protestas de estudiantes -

truth, tolerance, courage	la verdad, la tolerancia, el valor
will overcome no doubt	sin duda pronto vencerán
lies, fear, and silence	a mentiras, el miedo, el silencio

BREAKING NEWS!

Mexican Food banned From Tucson Schools

¡ULTIMAS NOTICIAS!

Prohiben Comida Mexicana En Escuelas De Tucson, Arizona

after dismantling	tras desmantelar
the Mexican-American	el Programa de Estudios
Studies program in its schools	Méxicoamericanos de las escuelas
and banning books	y prohibir libros publicados
by Native America authors	por autores nativoamericanos
and Mexican-American authors	y autores méxicoamericanos
the Tucson Unified School	la Junta del Distrito Escolar
District board went on to ban	Unificado de Tucson prohibió
Mexican food from all its schools	la comida mexicana en sus escuelas
the board indicated that they	la Junta Escolar indicó
just want to be in compliance	que sólo quería cumplir

with Arizona law HB 2281	con la ley HB 2281 de Arizona
Arizona Schools Superintendent	John Huppenthal, Superinden-
John Huppenthal and District	dente de Escuelas de Arizona y Tom
Attorney Tom Horne stated	Horne, Fiscal General del estado,
	declararon
in a joint press conference	en una conferencia de prensa
that the Tucson schools had	que las escuelas de Tucson tenía
to stop serving Mexican food	que dejar de servir comida mexicana
"tacos, enchiladas, guacamole	"los tacos, enchiladas, guacamole
tamales, quesadillas	tamales, quesadillas
are really divisive	crean mucha división
they have come under	y son merecedores
'reasonable suspicion'	de 'sospecha razonable'
for being anti-American -	por su anti-americanismo -
cheese nachos are excepted;	los nachos con queso están
'burritos' from now on will be	extentos; los 'burritos' desde hoy
known as American 'wrap-ups'"	se llamarán 'envoltorios' america-
	nos"
they indicated that they are	los dos indicaron que están

implementing Arizona laws

SB 1070 and HB 2281

supported by the majority

of Arizona Anglo residents;

that new laws are necessary

against other "foreign" foodstuff

like the pernicious Chinese food

and the ever suspicious bagels

implementando las leyes

SB 1070 y HB 2281 de Arizona

apoyadas por la mayoría

de residentes anglos de Arizona;

y que se necesitan nuevas leyes

contra otras comidas "extranjeras"

como la maligna comida china

y los siempre sospechosos "bagels"

IN IXTLI IN YOLLOTI

FACE AND HEART

ROSTRO Y CORAZÓN

may our ears

hear

what nobody

wants to hear

que nuestros oídos

oigan

lo que nadie

quiere oír

may our eyes

see what everyone

wants to hide

que nuestros ojos

veanlo que todos

quieren ocultar

may our mouths	que nuestras bocas
speak up	digan la verdad
our true faces	de nuestros rostros
and hearts	y corazones
may our arms	que nuestros brazos
be branches	sean ramas
that give shade	que den sombra
and joy	y alegría
let us be a drizzle	seamos llovizna
a sudden storm	tormenta inesperada
let us get wet	mojémonos
in the rain	en la lluvia
let us be the key	seamos la llave
the hand the door	la mano la puerta
the kick the ball	el pie la pelota
the road	el camino
let us arrive	lleguemos
as children	como niños
to this huge	a este inmenso

playground:		parque de juegos:
the universe!		¡el universe!

NEW SUN AT TEOTIHUACAN

to poet Raúl Sánchezwho took the banner of
"Poets Responding to SB 1070" to that sacred site

it is here	it is here	it is here
in Teotihuacan	in Teotihuacan	on the Pyramid
the City of the Gods	the City of the Gods	of the Sun
where the Sun	where the Moon	where once again
was born when	was also born	a new Sun
Quetzalcoatl	as companion	will be born
threw himself	of the Sun	the Flower Sun
into a big bonfire	and Queen	announced by
immolating himself	of all seas	prophet poets
emerging	where hope	an Era of Justice
as the new Sun	defeated fear	a redeeming
dispelling the darkness	and despair	rainbow

NUEVO SOL EN TEOTIHUACAN

al poeta Raúl Sánchez
quien tomó el estandarte lema de "Poetas
Respondiendo a la SB 107"0 a ese sagrado reciento

es aquí	es aquí	es aquí
en Teotihuacan	en Teotihuacan	en la Pirámide
la Ciudad de los Dioses	la Ciudad de los Dioses	del Sol
donde el Sol	donde la Luna	donde otra vez
nació cuando	tambíen nació	un nuevo Sol
Quetzalcóatl	como compañera	nacerá
se arrojó	del Sol	el Sol Flor
a una gran hoguera	y Reina de	anunciado por
inmo ándose el mismo	todos los mares	poetas profetas
emergiendo	donde la esperanza	una Era de Justicia
como el nuevo Sol	derrotó al miedo	un arco iris
dispersando la oscuridad	y la desesperanza	redentor

ROBERTO "DR. CINTLI" RODRIGUEZ

Roberto Rodriguez, PhD, -- or Dr. Cintli – is an assistant professor, Mexican American Studies Department, at the University of Arizona. He is a longtime-award-winning journalist/columnist who returned to school in 2003 in pursuit of a Master's degree (2005) and a Ph.D. in Mass Communications (Jan. 2008) at the University of Wisconsin at Madison. He is the author of Justice: A Question of Race; it documents his 7 ½ year quest for justice in the courtroom, stemming from a case of police brutality that almost cost him his life. His research focus at the University of Arizona is on Maiz culture on this continent, and its relationship to the Ethnic Studies controversies. He works with the concepts of elder-youth epistemology and running epistemology. He can be reached at: XColumn@gmail.com

IN LAK ECH, PANCHE BE & HUNAB KU

The Philosophical Foundation for Raza Studies…or What State Officials Don't Want Arizona School Children to Know

For the next few months, the world will be focusing on Arizona's SB 1070 – the state's new racial profiling law. However, in this insane asylum known as Arizona, where conservatives have concocted one reactionary scheme after another, another law in particular stands out for its embrace of censorship – the 2010 anti-ethnic studies HB 2281 – a law that seeks to codify the "triumph" of Western Civilization with its emphasis on Greco-Roman culture.

Unless it is blocked, HB 2281 – which creates an Inquisitorial mechanism that will determine which books and curriculums are acceptable in the state – will go into effect on Jan 1, 2011. Books such as Occupied America by Rodolfo Acuña and Pedagogy of the Oppressed by Paulo Freire, have already been singled out as being un-American and preaching the violent overthrow of the U.S. government.

Both laws are genocidal: one law attacks the physical presence of red-brown peoples; the other one, our minds and spirits.

Lost in the tumultuous debate regarding what can be taught in the state's schools is the topic of what actually constitutes Ethnic/Raza Studies.

The philosophical foundation for Raza Studies are several Indigenous concepts, including: In Lak Ech, Panche Be and Hunab Ku. Over the past generation, the first two concepts have become fairly well known in the Mexican/Chicana/Chicano communities of the United States. The third concept, Hunab Ku, is relatively less well known, though it actually forms the foundation for In Lak Ech – 'Tu eres mi otro yo – You are my other self' and Panche Be – 'to seek the root of the truth' or 'to find the truth in the roots'. As explained by Maya scholar, Domingo Martínez Paredez, Hunab Ku is the name the Maya gave in their language to the equivalence of the Supreme Being or the Grand Architect of the Universe (Hunab Ku, 1970). Such concept is an understanding of how the universe functions.

These three concepts are rooted in a philosophy based on maiz. Maiz, incidentally, is the only crop in the history of humanity that was created by humans. Also, the Indigenous peoples of this continent are the only peoples in the history of humanity to have created their/our own food – maiz – a food so special that it is what virtually unites not simply this continent, but this era. These three maiz-based concepts, in effect, constitute the essence of who we are or who we can be; human beings connected to each other, to all of life and creation. Part of creation; not outside of it. This is the definition of what it means to be human.

Despite the destruction of the many thousands of the ancient books of the Maya (along with those of the Aztecs-Mexica) by Spanish priests during the colonial era, these Maya-Nahua concepts were not destroyed, nor are they consigned to the past. Today, they continue to be preserved and conveyed via ceremony, oral traditions, poetry and song (In Xochitl – In Cuicatl) and danza. And they continue to be developed by life's experiences.

In Raza Studies, these ideas are designed to reach those that are unfamiliar with these concepts, in particular, Mexicans/Chicanos and Central Americans and other peoples from the Americas who live in the United States and who are maiz-based peoples or gente de maiz, albeit, sometimes far-removed from the cornfield or milpa. Despite their disconnection from the fields and despite the disconnection from the planting cycles and accompanying ceremonies – and in many cases the ancestral stories – their/our daily diet consciously and unconsciously keeps us connected to this continent and to the other original peoples and cultures of this continent.

In part, this effort to understand these concepts is an attempt to reclaim a creation/resistance culture, as opposed to viewing themselves/ourselves as foreigners or merely as U.S. minorities. It is also an affirmation that de-Indigenized Mexicans/Chicana/Chicano and Central and South American peoples are not trying to revive or learn from dead cultures. Instead, as elders from throughout this continent generally affirm, these cultures have never died and neither have these concepts; peoples have simply been disconnected from them. That is one definition of colonization and/or de-Indigenization. The effort to understand these and similar concepts and to embrace and live by them, is also one definition of de-colonization. And to be sure, it is elders from Mexico primarily, that have for more than a generation reached out to these communities, imploring them/us to "return to our roots."

Asserting the right to this knowledge that is Indigenous to this very continent is an effort to proclaim both the humanity and Indigeneity of peoples who are matter-of-factly treated as unwelcome and considered alien in this society. HB 2281 bizarrely treats this knowledge as "un-American."

Additionally, asserting the right to write modern amoxtlis or codices – is also part of an effort to proclaim that de-Indigenized peoples also have the right not simply to repeat (or recreate) things ancient, but to produce their/our own living knowledge, based on the lived reality in this country. And in the case of Arizona – with red-brown peoples continuously under siege – these concepts can help us bring about peace, dignity and justice, with the potential to create better human beings of all of us.

FROM MANIFEST DESTINY TO MANIFEST INSANITY

As a result of several recent draconian laws, Arizona's image has taken a drubbing internationally. And yet, Arizona is but the spear. In reality, its politics are not dramatically different from those of other states, or from Washington's. More than a dozen states are waiting in the wings with copycat legislation, and the Obama administration continues to view migration through the prisms of law enforcement and military might.

Fueled by hateful and cowardly politicians and the hate-radio universe, these new and emerging laws are undeniably anti-Mexican and anti-immigrant, but most of all, they are anti-indigenous. In effect, they are an extension of Manifest Destiny. Its modern expression is Manifest Insanity - an attempt to maintain, amid the "browning" of the nation, the myth of America as the pristine home God promised to English-speaking, white, Anglo-Saxon Protestants.

The new Arizona laws are part of a spasmodic reaction to the demographic shift that immigration sets in motion; they are an attempt to maintain a political and cultural dominance over indigenous peoples, who are seen as nonhumans from defeated nations. The laws seek to maintain the narrative of conquest, an archetype dictating that the deaths of some 5,000 primarily indigenous Mexicans and Central Americans in the Arizona/Sonora desert in the past dozen years mean little in this clash. It is the same narrative used to rationalize the recent killings of two Mexicans by US agents along the US/Mexico border.

For those who are attempting to uphold this dominance, the browning of America represents a time reversal - a cultural and political turnabout of the so-called triumph of Western civilization. This is what Arizona represents: a civilizational clash, and a clash of narratives over the myth of America itself - nothing less.

Rodolfo Acuña, author of "Occupied America," came to Arizona last week offering a stark reminder about this clash. His book - along with Paulo Freire's "Pedagogy of the Oppressed" - has been at the center of the anti-ethnic-studies firestorm that culminated when Gov. Jan Brewer signed HB 2281 last month. (She had signed SB 1070 - the racial profiling law - the previous month.)

The controversy surrounding Acuña's book has been fueled by an extreme Eurocentric ignorance. For several years, State Superintendent Tom Horne has been pushing an "Americanization" agenda, insisting that Arizona students be exposed only to "Greco-Roman" knowledge. Knowledge centered elsewhere, including the Mesoamerican, or Maize, knowledge that is indigenous to this continent, is generally considered subversive and un-American. This knowledge is at the philosophical heart of Mexican American, or Raza, studies. Arizona is not alone in this insanity; Texas education officials recently banned the inclusion of labor leader Dolores Huerta in the state's school curricula.

Horne has long claimed that Raza studies preach hate, result in segregation, and promote anti-Americanism and the violent overthrow of the US government. Truth is, he has had a vendetta against Raza studies since Dolores Huerta proclaimed at Tucson High in 2006 that Republicans "hate Latinos." Horne (who constantly denigrates Huerta as "Cesar Chavez's former girlfriend") and his allies have spent the past several years trying to prove her right.

As Acuña found out in Arizona, the mere act of embracing a different philosophical center constitutes a threat to those invested in the cultural and political domination that would negate inclusive worldviews in education. More than that, it threatens the national narrative of taming a wild, savage and empty continent and conquering, exterminating and civilizing "the Indians."

Occupied America upsets the carefully crafted myth of the United States as the land of freedom and democracy or Paradise on Earth.

Raza studies' critics in Arizona - including media professionals - are barely familiar with Acuña's book. (He matter-of-factly tells them to read his book before attacking him.) At best, they spar over its title and a few catch phrases (mistranslating "La Raza" to mean "The Race" as opposed to "The People") and attempt to denigrate an entire discipline on the basis of their ignorance. Yet, at the core of their argument, the critics are correct. Ethnic studies is indeed a threat to the mythical America where the genocide, land theft, slavery and dehumanization that are the foundation of this nation are denied, or are mere footnotes. (Unchallenged, this glossed-over view permits US citizens to view permanent war as a God-given birthright.) Such complete denial - accompanied by the complementary myth of an empty continent - renders the concept of occupied America completely unfathomable.

Raza studies' critics attempt to dehumanize Mexicans/Chicanos. In the critics' conjured narrative, Mexicans/Chicanos are neither legitimate Americans nor legitimate human beings, neither are they afforded the status of indigenous peoples. At best, they are mongrels, undeserving of full human rights. The survival of this narrative is dependent upon the process of de-indigenization and dehumanization. Those of us that cannot be deported (it remains to be seen what's in store during next year's battle in Arizona over the 14th Amendment and birthright citizenship) are welcome here - as long as we participate in our own assimilation - or ethnic cleansing - and accept this nation's mythologized narrative.

That's the definition of Manifest Insanity.

LUÍS ALBERTO URREA

Luis Alberto Urrea is an award winning Chicano poet, novelist and educator. He was born in Tijuana, raised in San Diego, and banned in Tucson. He is the author of several books, including Vatos, By the Lake of Sleeping Children, Across the Wire, The Hummingbird's Daughter, Into the Beautiful North, The Devil's Highway and Queen of America. Urrea was a Pulitzer Prize finalist in 2005 and is a member of the Latino Literature Hall of Fame.

ARIZONA LAMENTATION

We were happy here before they came.

This was always Odin's garden,

A clean white place.

Cradle of Saxons,

Home harbor of the Norsemen.

No Mexican was ever born

In our land.

Then their envy, their racial hatred

Made us build a border fence

To protect our children.

But they kept coming.

There were never any Apaches here -

We never saw these Navajos, these Papagos,

These Yaquis. It's a lie we cut from

Their history books.

But their wagons kept coming and coming.

And their soldiers.

We worshipped the god's great tree,

But he forsook us.

We had something grand here

We had family values, we had clean sidewalks.

Then these strangers came. These mudmen.

They invaded our dream

And colored it.

TYPEWRITER

we were poor enough

big deal

everybody

was poor

and we

among them

mom

watched me scrawl

poems

on butcher paper, notebook

drawing tracing

paper.

went

into the garage, dug

through boxes for her

WWII

typewriter.

it came in a beat box

w/ rusty hinges, had a black

and red ribbon tattered, some letters

came out two-toned, half red & half black -

that was all right with me:

it looked

like the words were burning:

fire above,

night below.

banging away in the kitchen, ratta

tatta like crazy hail

on a tin roof.

naked girls lived in my typewriter.

I pried ink clots

from the mouth of the O,

from the Q, the % and the B.

at night on our phone

I whispered my poems

to Becky

who cried into her pillow

all the way

across town.

I had a book by Stephen Crane,

so I clacked out second hand

Stephen Crane. Richard

Brautigan wrote really short poems,

so I beat out Brautigans.

Then I read Jim Morrison's book

& locked myself

in the bathroom, bellowed

second rate Morrison.

a $4.95 Bukowski.

a $1.98 Wakoski.

I hammered my way

through second hand books.

it was beautiful.

All of America, which I had yet to see,

lived in my typewriter. Then China.

Then Argentina. Then Chile. Then

Japan.

mom

sewed my manuscripts together,

kitchen books:

I was the most famous

author in my

dining room.

grime

slowed the keys - the R

stuck, the ~

wouldn't go

over the N.

then

one day,

trying to help,

mom

oiled the machine.

poured

cooking oil

into it - Wesson

in its dirty heart.

freezing the O.

Q was paralyzed.

the % fainted, the B

was in a coma.

words dusted over

and died.

Becky moved away from my typewriter.

oh well,

it was only fun, anyway, only

a goof.

every morning

I'd walk a mile

and a bit

through California fog

to my silent school.

I only cried once.

TEOCALLI BLUES

For S. J. Rivera

Dangling from this desvelada,

angling along this workday flojera,

navigating dawn-wet streets

brainwash myself again:

rain washed heaven's scent

down the sidewalk grates,

no smoke from the copal--

orale vato - got those Levi's apretaditos

musta lost ten pounds on that diet

got your new cowboy boots,

qué bruto, man, qué bárbaro 'mano -

hijole, today's your big

day, guey--

and I march

like some pinche mazehual

up the steps of the templo mayor:

all the sacrificial class before me

sees the blood come down

and tells itself it's paint:

those priests in black feathers

wait to cut out my heart, feed it

to the sungod mainframe.

But in eyedroop shuffle

of another 6:30, I have lost

my faith: birds

are buscando bronca

in every tree - I don't believe

anymore, I don't believe,

I'm not convinced

that the temple ever earned my heart,

that life isn't better than this sacrifice,

that I am a slave to be butchered,

that I am born to die up there like my fathers

who built the temple with stones

on their backs:

I cannot believe

not for a minute

that I must submit

and only ever hope

to leave behind me

this poem.

SIEGE COMMUNIQUÉ

In Tijuana

they said Juárez

was the pueblo where old

whores went to die, where

25 cents bought flesh

by the river, no

body loved you, Sister -

so close to Texas

so far from

Revolución.

Today, they say

you are the cementerio

of hope: the only crop

in your garden of Río

Grande mud is bullets,

is machetes, is

acid baths for bones,

choruses of prayers

from those in torture church.

Hermanita of Perpetual

Sorrow, what flowers

do we hand you - we

who die now too.

We who dangle nude

and burned from bridges,

we who hoped

to see our daughters

run through sunlight, only

chased by waves

not bleeding

yet,

but laughing.

BRAVO 88

July in the Sonoran Desert. The Jeep is dying.

So is the first marriage. Both

spew oil, poisoned fluids

on the hardpan. Both wrecks

ready for the scrapyard.

And here comes a fat Chevy

tow-rig, muscling up from wobbly

water-mirages on the blacktop:

driver has Red Man tatters threaded

between his teeth and his gut

hangs out a torn shirt, burned

crimson and spotted

with spit that flies

straight as tasers when the wind

don't hit. "You call me

Bravo," he says, and

peering in the open maw of the Jeep and

the wife standing ten feet away,

adds: "This here

don't look too god for you,

buddy. No it do not."

Lying underneath, busted windshield glass and pebbles

Pocking his back he says: "You wanna come

home with me tonight? Spend the night?

I got seven rooms. I got

A spare. Got a bed and a couch.

Got my dad in there. It ain't much I got

but it's a house."

We imagine chainsaws and

human sacrifice. The wife

backs deeper into the desert. Away.

Bravo

is not hurt.

"Tell you what."

He spits. He hooks the winded Jeep's lip.

Lifts it from the sand. Guts

the drive train out of it and tosses it

in the Chevy rig.

"I'll strike you a deal right now.

I'll tow you 40 mile out of here

For $90 cash money."

The Jeep fights the hook, bucks

all the way over Starr Pass,

rocks us like a rowboat in chop.

Bravo says: "You been to Ohio?"

Ohio?

"Ohio, man. They got a blue hole down there,

gobble you up.

Just this bottomless pit

fullup with cold water."

We could share with him something about

bottomless pits.

"One time they dropped weights down in 'at sucker -

they went down

and down

kept goin and goin.

Seems a fella tried to swim a team of horses

crosst there and they sunk to the bottom.

Come up ,later over to

New Hampshire."

He spits.

"I shit you not."

He shifts right between her knees.

"This guy I know, he ran into a fourteen foot

catfish in this one damn.

I gone down there fishin

and this dude pulls up in a tow truck

and slaps a bigass pot roast on the hook

and winches it out and drives up the beach

and pulls himself out a six-foot

bass."

Bravo breaks down

three times on the road.

He gets out and sticks his head

into the Chevy's mouth.

Inside,

we fight.

"I caught a jet-jockey over to my wife's place.

I threw his ass in the pond.

He's like, I don't want no trouble.

And he covers up like a boxer.

I'm like, Well trouble done come.

So I break his arm in three places.

And I break his jaw in two places.

And I say to my wife,

You better get out here - your boyfriend's

in the pond getting all wet."

Pulling into Benson, he tells me

the astounding news: "Mexicans

tear open their own shirts

as a sign of grief."

Bravo

takes all my money.

He unhooks the Jeep and leaves me in the sunset desert

with my drive-train still

in his truck.

Car hopeless-dead in the dirt.

Just like that first wife

drove off one later summer.

But that year

I would just start to walk.

I would walk till it was dark, dark,

until the stars sifted like sugar

down the naked peaks

And I would not pause

to tear my clothes.

LINES FOR NERUDA

Ay, mi Viejo…

We were the men who worked the machines

each anointed with oil on his knees -

when our families dreamed, machines came awake

to search us out. I didn't know, I didn't know where

poetry entered. The thousand smashed windows

that watched empty alleys, did the virus of verse

blow in them with the tubercular wind?

Or the poisonous voices of wet oleanders

on Interstate 5, were they calling my name?

The electrical smell, the machinery smell,

the cannery smell, the armpit smell,

the shoe polish smell, the bakery smell,

the gas station smell, the gunpowder smell,

the Thunderbird smell, the V-8 smell,

the dirt street smell after rain,

the bare belly smell, the open sex smell,

the hair tonic smell, the wood varnish smell,

the tortilla smell, the ashtray smell,

the Catholic smell, the Tijuana smell,

the refinery smell never hinted at poems.

The first poem I read

was the ragged *V* scrawled

in a brown sky by gulls

escaping the garbage dump at sunset

cutting under clouds

over the apartment blocks

going to a sea I knew

was there across the city

but never saw.

And then dear darkness.

Our lullabies were the inexhaustible keen

of overhot gears beseeching grease. Our fathers' nightlights,

40 watt bulbs strung up on orange power cords: lynched stars

that swung over their heads, their shadows flapped

like wings of the machines. Old angels squinting

at nude magazines they couldn't read -

coffee break black and white braille - the smudge of hard fingers on thighs,

Pall Mall ash speckling sad night nipples - a touch of paper skin

deader than snow.

How did the Word ever hunt down our hearing?

The engines of hunger drove us deeper to silence.

What was it that urged us to sing? What handle

disengaged the gears, by what chain were we dragged

from the brink? We lost singers every day:

one lost to pistols, one lost to flames, one lost to

coughing night sweats, one erased by the highway. Each one

wore black shoes,

workingman soles as rippled as waves with no shore.

The ironwrack pounded unceasing around us,

the glass crash, the tire burn, the shotgun,

the shouting. Blue exhalations sighed from our cars -

were the vowels of my song gasping into the air?

Was the ratchet of pistons this consonance drumming?

Why did poetry come forth from cables, from coils,

punctuated by nails in veils of rust

to the beat of Border Patrol helicopters

from words as simple as hermano, hijo, compañero,

esperanza, amante, dolor--

how did you come to me to lay mothwings of song to burn on my tongue?

DEFINITION

Illegal Alien, adj. / n.

A term by which

An invading colonial force

Vilifies

Indigenous cultures

By identifying them as

An invading colonial force.

IRRIGATION CANAL CODEX

Y los muchachos cling

To the cantina's jukebox heart, sing:

We never go nowehere we never see nothing

But work: these fingers bleed every daylong day,

Aching from la joda of the harvest -

Y la muerte, esa puta que nos chifla

From the bus station balcony, from I-10,

From Imperial Ave. Truck lot behind the power station,

From waterbreak delirium, from short-hoe

Genuflections down pistolbarrel fields -

And the canals green,

Pumping life into those chiles, los tomates, once

A year some poor pendejo can't take the grease-

Heat drudge, the life of a burro, the lonesome nights

Of sweat and harsh sheets and drinks

Tattered lips pulling tequila

Till el vato's so alucinado he thinks

He can run free, thinks

The trucks with spotlights are motherships, thinks

He sees Villa shooting cars on I-25, hears Tlaloc, god

Of storms, calling, water to water,

Rain to rain, mud to mud - feed me your tears - I

Thirst - I will feed your daughters, I will

Sweeten the fields, I will ease your heat - and

He runs

¡Ban This!

He runs

Se larga el guey

Down the alley, out

Dirt road, cuts

Under freeway, jumps

Barbwire

Where that homey last year drove his troca

Into the ditch

He's so pedo he can't see

If it's stars or distant windows, he

Can't tell if it's roadside crosses where some bus

Drove into a delivery truck

Or if it's a fence all white and crooked

Or a boneyard

Where his grandfathers fell apart

Beneath him, he runs--

Through Carrizo reeds, midnight sunburn,

Cane and chapulines dry as bones,

Rattling like deer hooves, like Calaveras on

The Day of the dead, like Yaqui rattles,

Like old Death snapping her fingers and then amazing

Green

Green, cold green of the canal: sun-scummed

But icy, fresh and still steaming through back-crack

Cabbage fields, from sunrise to el poniente,

Going going green endlessly going

Verde que the quiero verde going

He dips his head to drink

And it grips him: he slips: he's a watersnake, slick:

Drinks his way to the bed of the acequia

And spreads his dust there: he is become an offering

To the raingod and it is good: he breathes

The green into his lungs until his heart grows cool:

And he goes -

He flows west: frogs ping off his back: dragonflies

Part before him: Tortugas worry his shirt tails:

He flies mouth-down, arms wide as cranes' wings

Touching the rusted rims as he sails: miles

Slide along his callused fingers - across the land he goes, no one

Watching: he goes through the harvest: corn

Combs his hair: nights he goes, days, no patrols

Hunt him now: his lips never stop

Kissing his shadow.

And he touches earth

400 miles away, gone somewhere now

South of Calexico - almost home -

Nothing in his pockets -

Small fish

In his eyes

Like coins.

DARLING PHYL

July.

Fireworks tonight. This new life.

I remember now

That other life,

The life below.

Those ten

Ement years.

On our dead alley.

And Papá gone out to screw

Bowling alley waitresses

Again.

Mother too scared

Of pachucos and winos and

Gang-fighters and black men

To go into the dark

To the Shelltown park

To watch the rockets.

Papá had the 49 Ford

Though Mom couldn't drive

Ten feet.

So what

Were we going to do

Anyway, jump

In the junky bus

And ride one mile

Through the concrete night?

10 o'clock and Ma

Wrapped us in blankets

To keep mosquitoes off

And we snuck

Thru the bldgs to the

Outside stairwell to the land

Lord's place and climbed

Halfway up, cement

Landing as cool as grass anyway

And we ate ketchup sandwiches.

She, a step above me,

Head thrown back, eyes

Up to the sky,

Searching, seeing dead ancestors,

Dead friends, seeing

The mysterious man who

Sent letters she kept hidden

In her drawer - he called her

Darling Phyl.

Fireworks.

But this is the real world.

It's almost funny.

We couldn't see a single firework.

All we saw was the ghost plumes

Of smoke angling away.

We heard the thunder.

All we saw was the color of the bombs

Reflected in the smoke.

The color, oh

The color

Lit the sky

And Phyllis

Dark as sorrow against it--

The color

Man it almost seemed

Beautiful.

THE LUNA CODEX

My moon pulled a different darkness across the sky.

My unknown sisters tucked in the barbed embrace of

the borderfence saw a different face in the moon. Theirs

was a Luna Tochtli, a Rabbit Moon - moon of running,

fear, hiding.

My bed was soft. Their beds were stone. My moon

was origami floating in a water cup, a Japanese

artwork of ricepaper and pearls. A light to dream of

girlfriends. Their moon peeled a panicked eye, goggled

blind as they ran. Headlights froze them, twin moonbeams

ran them down, tufts of their dreams tangled in thickets

of border tumbleweeds.

My sisters brought undocumented scents to sweeten

the valleys. Their perfume settled on roadsides, misted

over bloodstain, rattlesnake, bootprint, guard dog, flash

light: illegal exhalations, unlawful breathing tainted

with cinnamon, coffee, filling cries like sugar in the bellies

of honeysuckle. Underarm sweat from running. Belly

sweat. Back of the neck sweat. Small of the back sweat.

Shoulderblade sweat. Brow sweat. Behind them, hunger.

Before them, night. Thigh sweat. Tang of terror under their

skirts, smell of hope burning like mustard blossoms in

the caves. Burning stink of running, Death smells of

squatting where where they hoped no one could see them.

Fertilizer. Lemons.

Black soap fresh hair flagged in the wire.

Sun smell of underpants once hung in the wind. Heavy

hopeless breast milk smell. Smell of Morelos gardens

still in blouses. Burning stink of running.

2.

I did not need to run.

I had a paper moon. Stamped and certified. Mine was

a colonia moon, a barrio moon, a suburban moon. I

knew where I was, where I was supposed to be, where

I was allowed to go, and that was anywhere. We lived

the outhouse moon, the tortilla moon, the channel

12 bullfight Tijuana moon. And then we migrated

north, like monarchs, following the light.

And my moon was a Boy Scout moon.

A campout moon.

A drive-in triple feature moon.

My moon remained poor as a rusted coin in a frozen pond.

But documented. The green men in the tan trucks could

read my belonging by this moon's light. Gave us the all-

clear to walk, work, die on ground our ancestors had

forgotten. Let us don Bat Patrol patches and Troop 260

uniforms and hike the ridgelines where the Mexica had

taken Huitzilopochtli in their arms and begun their 100 year

walk to the south.

My moon rose over tidy houses.

3.

She ran.

She ran all her life. She ran to stay ahead of charging

darkness, galloping hunger. She ran west to el poniente,

north toward winter and Mictlán, land of the dead. Worked

the light of the moon in her small hands the color of earth:

she molded moonglow into trinkets traded for coins the color

of sun. Wove moon into bracelets she traded for perfume.

Worked the ceremonial motel chambers, swept the floors of the

moneyed, folded bloody sheets and knelt at toilets, scrubbing

sins of the mighty from their seats.

Everyone moving north.

She was thirteen:

Mactactli ihuan yei.

I was ten:

Mactlactli.

Somehow

she came to rest in my house. Trucks could not track her

for an hour. Dogs could not follow her scent. She was on

that invisible railroad to Los Angeles. Enemy city of the Great

Walled City of Tijuanatlán. I was in the invisible mountains

of Cuyamaca, walking in the ghost footprints of vanished hunters

in their tribes, wondering where their arrows went. And she slept

in my bed.

Too tired to eat or join in the gathered laughter of my livingroom,

she slept in my bed. She lay in my sheets, smelling the odor of

Thunderbird and America and her eyes pulled themselves closed

To protect her. Dreams of home.

4.

I came in and found her.

I came in and found her.

Is there any other story? Any other legend to tell? I came home.

I found her.

Her head on my pillow.

The first woman to ever sleep in my bed.

Her hair

black across my pillow, spilling toward earth, reaching for the heart

of Ce Anáhuac, the One World. Her eyebrows shallow as streams

fringed in cress and licorice in Cuyamaca shadows. Her brown brow,

unlined. One hand, fingers curled, nails pale small shells against the

Chichimeca shore of her skin.

Her breath

making small melodies of breezes and tides.

And me, holding my breath.

The thrum and sigh,

thrum and sigh,

thrum and sigh

of her sleep.

5.

Then they woke her. She didn't want to wake. She didn't want

to rise. She didn't want to go. I didn't want them to wake her.

I wanted to sleep beside her. I didn't know anything else that

men wanted to happen in a bed with a woman. I wanted to sleep.

Beside her. I did not know the language of beds. I wanted to pass

through the door of her color. I wanted to pray in her temple of hair.

She knew more than I did about this new language. She blushed

when she saw me at worship. I blushed discovered in my beholding.

We touched hands. Hello. We touched hands. Adios.

Then they tucked her in the back seat of a 1964 car, smuggled her

under blankets through trucks up freeways laden with runners, north

north, where she'd bask in the light of a thousand toilets, where her

nails would break on their porcelain, where she'd sweep more sheets

off more beds where she could not afford to sleep, where helicopters searched her alleys with burning eyes all night, where she could speak

to no one and no one could speak to her

 except to give her orders:

Girlie get your ass over here and wipe this up. You come when I

tell you to come and you do it now. Have papers? Do you like this,

you do, don't you? You like this. I'll teach you a little something

right here and now.

That night I lay in her outline on my sheets.

She was hot as sunburn on the cotton.

I sank my face

into the imprint of hers,

her perfume

crept from the pillow,

the smell of her memories:

I smelled her mother

in a kitchen with clay pots

and cilantro on her hands:

it was all there: it is still there:

hibiscus

tea, a river, a handful of

shampoo falling to a drain

like melting snow drifts.

First grade, the Mexican anthem,

the snap of the flag,

chalk dust sneezes,

smell of library paste.

Village church.

Incense.

The crack of unopened Bibles

freeing their musk.

Laundry day,

the boiling.

Tamale day,

and the aunts with their

crow-voice laughter,

the meat, the masa, the

raisins, the cinnamon.

Morning glory

vines all tangled

through cheap Tijuana

perfume.

Just an illegal drudge

in crepuscular rain.

If you see her, protect her.

Revere her.

My unknown sister.

Light candles in her honor, you travelers.

She is the mother of my race.

JIM MARQUEZ

Jim Marquez was born & raised in East Los Angeles. He has published in local/national/international arts & culture magazines and has self-published 12 books in the past 6 years. Jim has also backpacked, solo, over the past decade throughout Europe & Asia. He earned a Bachelor's in English/Full Teaching Credential-English/TOEFL Teaching Certificate from Cal State University, Los Angeles. He has taught adult ESL for 15 years. Jim's next book, "Beastly Bus Tales", is due 2012. Jim's books in print & Apple itunes downloads @ www.LuLu.com/spotlight/jimmarquez. Social/Blog/Book Events @ www.facebook.com/JimTheBeastMarquez

'BEASTLY BUS TALE #2: DRUNK WOMAN ON THE BUS

(An excerpt from "Beastly Bus Tales")

Jack Morales had never been afraid of no woman before until he ran into the drunk, white trash chick on the bus going back to the Eastside after putting a load on in downtown one Thursday night. It's unusual for any woman to be on LINE 18 at this ungodly hour along 6th Street through Downtown Los Angeles and ending up in Montebello with stops throughout Boyle Heights and East LA; yes, definitely *two distinct* areas though some like to think different.

It's mostly men riding the line at this time of night; men smart enough not to drive after the boozing, or, just too damn poor to afford a car; or, lately, the gas that goes with it. Either way, this bus, at this witching hour, becomes a collective designated driver for those with a hankering for the juice.

But this was a *GOOD* thing for Jack because that meant he didn't have to deal with the pigs from behind the wheel. But, also, *BAD* because Jack would then go ahead and drink like a goddamn fish because he knew he didn't have to drive afterwards.

It's best to sleep on these buses though, to keep your eyes closed so you won't see the sad fucks all around you, mirroring, of course, the sad fuck *you* are at this very moment.

You don't want to see, but sometimes side glances catch fleeting, twisted images of the guy masturbating in his white linen almost see-through pants across from you, or the man singing in Spanish to a woman in front of him who is not there, tears drying on a leathery face, or another man arguing with ghosts, another so utterly alone the space around him is evaporating, turning cotton candy, wisps of ectoplasm leaving fingertip traces in the air, minute whiffs of a life that ended long before he stepped onto this bus, or another man snickering like a loon, another lost in space, and another and another and another, each man in a private hell that may come to an end when the headache pounds from the inside out and rousts him from his piss-drenched, nightmarish sleep and comes to, if he's lucky, at 4 p.m. the next afternoon, feeling like a truck has run over him, as if he's gone ten rounds with the devil, as if he's run a marathon, as if he's re-lived the worst moment of his life over and over again.

He wants to forget 'that moment', but it keeps coming back when he boozes, that moment in every man's life he wished he could do over again, and yet there it is, rearing its fangs and sinking into your cock and ripping it away because you drank again and you'll keep drinking until you don't feel anything anymore, but guess what?

That moment *will never* end.

And here this nasty-ass broad comes along, to mock your misery, to take you away from your well deserved prison, to tempt you, to alter the plan, *your self-loathing for the night*, she and her tight, black, pull over sweater, no bra, tits bursting-nipples piercing daggers-her long, dirty blonde hair flowing, smile tobacco-brown, 99-cent store imitation perfume, gum chewing, chortling, wicked, twinkling eyes, drunk, fuckable…until you see her stomach protruding from underneath the sweater, hanging over the belt.

Her stomach looked chewed up, as if she lost a tremendous amount of weight and the skin had nowhere to go but down, *sagging*, and was pockmarked with cigarette burns, purple stretch lines, and age; simply ravaged. How old was she? 30? 40? 50? 60? You couldn't tell. Maybe she had been a damn fine fuck years ago… but not anymore. She stood at the front of the bus and patted the crotch of her black jeans and she shouted, "Suck my pussy!" and laughed a drunk-in-the-bar-kind-of-laugh. "Who's gonna suck my pussy tonight?"

It takes a few seconds to register this, this phrase *'suck my pussy'*, it's not what you usually hear on this nightly Eastside Death March, so the men on the bus needed to shake the cobwebs out, those still conscious, adjust their eyes to the brightness of the overhead lights, try to focus, and strain to hear again:

"Who's man enough to suck my pussy?"

Yes, you heard right. There's a woman on board. Instinct takes over. You assess the risks to your person, the trouble you'd have to go through, the bullshit you'd have to put up with, how much cash you have left in your wallet, and then the quality of the merchandise being offered. *Oh God. No! What the fuck is that?*

She moved quickly for a drunk, stroking the inner thigh of a day laborer in his late 40s snoring in the seat closest to the driver and plopping herself onto his knee. "How about you, baby? You want some free pussy?" Startled out of his stupor the man screamed and pushed her away, *"Ay, bruja, no! Pinche pendeja!"* and got up and pulled the cord and rang the bell and just his luck the bus was coming to a stop and he hopped off, shaking his head, waving his fist, and cursing at the bus as it pulled away.

The next was a salary man; tie undone, shirt untucked, unshaven, reeked of good whiskey, head leaning against the window, eyes half open because the screams of the day laborer had awaken him. Drunk Woman slid into the seat next to him and grabbed his hand and put it on her crotch.

"Feel how hot it is! Feel the heat goddamn you! LOVE ME!"

"What the fuck lady?!" the salary man barked, pushed her back, stood up, stepped over her dirty flip flopped feet, and stormed to the back of the bus.

Another man already aware of what was going on jumped up before the woman could get into his space and rang the bell and made for the side exit, rushing away, but she scooted after him and reached out and slapped his ass.

"Where you going handsome?" she shrieked, and groped him again.

The bus came to a stop and the man jumped off without looking back.

She was now in the middle of the bus. And Jack was sitting alone. She was two other men and two seats away.

Oh God, now what? Jack moaned under his breath. *Just sit the fuck down, will ya lady? Sit the fuck down!*

What can Jack do? If it wasn't for the excess flesh dangling about he'd think about it. What the hell? Free is Free. But no, dude. Come on. Even if she *was* a hot piece of 19 year old drunk USC ass with a fake ID in a bar back in town the sex drive wasn't clicking of late. Taking care of his Mother after her accident and hospitalization at home-which entailed the disposal of waste, sometimes even the assistance of cleaning up after her, and just the sudden overall stark nakedness of his 78 year old mother, seeing things no man should ever see of his own mother-was enough to dim the brightest of red lights in his mind.

He could not bring himself to even the slightest of peaks - nothing. So again: what if she comes and sits down next to him?

Does he smack her a good one for bothering him? Teach her some manners, not to fuck with a man, drunk, on a bus at 4 a.m., who isn't screwing with anybody else, keeping to himself, who is lost in his own world, doing his beastly best to maintain the slightest bit of sanity long enough to get back to the room? Is that an option?

Does he do his best to politely demure from the advance? No matter how crude and on most other occasions welcomed? *Can he?* Is there anything that can stop this woman? Jack heard once a woman is only 'interested' when her body is ready to make the babies. Doesn't matter if she wants kids or not, old or young, ugly or pretty, skinny or fat, it's not up to her; the woman gets aggressive when the biology needs to replicate. Or, maybe that's complete horseshit.

The drunkard was now one man away. Jack noticed she'd only sit & hit if there was space for her to do so. Bags, packages, or two men slumbering against each other she passed up. *Jack needed a bus buddy fast!* There was one dude directly in front him. Hunched over though, couldn't make out if he was asleep or crying. Fuck it. Get up and sit next to the bastard, it was the only way. And apologize to the man too because usually a move this late at night can only mean one of two things: you're either making a pass yourself, or, you're gonna try to hit him up for cash.

Jack got up, almost tipped forward, caught himself, stepped out from his seat and fell in next to the guy who then raised his head. It was shaved under a hoodie and tattoos covered his neck. A sneer curled his lips - his upper torso one large muscle.

Oh God.

His tattoos contained street names and numbers Jack wished he didn't know existed.

Oh God.

A darkened, red rimmed scowl in his eyes told Jack things just got very much worse.

OH GOD!

And, the 'homeboy' was rolling a joint.

OHHH GOD!!!

Great, just fucking great. Jack had to deal with the 'homie' at *the most* inopportune time. What the fuck can you say at a moment like this? Suddenly the old broad doesn't matter does it? You have to try to talk yourself out of a beating now, or a blast from a stolen gun, or at the minimum a harsh rebuke filled with cagey threats, fuck-your-motherisms, and much hand & finger gesticulations that always looks like laughably bad marionette theatre from far but up close with the spit flying and the meth-breath inches from your face, it becomes a surprisingly effective & affective method of street terrorism. For that's what these inbred monsters are: the original terrorists, sans any real political or religious bent of course. Just selfishness…

For a good three seconds Jack and The Homeboy stared at each other, sizing each other up, grasping this new reality, not quite getting over the shock of falling into each other's lap so unexpectedly. Then, Homeboy grumbled something. Jack feigned not-understanding, shaking his head, eyes wide, shrugging his shoulders. Homeboy glanced up at Drunk Woman then looked back at Jack and he said in a gravelly hiss, "Just stay right there, Homes, don't go anywheres-A."

WTF?!

Good God, was Homeboy *protecting* Jack? Taking him under his needle-pricked wing? Allowing Jack to suckle off his man-teat of cloudy milk? To bask in the dimming glow of a wasted life soon to be snuffed out by yet another senseless shooting at a backyard party he wasn't invited to or a batch of bad drugs, anyway? A last and perhaps only grasp of a heroic act to save his own sad and misunderstood soul?

Jack could only reply, "What?"

Homeboy scrunched down in his seat, he lowered his eyes; he look *wounded*, like a pitbull beaten the fuck out of by a pissed off neighbor at 4am when nobody was watching and then cowers whenever that neighbor comes home late, pulls into the driveway and looks over at the dog sitting on the porch and dares it to come back out snarling and barking at the fence again. Yeah, you know your place now motherfucker. That's how Homeboy looked.

NO! *Waaaaaaaait a minute here!* Homeboy wasn't playing the valiant knight in shiny Raiders gear, no, no, no, he was *afraid* of Drunk Woman too.

Oh my God! He was just as petrified, he was just as oft put, he was just as much a pussy as Jack! And Jack had to grin ear to ear at that one.

Both Jack and The Homeboy looked to the left and out the window when Drunk Woman finally stumbled past, falling out of her caked-in-filth sandals, laughing at herself, then about-faced and tripped forward *back* to the front of the bus, crashing into two shaky old timers standing and ready to disembark and linked arms with them and all three spilled out onto INDIANA Street in front of the Wells Fargo Bank; the men howling, the woman cackling, Homeboy visibly more relaxed, Jack the same.

Homeboy then continued to fumble with the joint. Jack stared straight ahead. Wishing he could be lost on a book's pages, in the book itself, 'The Black Dahlia', maybe, staring over

Bucky's shoulder as he discovers Lee's chopped up body in a sand pit down in Ensenada, a fiery cross burning to mark the grave; Jack's body too wrapped up in a tattered and maggot-soaked American flag.

Jack stared straight ahead and sat and stared and sat until his stop came up on VAN-COUVER AVE across from the Jack in a Box on WHITTIER BLVD. He looked back as he left and hadn't noticed that Homeboy was already gone.

THE GIRL IN THE CAFÉ

-a portrait-

She sits in the corner of this Mexican café in Monterey Park; a sleepy enclave of Asian and Latino inhabitants blissfully ignoring each other in order to coexist just eight miles outside of Downtown Los Angeles in the West San Gabriel Valley.

A clean and fairly well lit place this is, this Mexican café, where this girl sits in the corner. At lunchtime she sits there. I see her after I get out of my morning class. I go there exactly twice a week for lunch. I would like to think she is there every day.

I neither love nor lust for her, merely curious; although she is somewhat attractive: a pale moon face peeks out from behind strands of light, brown hair. Her eyes are heavy, though not sad. More *resigned*. Her dress is plain, so plain that I never notice what she's wearing. The tilt of her head and body show me that she is in perpetual pain though, but it may not necessarily be physical in nature. She's maybe in her early twenties.

I've tried to say "hello" on numerous occasions whenever I walked over to the soda dispenser to get my root beer. I'd wave, or nod my head, always with a smile, never flirting; being kind.

Sometimes I'd mouth the words "Hey" or "Hi" or "What's up?" but she never returns the gesture. She does look *through* me though, this I know. This I feel. I feel her eyes and attention rolling through a stop sign and not bothering to look left.

Besides, I've had plenty of women look through me before. I know that look, usually of contempt, but this look, this girl in the café, not only did she see past me, but into the parking lot behind me and onto Atlantic Boulevard.

One day she did manage to crack *half* a smile at me as I lived dangerously and went up for a refill of a Diet Sprite, but she caught herself, moved her lips, cursed under her breath for doing so, then lowered her head and picked at the plate in front of her.

Hey, I'm not a leper. I've had my share of women, my confidence is not crushed by this, but it would be nice to get a smile every now and then. I mean, I wasn't going to take her purse or anything. Come on, lady; be nice. Would that *kill* you so much?

This went on for about six months. I'd come in for lunch, I'd see her, say "hi", she pretended I wasn't there, then, I'd grab the special of the day. OK, fine with me.

Whatever.

One day I went in and she wasn't there. I ate, read my paper then got up to use the men's room, which is at the end of the hall. I would have to walk past her usual spot. When I came back out, she *was* there.

I thought, oh, what the hell? Be a gentleman. I approached her table, she was already looking down, and I said, "How are you today?"

She whispered, "Fine. And you?" Eyes still averted.

"Good, good. Hey, I've seen you around here before."

"Yes, I know," she said.

"So what's your name? I'm Jim." I put my hand out.

She barely took it. "Nice to meet you," she said, and then she looked toward the front of the café, near the register area. Nobody was there. "I'm not supposed to talk to anybody," she said to me.

"Excuse me? What?"

"I'm not supposed to look at other men," she said.

"What?"

"My husband, he works in the kitchen…I wait for him."

"And…"

"And while I wait for him to get out of work I'm not supposed to talk to other men, or look at other men."

"Or what?"

"Or else he hits me."

"What? Oh God…I'm…I'm sorry."

She shrugged her shoulders, then, said, "That's the way it is."

"But what about your girlfriends, can't you at least talk to them?"

"Nooooo, *especially* other girls I'm not supposed to talk to."

"Why not?"

She said, "Because my husband says that women put ideas into other women's heads that aren't good. They're *worse* than men."

"He actually *said* that to you?"

"He reminds me all the time."

"Well, yeah, that's because women are smarter than men, that's why."

"My husband doesn't think so."

"Well, who manages the money once the check comes into the house?

You, right? Who pays the bills? *You*, right? Who makes sure his damn shorts are clean for work? *You*, right? He probably doesn't even know how to start a washing machine, am I right?

"I guess," she said, looking over at the register area again.

"Then who do you talk to?"

"Nobody. Now please go."

"Whoa, wait a minute, let me ask you: how long have you been married? How long has this been going on?"

"Since I was thirteen."

"How old are you now?"

"Twenty-three."

"And how old is your husband?"

"Fifty-one. Sometimes, in Mexico, we marry early."

My God, what do you say to that? What can you do? Ride in on a horse, slay the dragon, and rescue the damsel in distress? But then what? You take her home to meet your mother? Naw, that's not gonna happen, pal. Then again, she never asked to be liberated in the first place. (*Odd though, my own grandmother married at 14, my grandfather was 25, in Mexico City, before coming to the States, where she remained happily married for the next 65-years. Something I know I'll never be able to have because I'm too goddamn old already…..not fair*).

"You better go before he sees you. He'll *say* something to you."

"Yeah, right, he could try," I said. "Let him deal with a *real* man. But, I don't want to get you in trouble. I'll go now. I just wanted to finally say 'Hi' is all."

"OK, please go. Don't talk to me anymore."

Don't talk to me anymore. I never heard a woman say that to me before. *Drop dead*, yes. *Go to hell*, sure. *Fuck off*, plenty of times, but never straight out *Don't-Talk-To-Me-Anymore!*

And, so, I didn't. I pretended she wasn't there until, eventually; I stopped noticing her. I'd go in, eat, read my paper, though I never used the men's room there, then, quickly leave.

One time, a few months back, I had to glance over at this girl, just *had to*, as she sat in the corner of this Mexican café, and the first thing I noticed were the bags under her eyes. Crow's feet stamped on the edges of them too. There was also a blotchy rash on her neck. Her face had broken out. There were dandruff specks in her hair. She looked beat up, but not by any kind of fists, no, that's too easy and obvious. The *whole* of her was just a lot *dimmer* than before. Her life force was fading.

At 23!

I saw her pick through her food, sip at her soda, then, she looked out into the parking lot of the strip mall behind me; looking and looking and looking, but, then, not really.

Nothing was there…and never will be.

BEASTLY BUS TALE #5

This Is Not A Story, Maybe A Portrait…

(An excerpt from "Beastly Bus Tales")

Jack Morales didn't always catch the #18 bus back to East Los Angeles on 6th & Spring in Downtown LA; he used to get it on the corner of *Broadway* & 6th, about two blocks up where at one time it seemed a safer place to catch the bus in the dark after the boozing; 3am. 4am. 5am. Where there were more people. So, he thought that meant protection, or, witnesses to whatever bullshit the methed-out lunatics had in store for the overnight hours and possibly the innocent bus riders.

Jack had tried the corner of 6th & Spring a couple years before but he was attacked from all sides; it was closer to the "skidrow" area, and so that meant malevolent pan handlers, freaked-out, paranoid drug dealers *threatening* to flash their guns, and the looking-for-a-fight-because-I-am-not-a-real-man-and-I-cannot-handle-my-shit-drunkards congregated there every night.

Being new to the scene at that time Broadway & 6th became Jack's escape hatch.

There were regulars Jack saw at the Broadway stop on a weekly basis but he tried never to acknowledge them for fear that they would want to become his friend. Most faceless. Some formless; seething shadows. Silent. No eye contact. Whenever Jack approached he'd look away, the others would do the same; mostly brooding, intoxicated men, standing and waiting. Sometimes passing he saw the black, skinny, barefooted female prosty with- Jack assumed-her grandmother, dressed just as provocatively. A tag-team? Two for the price of one? *Christ*. And, there were always the Latino boys in drag.

Jack tried not to stare but in the moonlight you couldn't help but notice that the beard had come back after a probably tough evening's work. There was one who tried talking to Jack (very effeminate, fingertips on Jack's shoulder), saying something about how his cousin was Jennifer Lopez and that if he really wanted to he could call her and get his big break (at doing what?) but he choose not to because he didn't want to get too famous too fast.

Jack nodded, said, "I hear that", then, stepped off the curb and into the street to look, *pray*, for their approaching bus, then said, "I'm tired, man; *honey?* I gotta sleep this off when the bus comes."

And once on the bus Jack would close his eyes to forget where he was. One freak used to shout in the back of the bus, "Old MacDonald was a black man, me-o-me-o-my!" over and over and over again and again, and then, as most of the skidrow citizens who waited almost an hour for the bus, he'd hop off not even two stops later. Why not walk?

Jack ended up at this stop after one wickedly spirited Halloween night. He and a buddy had taken the bus from 8th & Spring earlier in the evening, headed west, and through a dizzying array of turns, short cuts, and L.A. traffic voodoo, they hopped off at Santa Monica Blvd, or was it Melrose? It was in West Hollywood. They then walked the mile or so of the gay Halloween frivolity route.

Hundreds of thousands of Angelenos from all corners of the freak-kingdom are blasted on liquor and drugs; open containers everywhere, nudity, fire breathers, bands, chaos, and not one spot of trouble. It's the only time in Los Angeles that this is allowed to happen. You can't do this on New Year's Eve, where L.A. is THE MOST BORING city on the planet, you can't do this on Super Bowl Sunday, or, on any other holiday for that matter. And you can thank the West Hollywood Sheriffs Department for that. For understanding that the people of this shithole need to blow off steam, they need to partake in the debauchery or else they'd go insane and take a rifle to the top of a building.

They, the WeHo Sheriffs, are trained, apparently, to understand the needs of its citizenry. Unlike the nearby LAPD, as led by an assistant to the old Daryl Gates Regime where the following must be written on a chalkboard either in roll call or in the locker room: "IT'S US AND THE REST ARE NIGERS AND SPICKS. CHINKS DON'T COUNT!"

After a two hour surly crawl back from the festivities on a bus sardined with every amateur-fucko drinker in the city Jack and his buddy are deposited at 5th & Hill (Pershing Square) where Jack immediately runs to the alley behind the Metro Station escalators and vomits blood. His friend, an avid photographer, is clicking away. That fucker. Said friend claimed later it was too dark to get anything good though Jack never believed him. They stagger down the alley and pop out on 6th where they quickly part company. Friend off to Tacos Mexico on 9th & Broadway-*fuck that, too far*-and Jack to his bus stop.

Which is where we see him now.

It is 3:30am.

He just missed the 3:12 home.

He has to wait until the 4:12.

And because it is Halloween, or, *was*, the streets are empty.

Except for Jack.

Leaning back against one of those roll-down doors they use to protect the storefronts. Jack's weight, his fat ass, is pushing into the give of the door and the door rumbles, wobbles like a wave. Jack's head is hung low. There are fresh strands of vomit lying over his fake red silk shirt, from the collar down to the ripped pocket. His jeans are scuffed at the knees. His black boots are also scuffed at the tips. He needs to get new boots soon. They look bad. He slaps the back pocket of his jeans to make sure his wallet is still there. It is. He slaps the right front pocket to make sure his keys are still there. They are. He hears voices, suddenly, not in his head, but fading laughter from far, far above through high in the sky loft windows. They're still having their Halloween party. Lucky bastards.

He feels hot though it is cold, the first of November it has become overnight. Jack's birthday is in 16 days. He is alone. Though *shapes* out of the corner of his eye catch his attention.

Rats.

Waddling from the curb to past his feet as they scurry under the door Jack is leaning against. He is not that alone it turns out.

Jack's mouth is dry despite the fact that he has been drinking all night and even on the bus back to Downtown. His legs are tired. His feet hurt. His back is sore. He is not hung over, not yet, that hell will be breached tomorrow afternoon. But his vision is blurry. His eyes are heavy. He wants to sleep. He should eat but there is nothing close. Perhaps he should have gone with his buddy, grab a plate of carne asada tacos, let those little fuckers soak up some of the booze; bring him around, get his senses back. But no, he is a lazy drunk; Jack is; too much running around tonight.

At one point dangerously darting across Sunset Blvd to retrieve his demon-mask that had blown off his head when a truck charged past the two of them as they stood on the corner outside Book Soup and leered at the scantily clad teenage girls, calling them over, asking if they could take their picture. Jack got the mask back after nearly getting obliterated by a Cadillac Escalade with its driver on his cell phone. "You know you almost got killed, right?" Photog Friend said, lit his hash pipe, and took a deep suck.

"What, again?"

"Don't worry, I got it," Friend said, tapping his camera. "Say, let's go to that liquor store over there; get something for the ride back."

"You're crazy," Jack mumbles, giggles. "You fucker." Jack raises his head to ask his friend if he could borrow a few bucks to buy tacos but his friend is not here. Another rat appears, *poof,* and, scurries past his feet. "Fucker," Jack giggles again. He is sleepy. Maybe he can sit for a bit. Yeah, he's wearing jeans, he'll wash them tomorrow. It's a long wait for the next bus. His back is killing him now. Yeah. Just a bit.

Jack lets himself slide down the length of the door, more rumbles & wobbles, sounds like distant thunder, and lands with a soft *plop* onto the glassy-looking asphalt. "Ahhh, that's better," Jack says to nobody and coughs. "I need some water," Jack says. "Couple Advil too."

Jack then drifts off to sleep.

Snoring.

Phlegmy.

The rat looking at Jack from the curb wonders if it makes that kind of sound when it sleeps too. He will try to remember to listen for it the next time he and his buddies bunk down for the night. He stands on his hind legs, as all rats do when there is no human-thing around. It would really fuck with them badly if the human-things saw that rats, like most animals, could actually walk upright with no trouble at all. Another human-thing has placed a votive candle, lit, on the ground, near Jack. There is no explanation for this, maybe as a warning to other human-things to be careful as they pass on the sidewalk.

The flickering glow of the fire bounces off Jack's face. He can see wisps of grey hair at the sides of his temple. He can see Jack's pug nose crinkle as he snores. He can see dry lips. Protruding tongue. Eye sockets dark. Rings under the eyes. Hair askew. Spiky probably once earlier in the evening but now matted down with sweat and grime. Cheeks bloated. He can see Jack's shirt untucked, the buttons on top missing, the pocket ripped, dangling, his legs, the left straight out, the right at an angle creating a triangle shape over the other. He looks fat and stupid. No wedding ring. What a loser. Pathetic. What would his father think? He can also see that there is a wet spot on Jack's crotch. The rat can smell urine. He knows that scent very well. And he can smell something else. The rat twirls his whiskers, licks his paws. He doesn't want to disturb the human-thing, he senses that it poses no threat, but, still, it's time for a closer inspection.

The rat walks over to Jack, falls forward and uses all four legs to step onto Jack's boot, then, ankle, then, quickly up Jack's leg, to his inflated stomach, over his torn pocket and stops at Jack's throat.

He sniffs at the strands of drying vomit on Jack's skin. He lets out his tongue and tastes. Hmm, interesting. The rat begins to lick at Jack's vomit from his throat down to the pocket. And abruptly stops. The rat feels a sensation he has not felt before; he feels woozy, a little dizzy. He must rest his head against Jack's rising chest. Jack feels warm. The rat feels safe. And excited.

His whatever-it-is *down there* under his ass and tail gets hard. He feels it vibrate. He needs to mate. Fast. The scent coming off Jack's urine soaked crotch is now sweetly attractive. The rat cannot wait. The rat leaps and lands with a heavy *thump* onto Jack's semi-hard and wet package. Jack does not stir. But *his* whatever-it-is *down there* is bulbous, and throbbing, the rat can feel it getting bigger as the rat thrusts against the bulge covered in blue denim. It is responsive to the rat's touch. The rat is happy.

Jack is happy too. He can see the girl he met at a New Year's Eve party a couple years back here in downtown. They are both seriously drunk. Barely walking back to her place a few blocks down from the underground afters. Up the stairs. Clothes off. Making out like teenagers for the first time. She turns up the TV loud so her housemates can't hear them. This bothers Jack. She has great tits. Hard, black nipples. He partakes. She moans and giggles. They are on the wooden floor in her room. She's wearing Wonder Woman panties.

He yanks them off.

She has just finished her period, she says, you're going to have to pull the tampon out if you wanna fuck me. Pull the string, go ahead. Pull it. Jack does. Slowly. Looks like a tail, he says, and laughs, and pulls the tampon out, wiggles it in the air and he says, what the fuck, you got a mouse up your snatch or what? And they both laugh and Jack tosses it across the room where it lands with a *splat* against the TV screen.

You going to fuck me now, baby? Yes. She has a mass of tight, curly black pubic hair; it scratches Jack's cock as he enters but then tickles as he begins the rhythmic thrusting. Feels furry. Next time wear a condom, baby, she says and moans and bucks against him. Yes, right, next time. Sure. And Jack fucks and fucks and fucks. She digs it. He can still hear her squealing, even now.

LIZZ HUERTA

Lizz Huerta is a poet, fiction writer and memoirist who was born and raised in Chula Vista, CA. She currently works with non-profit So Say We All, teaching creative writing to homeless teens and owns a business called Wrought Iron Maiden. She's currently working on a YA fantasy novel.

THE GAME

Our bodies are pressed tightly against the side of a parked car. We hear the border patrol agent's footsteps approaching. I motion for my little sister to be quiet, to not breathe, not make any noise. The United States of America is within reach, we see its yellow light in the dark night. The border patrol agent has reached the car. In our veins out blood turns to ice. It's no good, we're as good as caught.

I contemplate running, leading him away so that my little sister has a chance to make it across the border, but a few feet away from where we're hiding someone else starts to run and the border patrol agent is off, yelling at the kid to stop. I yell at my sister to go - I grab her hand and we run as fast as we can and we make it. We reach the light and celebrate! We've made it to the United States!

One by one the others straggle in, some on their own, jubilant they've made it too. Others are brought in by Border Patrol Agents, they've lost this round and will have to be in the Border Patrol the next round. Agents who have caught someone get to hide with the rest of us.

The street we live on, Barrett Ave, is a long s-curved street lined with Jacaranda trees. The houses are small but the yards are large. Most of the families on the block are Mexican, but not *Mexican*-Mexican. We say "Yeah, I'm Mexican, but not *Mexican*-Mexican." We are the children and grandchildren of immigrants. All of us know Spanish but we speak English. We hiss and cuss in Spanish, cry and are soothed in Spanish but our conversations are in English. We're a mixed bunch. My sister and I are goody-two shoes, the daughters of a pastor and we can be annoying in our *"I'm telling!"* But we have the only swimming pool in the neighborhood so we're tolerated. Across the street live the boys - the children of farm workers who marched with Cesar Chavez. The down-the-street kids have weird Aztec middle names and call themselves Chicano. On weekends they dance with their parents in feathers and rattles. There are also a couple of white girls who moved here from Tennessee; Tybee Harmony and Bobby Jo. We like to laugh at their funny accents and their horrified faces when they try our Mexican candy covered in chile.

Six miles to the south, Tijuana and the real border glitter visibly at night. We are kids who cross back and forth easily, between cultures and languages. We go to Tijuana often; for groceries, to eat with family…we don't understand why some cousins can't come over to play…it is just a part of the larger universe that we just don't get.

When we play Border Patrol there are two teams. The stakes are high. Territories are defined by streetlights and the yards of mean neighbors. There is one streetlight more important than any other streetlight. That street light is the United States of America We gather at night, every summer night. We are dead serious.

The rules are simple - the team who is the Border Patrol (or La Migra), waits by the USA streetlight. The other team, the Mexican immigrant team (we call them the Wetbacks), hides in the territory that is defined as Mexico. When the count is finished La Migra comes looking for the Wetbacks, to catch them and prevent them from getting into their country. If you're a Wetback you do whatever you can to make it to the United States without getting caught. You sell out your fellow mojados, you hide under cars, you push and shove away La Migra who are hunting you down. You have a goal.

If you're La Migra you just want to keep the Mexicans out of your country. It isn't easy, your eyes aren't completely adjusted to the dark because you've been standing under the light that is the United States of America. When you head out into the night to find the immigrants it is hard to see, and there are so many of them.

*

We love this game. We play it as late as our parents let us stay up. I'm much better as a Wetback than Border Patrol Agent, I can't run very fast but I can hide. I can see well enough in the dark to position myself between more vulnerable Wetbacks and the Border Patrol. When I make it under the light that is the United States I am jubilant and cry out "America! I made it to America!"

It wasn't until I was older and stopped playing Border Patrol that I began to think about the game. We never thought about the political significance of what we were playing, just like the kids who grow up playing Cowboys don't stop to think: *Oh, hey! I'm representing manifest destiny and colonization! Bang-bang you're dead!* while the kids playing Indians don't stop to think: *What the fuck?*

Every night while we were playing Border Patrol, what we were playing at was being played out with real lives, by humans beings, a few miles from where we lived.

Children have been mimicking the world around them since the beginning of time. It's how we learn. We play house, we grow from the fantasy world of early childhood to reenacting the world we see around us. The Border Patrol was real in our lives, as were immigrants, documented and otherwise.

A couple of years ago I was walking through my San Diego neighborhood and I saw the Mexican kids who live behind my apartment building playing in the alley that separated our homes. There were always playing, screaming at each other, and even though it annoyed me at times I was happy they lived their afternoons outdoors, away from television, computers and video games. But this time the little girl, about five years old, was standing prostrate with a pillowcase over her head. One of her older brothers was standing beside her, the orange muzzle of a toy gun pressed firmly against the side of her head. A few feet away their other brother was smiling, pretending to take pictures. The image was horrifyingly familiar as it had been on the news channels for days. They were reenacting the prisoner torture and humiliation at Abu Ghraib prison in Iraq.

Seeing the kids play Abu Ghraib made me feel sick. Didn't they know? Hadn't anyone told them it wasn't right? That what they saw on television was sickening - the treatment of people as playthings - the value of being seen as human stripped away.

Then I thought of my childhood. I wonder if anyone who saw us playing Border Patrol had the same feeling. Playing a game that set brother against sister; those who lived in the light and those who would do anything for a chance to feel it on their faces.

Sometimes I wonder if the games kids play tell us more about our society than we would like to admit. It isn't just our kids who are comfortable playing the roles of jailer against inmate, cowboy against Indian, immigrant against Border Patrol Agent. We live comfortable in the light and in the roles that society sets out for us, but we too often miss the truth hidden in the shadows our actions leave behind. Our eyes have trouble adjusting to see the wider reality, that those people in the shadows are also people; and that it isn't a game.

TOMÁS RETURNS

Tomás, tell me the stories of your solitude

the city sinking backwards into memory

every passing truck a missed opportunity

the security in a well-placed home beneath a bridge

if only for one night's sleep in a fumed, grey veil.

tell me of your troubles, the music of the last seven cents,

the edible plants rinsed of animal urine

spiritual bounty under shelters of stars

water collected off of the windshields of sleeping vehicles

truths I never wanted to recognize.

speak to me of the righteous, Tomás

the back mountain women and their resistance stained smiles

dead groundhogs who never made it above after,

how fruitful American garbage is to the hungry,

the capacity and limits of fear, the disconnect of memory.

tell me of hunger, beloved.

the distinctions between wild mushrooms

of being belly flat on a sandbar sucking the empty shells of crabs.

I want to know how you wrote off life for experience

the roads I never even knew existed.

sing me the songs of migrant orphans

how to spin one dollar into thirty then one hundred

the ways of walking invisible

washing the days off in the gutters

segments of fruit and patterns of consumption.

feed me the weariness of your possessions

your freedom handcuffs and their scars

what was ever your destination, lover?

vicious mosquito thirst for knowledge

country spread open like a wound?

WORKING TO UNDERSTAND

Little Hector and I were wire

brushing the wrought-iron

fence that surrounded the

graves of Otis, Miles and

Dolly, all award-winning

beauties; blonde, postured,

blood-lines of royalty if

the humans who owned

them were to be believed.

Little Hector was telling some

tale or another of back in

the day when he drove for

the cartels until he fell

in love and didn't want to

end up headless or raising

pigs to sell for slaughter

to the corrupt, so he

followed the trails north,

passing more dead bodies

than he had ever seen while

working for the men the

songs on the Spanish station

were written about.

He asked me why people

in this country I was born

into erect fences for their

dead animals but those

who built the fences and

dug the graves received less

respect than the piles of

fur and bones decomposing

beneath our feet. He asked

who would bury him if he

died in the canyon or fell

from a roof he was tiling.

I had no answers.

He half-joked if he were a

dog he'd have papers, a home

to live in, he wouldn't be seen

as a beast of burden anymore,

strangers on the street

would stop to love him.

SARA INÉS CALDERÓN

Sara Inés Calderón is Latina a writer, journalist, bloguera and editor who has worked for the past decade at various newspapers in Texas and California, and has written for various blogs, and most recently was the editor of NewsTaco.

WHAT'S A MEXICAN "SUPPOSED" TO LOOK LIKE?

"You don't look Mexican."

That's a phrase I've heard many times from many people in many different situations. As a light-skinned and green-eyed Latina, people say this to me in a variety of contexts, and I'm not always sure what my response should be - or what response they expect. Would you ever tell a white person that they aren't white? Would you ever tell an African-American that they weren't African-American? I hear the question from whites, African-Americans, Asians, Mexican nationals, Latinos from Latin America, just about everyone - race has no effect on who's asking the question.

Every time I'm asked a flurry of thoughts come to mind. First, I don't understand the question; I don't go around telling people who they are, or who I think they are, so I don't understand why people would do the same to me. I don't know what a Mexican is "supposed" to look like, but I assume the authors of this question have a very particular image (or stereotype) in mind. I wonder how it is that the entirety of my cultural experience can be dismissed so completely in the span of four words.

What, exactly is a Mexican "supposed" to look like? Am I supposed to be wearing a poncho? Am I to be astride a donkey? Do I need a black mustache? What about a sombrero? Shall I be barefoot and pregnant while I'm at it? Once I go down the road of trying to guess the stereotypes of others, the possibilities are limitless.

The point is that, behind that statement are a lot of unfair, prejudicial, perhaps even racist assumptions not only about me, but about anyone who would call themselves Mexican. I've even argued with people who, after I tell them that I am in fact Mexican, insist that it simply cannot be, and drag out the conversation by insisting that I simply cannot be who I say I am. If I can't look Mexican - because my eyes are the wrong color or my skin is not telltale enough - then who *does* get to look Mexican?

If I don't get to be who I say I am, then who does have the power to make those designations?

For the sake of ease, I usually respond to this question by insisting that I am actually Mexican, or saying something like, "Oh, yeah, I get that a lot." Other times, the conversation turns into the "Let's Guess the Race" game, where people try to assign me to an ethnicity or nationality that makes them more comfortable. Sometimes over the phone it's French, other people assume I'm from Argentina or Chile, some people want me to be Spanish or Italian. And there's nothing wrong with being from any of these places. Rather, I don't understand why it makes more sense for me to be from somewhere far away than to be who I say I am.

I personally feel no shame about my ethnicity, culture, family, ancestry, heritage, or whatever you want to call it. I feel no need to lie to people about who I am. On the contrary, I feel proud - especially when I think about my parents and grandparents and ancestors who lived much more difficult lives than myself so that I could live in a world where I could insist that who I say I am matters.

And perhaps this is why I am so bothered by this questioning of my ethnicity: I want everyone else to be as accepting and proud of who I am and where I come from. Every time someone denies who I am, it's more than just a stereotype; it's insistence that who I am is not valuable.

I know we don't live in a perfect world, and I think the fact that we talk about race is important, even a step in the right direction. I don't expect everyone to know everything about me off the bat, but I do expect them to take what I say about myself at face value. I want to live in a world where it's not incredulous to be matter-of-fact about who you are, where the last battle we have to fight is that of being able to just be.

ANDREA J. SERRANO

Albuquerque native Andrea J. Serrano has been writing and performing poetry since 1994. Andrea has been published in various publications including Cantos al Sexto Sol: An Anthology of Aztlanahuac Writings (Rodriguez/Gonzales). Andrea is the youngest of six daughters and credits her family, her ties to land, language and culture and the experience of growing up Chicana in Albuquerque with influencing her writing. Andrea is a member of the band Cultura Fuerte, and is the creator and host of Speak, Poet: Voz, Palabra y Sonido, a monthly poetry venue. Her book, 'My Ranchera Hips Can't Dance Salsa and Other Poems' will be published in 2012.

LAMENT

In response to the Tucson Unified School District's ban on Chicano Studies. All respect to those who fight for freedom.

I want to write angry words about Arizona

fill up line after line of my notebook

with words like hate, ignorance, disbelief and fuck you

poetry filled with bravado

daring Arizona to pick a fight with me

I want to throw a finger at Arizona's villains

the culprits who wish to ban

our history

our books

our people

I want to pen a hateful masterpiece

but the words don't flow

my thoughts are muddled

my voice is frozen

as if Arizona's censoring hand

is gripping my throat

fingers wrapped tight

wanting me to remain silent about the war

that has been waged against my people

This poem is supposed to be about

the Tucson Unified School District's ban of Ethnic Studies

this poem is supposed to be lines of outrage over books

so subversive

they have been banned

Shakespeare, Zinn, Cisneros, Urrea, Alexie, Hooks

and countless others

were shoved into boxes

because they wrote books

by

about

for

Brown people

all people

Opening my US history book in the 11th grade

and not finding a single person who looked like me

felt like a slap in the face

reminded me I am invisible

almost made me lose all hope

until a mentor placed *Occupied America* in my hands

the title alone gave me power and courage

and I was reminded that I am an important part

of this country's history

this poem was meant to be angry

but instead

is bewildered, disgusted, shocked, hurt, sad

this poem is a very confused poet's lament over hate

specifically

hatred of Chicanos and Mexicanos

I don't understand why my people

like so many others

have been targets for violence

since the beginning of our existence

I am not a resident of Arizona

but borders and state lines do not exist

for Indigenous people

we are meant to walk wherever we wish

still, Arizona's influence

spills over to New Mexico

boils over to Texas

seeps into Birmingham

where four little girls

were martyred on September 15, 1963

because they were defenseless

because their lives were deemed worthless

because they were Black

I wait in fear

for four more to die

because they are Mexican

I wait in fear for another Brisenia Flores

a nine year old girl slaughtered in Arizona because

she was Mexican

I wonder why President Obama didn't attend her funeral

I wonder what her killers thought

when they looked into her eyes before ending her short life

I wonder why no one made a big deal about her murder

I wonder why the pro-life right didn't protect her

¡Ban This!

I want to shout my angriest words

but they don't come

maybe because they are being

shouted by the governors

and the tea partiers

the minute-men

and every day folks who have no idea why they hate Brown
people

they just do

I have to pause

because shouting over ignorance

only sounds like more shouting

My words are scribbled in margins

and scrawled across the middle of the page

my throat may be gripped

my history may be banned

but it is not erased

and like the relentless sun beating down on the Arizona desert

we will not be ignored

- Burque, Nuevo Mexico, Aztlán

ΠOEMI MARTINEZ

Noemi Martinez is a Chicana/Boriqua writer, blogger, activist, mother, poet, mixed media artist and superhero sirena living in deep South Texas.

REALITY

The browning of America they say

but it's not evident

until you see who's cooking

your Zen garden bowl of noodles

when we see brown brothers

working in snazzy yuppie catering

establishments on 6th & Congress.

The browning of this meat

can't be seen in the strawberries,

grapes, oranges, onions that

we consume with no

second thought on the thumbs

that blacken

and burn.

The browning in El Paso sand

where voiceless bones are bleached,

the sun tenderly loving the already dead.

Tell me when
when this fucking new dawn

age of revolution will come

tell me when this take over

is scheduled to appear

we've been waiting

for 500 years

with no release in sight.

We've seen too many - too many

raza, the brown folks,

killed, scalped, beheaded, handcuffed, raped, gutted.

Too many of us sent, trained to kill

kill ourselves with lies

of a better tomorrow

a steady paycheck

and we have fucking killed ourselves,

killed each other, misled

signed up for a rich man's war.

We have this history in our blood

of assimilation, acculturation, murder and revelations

cultural genocide, ethnocide

riding on three white horses

yet we repeat the process
ingest, repeat

ingest, repeat

When will this browning of amerikkka

be here

because I am so tired

so fucking tired of

having to reteach to my kid

who Christopher Columbus really was

and what really happened to the "Indians"

and how being brown is not wrong

and there being one black history month

and one "his-panic" month

but I'm trying to teach him

to be a proud Chicano

12 months out of the year.

Calma, Mimi, Calma.

Because I'm trying to teach him

to be nonviolent,

nonsexist,

unmacho

in this fucked up society

where our voice is constantly

being silenced,

repressed,

oppressed.

When the color lines became apparent

to him at two, the class lines at four.

Reality

we were never meant to survive.

HOUSES

all the houses we've lived in have been torn down

the crack house on the corner of 7th and Canal

Street

with the caving in walls,

mice in the fridge.

That baby swing hung

from the tree

years after I left

all the houses

we have lived have been

torn

      down

the lean-to in La Blanca

attached to the owner's house

 my car was leaking gas

we fixed it with a pano

 pregnant me with baby girl

driving a car with leaking gas

handkerchief dangling from

undersides, trailing potential

hazards

it doesn't stand anymore.

all the houses

where we were

have been torn down

the old house next to the church

across the street from Rainy,

who killed himself

that house with two living rooms

from different centuries

the only time

anyone's every taken me flowers

afterwards we fucked in the shed

that house, I saw ghosts

everywhere.

all the houses

where we

were

have been

torn

down

and this ain't a poem

for you

the dead dad

or for you

who's been missing since

that last phone call in 99.

¡Ban This!

This ain't a poem

about the memories

created in houses

you couldn't build up

and this ain't a poem

for you, the dead

my friend from Durham

tried to convince me

some folks are black holes

and tunnel everything

with them-

and did I even see it then

and this ain't a poem

for the dad attached

to the boot that attached

to belly or the words

powerful punches with poison

that try to trip me up

this ain't the poem

for the father

who tried to marry me off

at 17

who with implicit words

said I deserved it

this ain't for the dad

who fucked me up at 9 or 10 or 11

either

this poem is about the crack house

where lines were made

baby girl rooted

deep

blows couldn't shake her

it ain't there no more.

this poem is about the lean-to

in La Blanca-where you

packed your jeans

all tidy and nice

I watched the swaying

of the trees

danced outside

to the moon

with the kid

And I was saved.

this poem is about that house

on 21st with two living rooms

too many doors

too many ghosts

baby girl

still wrinkly

my cuts hadn't healed

the landlady

told me to leave

and you laughed

it's gone

AT THE DRIVE-IN

The county line

Baseline Road east of Cameron County,

towards Mercedes

Frontage road leads

further south

escaping a checkpoint

with no access road,

but us-we go around

hit 3 mile line

halfway between the cities

of Weslaco, the land of

gold untold

and Mercedes, la reina del valle.

we park, at Wes-Mer Drive In

the lot half-filled already

vans, trucks, families with lawn chairs

someone in back has started

a fire, here

they don't check my backpack

 don't ask to look

in my purse-like they do

when we go to the zoo,

museum, or to visit

an exhibit at the chamber

of commerce, of cities

where we've paid taxes,

bought gas for twenty years,

a dining room set on credit

I pretend these

shadows don't exist,

don't mention the yellow

dividing lines to the kids

do they notice?

at checkouts they ask

if I'm paying with food stamps

if I have my Medicaid card

at the doctors--

because I have that look

that is not set but

moves, drives, jumps

at the drive in,

3 vans down, a pregnant teen

sits on an ice chest, her dad

holding hands with mom,

on lawn chairs from Wal-Mart

seven dollars each.

FOR YOU AGAIN

Keep thinking of those holes

you dig for ten bucks each

deep drenches for ranches,

a bandanna in your back pocket.

 The sweat falls

into the sweet earth

seeps, waits for

blood or tears,

sees your years

waits for you

Is your tongue touching the

corner of your lips

like you did when

fixing computers and cars,

when concentrating on

wires

trumpet solos or

el guitarrón

What goes through your head now

living east of the valley

displaced home of ours

twenty sum years

the threads of our roots

spread out thinly,

our names mean nothing

deep in earth,

mean nothing

You travel back

to that place,

a room 10x10

you never say

    much

these lives

overlap

your story

waits

PHYLLIS VICTORIA LOPEZ

Phyllis Victoria Lopez is a Chicana writer who has previously published work in Xalman, Comadre, and the Bilingual Review. She has a BA in Chicano Studies from UC Santa Barbara and an MA in Clinical Psychology from Antioch University, Santa Barbara.

THE POOR

Today, I heard you call

my name, hermano

And for a brief moment

I thought you had returned

to the two-room shack

that we had grown up in

There were no white picket fences

to greet you outside

Only weeds that had grown

waist high

and a '57 Chevy

that groaned

every time the starter was turned

with a key

¡Ban This!

Years ago,

we squatted under Tia Chuy's

front porch

and unearthed

a leash of worms

with our bare hands

When the heat

flared

like a match,

we scaled a tree

in the back yard

and hid under a cluster

of leaves

Peering through the lens

of a rolled up newspaper,

we saw a carload

of brown faces

pull into town

with their car windows rolled down

Mumbling in Spanish

a neighbor

pointed them in the direction

of the labor camps where

brown-eyed children

sleep side by side

And field hands

stoop over

long rows of cotton

with sacks

slung over their shoulders

and handkerchiefs

tied around their necks

like winter scarves

Soon, swirls of dust

will gather like lint

around their ankles

and beads of perspiration

will drop from their foreheads

as they shuffle

from one row to the next

When this hour

comes to a day's end

we leave this place

in the same dirty clothes

we had arrived in

While the prayers

that we offered on behalf

of the poor

rose like a deep sigh

high in the heavens.

THE JOURNEY

As I stand before a window

and watch the evening's darkness

spill Eastward, I remember

how we gathered

before the crack of dawn

with our hands

in our pockets

and our eyes half shut

beneath a cloak of chilled air

Every day was the same

a flatbed truck

would pull up beside us

to carry us

across the tracks

to a field that blossomed white

with cotton

The front door would open

like a hungry mouth

and a driver would greet us

without words.

with a nod of the head,

we climbed into the back

where we sat, shoulder to shoulder

and listened to each other sigh

as the cold slowly descended upon us

like an army of soldiers

pursuing an enemy

in a foreign land

we pressed forward

with our headlights

clearing a pathway

beneath an umbrella of stars.

PICKERS

When the sunlight seeps through

my window

to shimmer on the floor

Trucks rattle down a

trackless road

and only a whirl of dust

is left behind.

in the back, familiar

faces nod like broken candles;

Newcomers sit quietly

like sacks on a shelf, waiting.

It won't be long until they scatter

like a handful of seeds

from one field to another,

and cut across summer-long

rows of cotton.

RODOLFO ACUÑA

Dr. Rodolfo Acuña is a Chicana/o historian and professor emeritus at California State University, Northridge. He is the author of Occupied America: A History of Chicanos, which approaches the history of the Southwestern United States that includes Mexican Americans. Dr. Acuña is also an activist and he has supported the numerous causes of the Chicano Movement. He has also written for the Los Angeles Times, The Los Angeles Herald-Express, La Opinión, and numerous other newspapers. His work emphasizes the struggle of the Mexican American people. Acuña is also the author of The Making of Chicana/o Studies: In the Trenches of Academe , Anything But Mexican and Corridors of Migration: The Odyssey of Mexican Laborers.

WORSE OFF TODAY THAN IN THE SIXTIES:

WHO GIVES A DAMN?

Teresa Wiltz in *America's Wire* writes that despite claims of increased educational opportunities for minorities that the performance of black and Latino teenagers remains the same or lower than 30 years ago. In fact, the math and reading performance of black and Latino high school seniors equal that of 13-year-old white students – so much for the post racial society.

Educators and liberal politicos point the finger at low expectations, inequality of resources, less qualified teachers, the income inequality, teacher bias, and inexperienced teachers. They throw in the tracking of black and brown students into remedial class while whites are put into university bound classes.

Further, minority students are more likely to be given "A's" for work that would receive a "C" in a rich school giving the illusion that they are being educated. Society would not tolerate this record in a football team at any level, or for that matter if we had fewer weapons of mass destruction than 30 years ago.

However, in my view, the major reason for the lack of progress of Mexican American and other minorities is society's historical amnesia or more aptly its Alzheimer disorder that erases the memory of previous efforts or commitments to bridge the gap between black, brown and white – rich and poor.

The truth be told, educators pay less attention today to Mexican Americans than they did 50 years ago. In the sixties educators and reporters at least talked about it. The late *Los Angeles Times'* columnist Ruben Salazar attacked the dropout problem and the failure of the schools to devise a relevant curriculum, as well as the failure to recruit and train effective Mexican American teachers.

In February 1963, Salazar began a series on Mexican American education. He titled his first article, "What Causes Jose's Trouble in School?: Mexican-Americans Problems Analyzed." Salazar begins,

"Kicked out of school, Jose Mendez at 16 has been trapped in a peculiar twilight zone of American life. They tested him, graded him and pigeonholed him…say some educators, the fault may lie in the tests and the teachers – not in Jose. Educational policy and curriculum are oriented towards the education of the middle-class, monolingual, monocultural English-speaking student … [Jose] is at a great disadvantage…[he] is a hyphenated American, a Mexican-American … he is culturally confused."

Salazar interviewed educators, Drs. George I. Sánchez, Paul Sheldon, Julian Samora and high school teacher Marcos de Leon on why José was dropping out of school. They attributed the dropout problem to the Mexican American's inferiority complex, which has intensified his marginalization.

Salazar blamed the schools for the Mexican Americans' failure. Schools nurtured a negative self-image, which was reinforced by the movies and literature, and failed to correct the stereotyping of poor Mexicans. It was a vicious cycle: the schools did think Mexicans could not learn, students developed a low esteem, they failed and dropped out.

The experts advocated bilingual-bicultural education, and initially there was a consensus for these programs, from President Lyndon B. Johnson to Republican St. Ronald Reagan. Yet, the Greek Chorus gained traction and labeled the programs separatist, un-American and racist. This nativist movement allied itself with right wing think tanks and foundations, and by the beginning of the 21st century, bilingual ed died a violent death.

By and large educators were mute as bilingual programs were wiped out and university based teacher training programs specializing on Mexican Americans were eliminated. At teacher training institutions grade point average was favored over knowledge of the child's background. Although Latinos comprised 75 percent of the Los Angeles Unified School District, student teachers were given minimal preparation on how to teach Latino students.

The dropout was one of the major reasons for the development of Chicano Studies in 1969. A solution was sought for the high dropout problem that was overexposing Latino students to a life of poverty and, not incidentally, to the Vietnam draft. One of my first books *Cultures in Conflict: Case Studies of the Mexican American* **was written for fifth graders. The purpose was to build a positive image in order to facilitate the acquisition of skills. These skills would prepare students to enter which ever field they wanted.**

The importance of self-image is common sense. I remember looking for engineering computer lab with my future wife at UCLA in the 1980s. We asked several students if they knew where the computer lab was. They all gave us blank looks. Finally, we asked a Latino student who told us to ask an Asian. We did and she told us where it was. Talking to Asian fiends they told me that they exceled in math because the teachers expected them to.

Looking back at my own life, I was fortunate that I ended up in a Jesuit high school where I had to take four years of Latin. My relatives would notice my Latin book on the table, would ask my mother who it belonged to, and they would remark that Rudy must be smart. In contrast, in the first grade, before I knew English, I was pushed out of public school as mentally retarded.

When I became smart, that is adhered to their rules, anytime a Mexican student would act up, other teachers would ask me why? When I told them, they generally did not like the answer. They thought I was flip when I said that my solution for the marginalization of Mexicans was to rewrite the bible and substitute the word Mexican for Israeli. In a couple of decades, Mexicans would start looking at themselves as the "chosen people."

This identity has helped Jews survive and endure over 2,000 years of persecution. In my view it comes down to self-image.

This was the premise of the Tucson Unified School District's program. It was the repairing the damage done by marginalization – of being written out of history. The thinking was that learning history, literature and the arts though their viewpoint would repair the image of the greaser, the loser and the numerous other stereotypes.

From the beginning, the xenophobes tried to send the Mexican American Studies program down the same path as bilingual education. It was unpatriotic to learn any language other than English, it was un-American to learn history other than the American way.

The reasoning ignored the past; it was as if the debates of the sixties and seventies never occurred. They disregarded pedagogical principles that even St. Ronald accepted.

One of the books banned in Tucson was Paulo Freire's *Pedagogy of the Oppressed*. It was based on a highly successful literacy campaign conducted in Brazil. The xenophobes' main argument is that Freire was a Marxist, which is ridiculous since the pedagogy goes back to Socrates. With that aside, would we cast aside a cure for cancer because the researcher was a Marxist?

The Cambium Learning Corp's Curriculum Audit of the Tucson Mexican American Studies Department which was commissioned by Arizona Superintendent of Schools John Huppenthal and cost the $177,000 concluded,

> *"No observable evidence exists that instruction within Mexican American Studies Department promotes resentment towards a race or class of people. The auditors observed the opposite, as students are taught to be accepting of multiple ethnicities of people. MASD teachers are teaching Cesar Chavez alongside Martin Luther King, Jr. and Gandhi, all as peaceful protesters who sacrificed for people and ideas they believed in. Additionally, all ethnicities are welcomed into the program and these very students of multiple backgrounds are being inspired and taught in the same manner as Mexican American students. All evidence points to peace as the essence for program teachings. Resentment does not exist in the context of these courses observable evidence exists that instruction within Mexican American Studies Department promotes resentment towards a race or class of people ... No evidence as seen by the auditors exists to indicate that instruction within Mexican American Studies Department program classes advocates ethnic solidarity; rather it has been proven to treat student as individuals."*

There has not been any credible proof to refute claims that the program has improved chances of graduation, improved the students' self-images, and motivated them to pursue a higher education.

A society that has historical dementia or Alzheimers cannot correct the defects of the present just like it cannot correct racism, sexism or homophobia.

Stupidity and fanaticism led to the destruction of the most transformative movements in Latin American, Liberation Theology. The forces of reaction in order to protect the large landowners redbaited Liberation Theology and substituted a reactionary evangelical Christian movement that promised that their reward would come in the next world. So it is in Arizona.

With the destruction of Mexican American Studies and the banning of the books, Mexican Americans are being put in their place. Vicariously, they are burning the infidels. The difference is that students are fighting back! They are reading books and will remember that anybody can learn.   It is their right.

GIVING HYPOCRISY A BAD NAME

Censorship in Tucson

For the past six years or so I have heard constant threats from Arizona Attorney General Tom Horne (Canada) and Superintendent of Schools John Huppenthal (Indiana) that they were going to ban, destroy and wipe out Mexican American Studies, as well as Occupied America. Now after disregarding a $177,000 report that refutes their charges that the program and the book are racist and un-American, the nativists carry out their threats. They destroy MAS and snatch the books from on looking students. Their stupidity exposed them, so they now say it wasn't so.

The problem is that witnesses saw Tucson Unified School District Superintendent John Pedicone's (Illinois) swaggering thugs "remove" the books from MAS classes as students looked on.

Their cowardly behavior reached new lows when blogger Jeff Biggers wrote that the books had been "banned." They protested that they were not "banned" but only "removed."

Let me see if I understand: If the books would have been put on a prohibited list of readings they would have been banned, or better still censored. But, because they were already there and ripped from the sight of students, they were removed.

I have been visiting Tucson for the better part of my life. I could always understand white folk there, although I did not always agree with them. For example, Barry Goldwater was my ideological opposite, but he had an affinity for Arizona that few of the carpetbaggers such as Pedicone have today. He knew many of my relatives, and recognized that you better talk the talk.

Not so with the Arizona carpetbaggers (as distinguished from those of the 1860s who had a purpose). This recent bunch has moved there for the sun and the cash. They do not respect the environment, its traditions or the people. Witness the systematic destruction of Mexican American barrios. What is Old Town Tucson but a pseudo replica of Disney Land?

It is difficult to dumb down language to the level of the locust. So to start with, censorship is thought control. The First Amendment reads,

> *"Congress shall make no law respecting an establishment of religion, or prohibiting the free exercise thereof; or abridging the freedom of speech, or of the press; or the right of the people peaceably to assemble, and to petition the government for a redress of grievances…"*

Thomas Jefferson and James Madison argued that this freedom was critical to a free society.

What is happening in Tucson is a political act designed to control what students and the community read and think. It is not a question of good taste or what is true or not. It was the intentional use of naked political power to suppress a particular people.

Huppenthal was elected on the platform of "stopping La Raza [the people]."

On May 12, 2010 Horne said, "The bill [HB2281] was written to target the Chicano, or Mexican American, studies program in the Tucson school system." According to the Los Angeles Times, "He singled out one history book used in some classes, 'Occupied America: A History of Chicanos,' by Rodolfo Acuna, a professor and founder of the Chicano studies program at Cal State Northridge."

Horne continued, "To begin with, the title of the book implies to the kids that they live in occupied America, or occupied Mexico." Horne's language was pretty clear. He did not say remove but targeted the book and MAS.

As with Horne, others have labeled the book Marxist. A prominent scholar of European history labeled Occupied America, a Marxist book. When pressed on what he based this assumption, he fumbled around and finally said in a deposition that I used the term "hegemony" several times in the text.

In Horne's case, he did not like the title because, according to him, it "implies" that the United States invaded Mexico – a historical fact. Evidentially, Horne has not read the autobiography of Ulysses S. Grant or Abraham Lincoln's take on the war.

The truth be told, Occupied America does not refer to occupied Mexico; it refers to occupied America. If Horne had a grasp of Latin American history or geography, he would know that Argentines, Peruvians, Cubans, Central Americans and Mexicans are Americans. Indeed, U.S. secretaries of state have exploited the notion of Pan Americanism for economic advantage.

Thus the occupation began in 1492 not 1836 or 1848.

The touted Cambium Audit, which Horne's successor Huppenthal ordered and the citizens of Arizona paid for, said, Occupied America: A History of Chicanos is an unbiased, factual textbook designed to accommodate the growing number of Mexican-Americans or Chicano History courses. It is the most comprehensive text in this market according to Amazon. The Fifth Edition of Occupied America has been revised to make the text more user-friendly and student-oriented., while maintain its passionate voice. This text provides a comprehensive, in-depth analysis of the major historical experiences of Chicanos that invokes critical thinking and intellectual discussion.

The curriculum auditing team refutes the following allegations made by other individuals and organizations. Quotes have been taken out of context. Therefore, the 'controversial' aspects are indicated in italics to demonstrate the claims made by concerned constituents.

Thus the nativists' hypocrisy gives opportunism a bad name. They care nothing about the truth, they care nothing about Latino students, what they care about is controlling thought by "removing" books and killing a highly successful program.

They want to specifically suppress the thought of Latinos. The reason that they have not targeted Native, African and Asian Americans is that these groups are smaller and consequently more manageable. Latino public school students comprise 43 percent of the public schools, and they want to genetically engineer them.

Everyone in this country should be concerned about the removing or banning of books. They are euphemisms for censorship. What happened in Tucson constitutes an attack and constraint on everyone's freedom.

The locust have a history of trying to control Mexican American Studies through prior restraint. When this did not work, they demolished the program and banned the books. This banning will have a chilling effect on the publication of future books. Usually, there is the opportunity to dispute the charge in court. This has not happened in Arizona – there was no trial.

Aside from Occupied America, Critical Race Theory by Richard Delgado, 500 Years of Chicano History in Pictures edited by Elizabeth Martinez, Message to Aztlan by Rodolfo Corky Gonzales, Chicano! The History of the Mexican Civil Rights Movement by Arturo Rosales. Pedagogy of the Oppressed by Paulo Freire, Rethinking Columbus: The Next 500 Years edited by Bill Bigelow and Bob Peterson, William Shakespeare, The Tempest, more than a dozen other books have been banned.

The charges of censorship have shaken the administration. After acting brazenly they are drawing the distinction between "banned" and "removed." However, the record is the record. The banning of the books did not occur in a vacuum.

I have personally never experienced this level of hypocrisy in over fifty years of activism. It seems as if the locust and I do not speak the same language. It is also frustrating because up to now no one seemed to be listening. How do you deal with people who lie with such impunity?

As for me, it is a badge of honor to appear on the same list as the other banned authors. But what I resent is the draft dodgers, Pedicone, Horne and Huppenthal questioning my patriotism. I volunteered draft during the Korean War although I had a student draft deferment. They should check the records; they will learn that Mexican Americans served at a much higher ratio than any group in Tucson.

So my advice to them is not be so be opportunistic and hypocritical. The Tucson cabal is giving these words a bad name. Horne said that 2281 targeted Mexicans and specified which books it was going to get rid of. Huppenthal has not listened to facts and pressured the TUSD to ban MAS and the books. As for Pedicone, he is the bagman.

SANTINO J. RIVERA

Santino J. Rivera (aka S.J. Rivera, S. Joaquin Rivera), is an independent publisher, author and editor. Originally from Denver, Colorado, Rivera now calls Saint Augustine, Florida home. He is the owner of Broken Sword Publications, LLC and his books include 'Demon in the Mirror', 'Amerikkkan Stories' and' ¡Ban This! The BSP Anthology of Xican@ Literature'. Rivera is a former EMT and journalist. He is a regular contributor to Pocho.com and Aztlán Reads.

THE BALLAD OF TROY DAVIS

Death looms in Georgia

like a ghost from another era

welcoming parishioners, protesters and producers

to taste yet again

the strange fruit

Live from the set of death row!

and sponsored by doubt, rage and indifference

it all goes down on a Wednesday evening of censored truths

and ill consequences

where we learn time and again

there is no justice

just us

If all the world's a stage

then all eyes on the Peach state

on this date: 09:21:2011

where a man waits to bate his last breath

face his accusers and say:

I am Troy Davis and I *am* a man

Just like countless others who held signs

and marched

and said the same thing

until they died with a glimmer of hope

in their eyes

and cold doubt in their still hearts

I am Troy Davis

and I am a man

despite anything you say

there is more than a *reasonable* doubt

I am not guilty of this crime

blood be on *your* hands this night

and may God have mercy on *your* soul

and teach the world that

not all the king's lawyers

nor all the king's men

not even countless supporters, webcasts or media sharks

could put Troy Davis back together again

because it takes a nation of millions to prove that

though the days of tree hangings may be in the rearview mirror

when They want you dead

you will die

not only three times

but 1,000

and again until

the crowd is pregnant with doubt

of there ever being such a thing as justice

And so everything turns dark

and we all die a little this evening

full dark, no stars

full dark, no stars

full dark, no stars

nor soul

KILLING THE MESSENGER

(For Gary Webb)

Sometimes, when you dig deep enough
people are kind and write suicide notes
so that you don't have to

And you get not one
but two bullet holes in the head
in the wake of what they will say was depression

Because dead men know all too well
that when you find yourself covered in enough dirt
someone always comes looking to fill in the holes

Left by those who would rather
die standing on two feet
than survive kneeling on a rotting body of lies

And though the news would rather spin a tale
of government assassination as something new under the sun
dead men with stories to tell know better

Stories of desert drones with corporate loans

of magic bullets and liars pulpits
stories with code name killings and Faux news cheering

stories from the Audubon Ballroom
stories from the Ambassador Hotel
stories from the Silver Dollar Bar
stories from the Lorraine Motel
stories of CIA conspiracies,
crack cocaine and secret wars
stories live from Georgia's death row,
justice nevermore

And so they preach that the truth shall set you free!
(Hall-lee-lou-al-yehh!)
if sometimes that freedom means death
(and a last minute plea)
for the killing of the messenger
let's everyone sleep better at night in these United States
 of deaf, dumb and blind
where convenience rules
and no one minds
a little lie,
a giant lie,
an endless lie
it's all the same
here where the dark alliances
control the game

NEVER FORGET

Never forget!
(or so they say)
that's exactly what it says on the bumper sticker
on the pick-up/SUV/sedan/beater/cop car
in bright red, white and blue letters
but maybe just a little more red...
  the t-shirt
  the tattoo
  the timeless classic on network TV
  the banners
  the ribbons
  the parades
  the monuments
  the pages of the rewritten history books
  the speeches
Never forget!
the day the towers fell and buried
the rest of history underneath it
never forget wounded knee
never forget the emancipation proclamation
never forget 3/5ths of a man
never forget the Treaty of Guadalupe Hildalgo
never forget slave plantations and human bondage
never forget small pox infected blankets
never forget sour deals, free lunch meals
or public school no. 23
never forget Joaquin Murrietta's head in a jar
native skin with battle scars
the assassination of Che
of MLK
of Malcolm X and all the rest

never forget manifest destiny
never forget Timothy McVeigh
never forget all the bodies buried
in the Aztlán desert
never forget lines drawn in the sand
stolen land
shackled hands
never forget 1492
or 1942
the demonization of so-called savages
and invented gods and rules (and rulers!)
never forget bombs over Bahgdad
over Japan, Iran, Afghanistan and abroad
never forget the secret wars
the crack cocaine
nor the profits reaped from them
never forget the lynching
the wholesale murder of the People
never forget the people of the sun
never forget sb1070
the internment camps
never forget Wounded Knee
never forget Leonard Peltier
or Mumia Abu-Jamal
never forget Subcomandante Marcos
or the EZLN
never forget Troy Davis
Oscar Grant
Trayvon Martin
Brisenia Flores
Or countless others
never forget Operation Northwoods
never forget Operation Wetback
never forget the Chicano Moratorium
never forget the police brutality
never forget the casualties
never forget the Patriot Act
nor the lies perpetuated to pass it into law

never forget the original occupation
the indoctrination
the riots
the tear gas
or the wool being pulled over the eyes of the nation
never forget the liars
the killers
the rapists
the colonizers
never forget the inquisition
never forget that they have never let go of their hatred
never forget the white-washers
never forget the book banners
never forget the silencers
never forget them
never forget their inhumanity

never forget!
never forget!
Never Forget!
never
forget
ever

because the first casualty in any conflict
is always the truth

remember that

THERE'S NO SUCH THING AS REVERSE RACISM!

There's no such thing as reverse racism!
said the White slave to the Black plantation owner
Yeah, that's true, boy
the Black plantation owner said
Now get your White ass back work!
Crack goes the Master's whip
and away we go

There's no such thing as reverse racism!
said the White indigenous tribal leader to the Red colonizers
We know!
they said in turn and smiled
and burned several of the White people in a fire
Crackle goes the wood burning in the fire
and away we go

There's no such thing as reverse racism!
said the White kid who was face down on the concrete
with the knee of a Black police officer in his back
I know that, bitch
the Black cop said
as he shot the White kid in the back
Blam! goes the round from the barrel of a gun
and away we go

There's no such thing as reverse racism!
shouted the White indigenous farming community in Iraq

We know!
said the Middle Eastern pilots who were dropping
several tons of explosives on the White man's land
Boom goes the ignition of a warhead
and away we go

There's no such thing as reverse racism!
said the deformed White fetus in a jar to the Vietnamese scientist
I know that already, he said
and turned to burn more evidence of chemical warfare
Flash goes the volatile chemicals in the blaze
and away we go

There's no such thing as reverse racism!
screamed the White Zoot Suiter to the Mexican Navy Men
We know that!
they said and chuckled
as they beat him, stripped him and raped his wife
Snap goes the sound of a cranial fracture
and away we go

There's no such thing as reverse racism!
said the White Natives as they gasped for breath on dying land
we know said the Red military men
as they bulldozed a row of shitty government housing
to make room for a mega-mall
Smash goes the sound of 'free' housing collapsing
and away we go

There's no such thing as reverse racism!
said the elderly White man carrying his groceries
we know, honkey, said the jack-booted kids
from the Black supremacist gang
as they kicked the shit out of him and spray painted
'Whitey Go Home' on his garage

¡Ban This!

Psssssst goes the paint from the spray can
and away we go

There's no such thing as reverse racism!
said the elderly woman boarding the bus
the Black driver looked at her and said:
I know, Cracker! Get in the back of the bus!
The wheels of the bus go round and round
and away we go

There's no such thing as reverse racism!
said the little White girls burning to death
in their church
We know that!
said the Black KKK men throwing the Molotov cocktails
The wind carries the cries from the White church
And away we go

There's no such thing as reverse racism!
whispered the White man hanging from a tree
I know, said the all Black jury that convicted him
of a crime he did not commit
as they tied the noose round his neck
Shhhhh whispers the strange fruit
and away we go

There's no such thing as reverse racism!
cried the White man on death row
who was refused clemency
We all know that already
said the Black warden
As he pulled the switch
BZzzzzzzzt goes the sound of justice system
and away we go

There's no such thing as reverse racism!
yelled the crowd of White people
detained for not having their papers

we know that already, shut the fuck up!
replied the Mexican guards readying the trains to take them
away
Toot-toot goes the sound of the train whistle
and away we go

There's no such thing as reverse racism!
cried the disproportional number of White men in jail, in unison
We know that!
replied the chorus of Black and Mexican judges
Boom goes the sound of the Judge's gavel in court
and away we go

There's no such thing as reverse racism!
moaned the students in the Amerikkkan history class
we know that already!
said the Arizona school board
as they boxed up their books and put them away
for 'safe keeping'
the sound of censorship was so loud
that the silence was deafening
and away we go…

OF CODICES AND CULTURE

The stone is cast

what we do now

is pick up

the pieces

of broken glass

and try not to bleed to death

from wounds

opened by extreme

prejudice

and the censorship

of an invisible people

who walk the lines

between a pejorative

and a falsehood

still lost in a world

of confusion, scorn

and manipulation

the paradox

endures!

You can fire a bullet

into my head

with weapons fashioned from

hate

you can lock me up

under charges of

dissent

¡Ban This!

ban my books, pictures and art

seal them away in boxes

to collect the dust of bigots
lie, cheat and steal

as your ancestors before you

but nothing you do or say

will erase these words

this history

these stories

this culture

La Raza!

Our modern codices

will not be burned

no history

is ever

illegal

We *will* endure!

COME TO HEAVEN (IT'S WHITER HERE!)

Come to heaven

It's Whiter here

¡Ban This!

(Psst...*nicer* here)

No Blacks

No terrorists

No Indians

No Chinese

No illegals asking: por favor (that means 'please')

Steve Jobs is here!

The Macho Man, Ryan Dunn

Elvis and John Lennon too

Ronald Fucking Reagan, Liz Taylor

John Wayne and Charlton Heston

All have paid their dues

Pearly gates, pasty cherubs and wait...

(*Um, no...those people are down there. Yes, there...*)

Anyway, rejoice!

Hallelujah! We have Wi-Fi

And Starbucks

And pie!

And of course, the iPhone 5

And all the privilege you can shake a cloud at

It's really, really, *really* nice

We all sit-in and laugh and dance

and craft and play forever and a day

we are the people who keep heaven bright

We, the 99%

who are always White (and right!)

so when it's your turn to enter the gates

make sure your skin is just the right shade

for we all know that those who's pigment is less than perfect

are never seen (and never heard from)

White is divine

White is sacred

White is eternal

White is sated

Amen.

THE ST. AUGUSTINE MOVEMENT, 1964: A POEM

I live here

I've fished here, surfed, broke bread

started a family

here

where there are ghosts everywhere

and not just of civil rights warriors

but of conquistadors and slaves

heartbroken Natives and gleeful mass murderers

domestic terrorists in white sheets

all trying to tell you their history

because civic leaders have tried to

hide it

bury it

drown it

erase it

change it

put in on the so-called bad side of town

while hawking trinkets

maps and train rides

creating a tourist industry around a place

that conquered

divided

and saw not so human people

sell human beings like cattle

and so we continue on in this so-called paradise

blind, deaf, dumb

watching not so historical reenactments

soaking up the rich HIStory

while tossing wishful coins into fountains

and dining where bloodshed and tears have stained the earth

waiting for the hand of God

to wash it all away

NOTHING TO SEE HERE

The police DO NOT want citizens recording them

The police DO NOT want the media recording them

The police will police themselves

The police will replace the media in all instances of:

broken law

broken bones

and broken homes

The police will disperse:

Accurate

reliable

and timely information

in accordance with the standards

we have come to expect from them

The police WILL NOT be subjected to your scrutiny

The police WILL NOT be under the watch of anyone's eye

they have their own and it is watching you

right now

The police know what's best for the populace

The police department does not require transparency

The police would never try to cover up

anything

The police are not in the business of controlling information

The police

are

in

control

Carry on, citizen

NOTHING TO SEE HERE.

LITERALLY.

I AM NOT A TACO

I am not a taco

I am not a burrito

I am not a plate of nachos

with pickled jalapeños and black olives

I am not a bottle of Tapatío

I am not a bottle of Cholula

I am not a packet of hot sauce with a catchy phrase

on it telling you what an asshole you are

I am not a Corona,

a Tecate

or a bottle of Cuervo

I am not a daily especial con frijoles y arroz

or con goddamned sour cream

I am not illegal

I am not Hispanic

I am not Latino

I am not a voting bloc

I am not here

I am not there

I am not a statistic

I am not undocumented

I am not on the news

I am not at Home Depot

wearing tattered clothes

smeared in the dirt

waiting for the call of hard labor

to cut your fuckin' grass

lay the foundation for your dream home

or build your pool

I am not invisible

I am not in the fields

I am not putting food on your table

I am not cleaning hotel rooms

I am not cooking food at a trendy franchise restaurant

I am not first generation anything

I am not a dreamer

I am not a demographic

I am not a chess piece

I am not voting for you

I am not banned

I am not a big butt and a smile

I am not a firecracker

I am not hot-blooded

I am not in a gang

I am not in a cartel

I am the not a scapegoat

I am not a token

I am not a savage

I am not White

I am not uneducated

I am not on a hot new network sitcom

perpetuating ages old stereotypes

I am not a specialized website

I am not a Twitter account

I am none of these things

I simply am.

Xicano

LIBRARIAN'S CREED

This is my library. There are many like it, but this one is mine.
My library is my best friend. It is my life. I must master it as
I must master my life.

My library, without me, is useless. Without my library, I am useless. I must use my library true. I must read better than my enemy who is trying to ban my books. I must read, write and educate minds everywhere before he succeeds.

I will…

My library and myself know that what counts in this war is not the shows we watch, the noise on the radio, or the buzz online. We know that it is the books that count.

We will read…

Before God, I swear this creed. My library and myself are the defenders of my country. We are the masters of our enemy.

We are the saviors of my life.

So be it, until ignorance is conquered and there is no illiteracy, but knowledge!

LALO ALCARAZ

Born in San Diego and raised on the border, Lalo Alcaraz is an award winning artist and has been dubbed the most prolific Chicano artist in the nation. Based out of Los Angeles, he is the creator of the first nationally-syndicated, politically-themed Latino daily comic strip, "La Cucaracha," and co-host of KPFK's 'Pocho Hour of Power'. Alcaraz co-founded the seminal Chicano humor 'zine, 'POCHO Magazine' as well as the political satire comedy group 'Chicano Secret Service'. He is also Jefe in Chief of the infamous satirical website, Pocho.com. Lalo's books include 'Migra Mouse: Political Cartoons On Immigration, 'La Cucaracha' and 'Latino USA: A Cartoon History'. Alcaraz can be found online at @ lalolcaraz and at LaloAlcaraz.com.

XICANO X

Xicano X is a self-proclaimed writer and a thinker on a variety of issues related to Xicano/a culture, popular or otherwise. He is also a self-proclaimed insurgent within the university's educational system. On his free time he continues to search for Aztlan via archaeological digs. Xicano X keeps a blog at: xicanox.blogspot.com.

OF TOILETS AND BASKETS

Or a Piece of Cultural Studies Scholarshit

Today, after I finished giving my toilet a good scrubbing, I tried to flush it to dispose of the toilet bowl cleaner and grime, but the handle on the toilet broke. Luckily, I didn't leave a huge floating leñazo in the water, because the stench alone probably would have been enough for the people coming to fix it, to wear hazmat suits before going in. Well I guess more like luckily for them, all they need to do is go in and fix the handle and not worry about handling any toxic material (I had frijoles with chorizo this morning).

Anyhow, after putting in the maintenance order I began to reminisce about my history and toilet paper disposal. Along with this I thought about our culture as Chicanos/as and/or Mexicanos/as. There are some things that we grow up with and that's how we experience them. I started thinking about Chicano/a Studies and the many scholarly articles on Chicano/a culture that are published in respected journals.

I wondered if anybody had written about the cultural experience they've had with what happens after they wipe their ass? I'm not talking about washing your hands, but before that. The academic question plaguing me today is: Do you toss your soiled toilet paper in the basket next to the toilet or do you flush it down the toilet?

I know - I'm sure there are many great minds that discussed and argued this going back to the philosophers Plato and Socrates. A debate that I'm sure many current Chicano/a Studies scholars also argue over and probably discuss before and after sessions (probably even during) at the National Association of Chicano and Chicana Scholars Conference. There has to be someone, who has commented on this, maybe Jose Antonio Burciaga who wrote some humorous stuff about Chicano/a culture in his now canonical *Drink Cultura*. I think that maybe Gustavo

Arrellano of *Ask a Mexican* might have written about this in response to someone who asked about this situation.

Regardless of whether one of the great Chicano/a minds has written about it yet or not, I began to reflect on my own cultural experience. Growing up, my family had gotten all of us to toss our freshly soiled tp into a basket - a basket that usually had a plastic grocery bag sitting inside of it. As far as I knew, this was how everybody did it, regardless of race or creed. But it wasn't until I arrived at college that I found that we Mexicans were wrong in practicing this in a more civilized country!

I found that I was wrong during Spring Break down in Rosarito, Mexico. A few friends and I were sharing a hotel room and I proceeded to put in work on the toilet. After, I tossed the used toilet paper into the basket next to the toilet, washed my hands, felt my stomach more at ease after long night of beer and tacos, and stepped out to get ready for a night of binge drinking.

Not long after, I had a friend go in and do the same, except that after stepping out he said, "Ewww, did you toss your nasty ass brown shitted-on toilet paper into that basket?"

My response was pretty much, "yeah," and I looked at him like he was crazy for asking, or like he had done something wrong. But I guess my toilet paper was shit-side facing up, so it was hard for him not to notice.

Nevertheless he said "Ew, that's nasty!"

"Why?" I asked, still not understanding the problem and having always tossed shit-encrusted toilet paper into the basket at my parent's home and at my aunt's and uncle's places as well.

"You need to flush that shit down the toilet! You nasty!"

I laughed and said, "Shut the fuck up."

I seriously didn't believe him. It's not like we discussed how to get rid of ass-wiped toilet paper in grade school. I never even used the stalls at school; I'd wait till I'd get home. The only thing I'd do at school was take a leakiazo.

He started laughing and then asked if that's what I've always done. Which I did…up until I'd arrived at college.

The first year I lived in the dorms I used the stalls and flushed my tp, as opposed to walking out of the stall with my pants half way down my ass just so I could toss the tp into a bin. Apparently common sense hadn't really kicked in outside of the dorms.

Eventually, I got into this discussion with a friend about proper shit-smeared toilet paper disposal etiquette. I thought my friend got rid of his tp the same way I did but he said, "Hell nah!, My parents woulda' beat my ass if I put shit in the basket!"

Then I asked him why have a basket next to the toilet?

"To throw away tissue when you blow your nose, or when women do their makeup and use tissue to wipe away their mascara n'shit. Or like if you pluck your nose hairs! Fuckin' Mexican!"

I *still* couldn't fully believe my friend; he was trying to dispel something that for me had been not only a habit, but (gasp!) a cultural thing as well.

Ultimately, as we walked through the lobby to go get some dinner, my friend stopped and asked the woman at the desk if all Mexicans tossed their toilet paper into a basket after they wiped their ass.

She kind of laughed and realized that wasn't an attempt at a pick-up line (not that she would appreciate being picked up with an opening about fecal matter and toilet paper), but she answered his question nonetheless, saying that it was common, but usually or only in poor neighborhoods that didn't have appropriate plumbing. She told him that flushed tp can cause a backup in the septic system, so they tossed the paper into the basket. Then, when the bag was full they'd toss the bag out into a larger dump.

My friend couldn't really help laughing. I couldn't either to a certain extent, because there was some irony in all of this: mainly that what the woman was saying was that everybody in my family (and extended family) were poor or lower class because we did this.

I grew up tossing my tp in a basket - it wasn't questioned - and Mexican kids weren't taught to question. If for some reason, we tossed our tp into the toilet and it got backed up, we'd get yelled out or we'd get a chinga - and that's how we would eventually learn why we don't put anything in the toilet but our mierda.

The lesson was hard and well learned but I had to unlearn it in college. What that woman said wasn't really surprising, but I apparently had not realized the implications class had in all of this.

Upon returning to our college town, my friend couldn't stop talking about the tp incident. We went to stay at a another friend's place because the semester was going to commence in a couple of days, so he brought up the subject matter to the roommate of our friend who replied, "No man, we always flushed our toilet paper. But I'll kick your ass if you leave your toilet paper just lying outside."

We kept talking about this and laughing about it.

I would eventually discuss this with my family, but for them it was a nonissue, we just didn't flush our toilet paper, but we did try to pick up the new habit. It didn't work out and our toilet got backed up right away (and this was in the U.S.). Then again, it could have been that there were about seven us living in the house - imagine the variance of tp that each person used, and how many times that toilet was flushed. It created a volatile situation for our poor toilet.

Our aunts and uncles were in a similar dilemma because they lived the Mexican interpretation of the American dream; purchasing a home, but having about three or four other families living in the same house and at times, out in a smaller trailer in the back to make the mortgage payment. Our toilet was lucky compared to the toilets in those homes.

The more I thought about it, I realized there were probably times I went to the homes of distant relatives and left a nice scrunched up wad of toilet paper with a smattering of brown juxtaposed against the white, making the room smell like something that you could only imagine coming from the Saw film franchise.

That family might have taken offense to having my shitty tp in their basket and I didn't even know it because I was taught that that was what I suppose to do. But then again, a family would be equally offended if you clogged up there toilet not because of your massive leñazos, but because you decided to flush your voluminous wads of toilet paper down their weak plumbing system.

Flash forward to Fall 2009 - I'm in grad school and I get a call from a fraternity brother asking how I'm doing in my program. After some small talk he asks me about the tp etiquette of a former roommate of mine.

"Hahaha! Hey bro, did that fool always leave his toilet paper cagado next to the toilet in the basket when you lived with him?!"

"Well…I didn't share bathrooms with him, I had my own, so I don't really know what he did."

"Ese buey, aahaha, he leaves his toilet paper ahi todo cagado! One of the bros from Davis was up here, and he went to take a shit and he saw that. It's pretty gross bro."

Mind you, the fraternity brother from my chapter that called me is actually originally from Mexico, but I guess he must have been from the upper class of Mexico that had plumbing working at maximum capacity. I don't know who the fraternity brother from Davis was but apparently he also had great plumbing.

My fraternity brother found the tp in the basket inappropriate yet hilarious, I'm not sure if it crossed his mind that we were in a fraternity, and that one of us leaving our green shit stained tp in a basket wasn't the worst of offenses. Our fraternity brother that had green feces was actually from Mexico and had only arrived a few years ago in the states, and as far as I know, like many of us, he was from a rancho that didn't have appropriate plumbing.

My response to the issue of the green shit covered tp?

"Uh, well you know what it is. He's from the old country and if he's doing that it means that that's how he grew up," I said.

"I know bro, but it's still pretty gross."

"So talk to him about it and tell him it's okay to flush the toilet paper here, because our toilets won't get clogged as easily," I replied.

I unofficially became a toilet paper disposal etiquette liaison.

I remember flying to Queretaro, Mexico for an internship during the summer of 2007. I was fortunate enough to get a studio-type place in the back of my host family's home. I even had my own bathroom but when I went to take a shit, I had s serious conundrum; do I flush or toss the paper in the basket?

I was too embarrassed to ask the family what they wanted me to do. The fact the entire family was made up of women didn't help matters either. You just don't really discuss this. In my own apartment back in the states I would flush my tp, but I was now in Mexico where disposing of my tp the wrong way could lead to another embarrassing situation.

There was a basket next to the toilet, but did that mean I was supposed to toss my tp in there or was it for other uses like the tissue paper I used to pick my nose or for my cum filled condoms? If I flush my tp, I risk it backing up the toilet in my room but also in the plumbing in the main house, which leads to an uncomfortable situation and my possible exile from their home as well as all of Queretaro.

I eventually said fuck it - I need to take a dompe - I'll just do what comes naturally after I wipe my ass. I closed my eyes and dropped the kids off in the public swimming pool, reached backed with the toilet paper and wiped. I repeated this a few times and finally flushed. What did I do? I tossed the toilet paper into the toilet.

After flushing, I was still nerve wracked waiting for the toilet to overflow with my toilet paper and my kids floating over the rim and onto the light blue linoleum floor. I went to the bed, laid down, turned on the TV and glanced occasionally at the toilet, waiting for it to eventually burp and upchuck all of my contents.

Two hours later and still nothing. A few hours more and still nothing. I take a leakiazo, almost expecting to bring about my worst fear to life, and then having that be the determining factor in having it all surge upward. I'm almost daring it to happen. I grab the handle and flush, wait to feel the floor get wet as it soaks into my socks but nothing happens.

I went to bed and prayed to god and whatever Aztec and Mayan Gods I don't really know about. I slept expecting the worst but hoping for the best in the morning.

In the morning, there was nothing, no floaters, logs or drifting toilet paper. This still didn't assuage my conscience though, it took a couple of more times of this routine for me to finally realize that flushing my tp would be okay.

Which then lead me to realize: this must be an affluent family or just an affluent neighborhood if their plumbing system can handle both my shit and my mierda covered toilet paper.

I was relieved but then again, I was eating from many taco vendors in the area, and my stomach may not have been ready for that type of culinary treat, because I noticed that I wasn't shitting as solidly as I would if I were back in the U.S. chowing down burritos and burgers.

It was between solid and the type of watery stuff that comes out of you when you have the runs. So that might have helped my waste flow through that family's plumbing, ergo avoiding a localized international incident. Imagine having to discuss with them toilet paper disposal etiquette and reciting the origins of what I considered normal growing up, and then what I learned during college. Luckily that didn't occur, I returned to the States with no incidents.

If nothing else, I can say that college paid off, because my financial aid didn't all go to Pale Ale or tequila, it also went towards my education because I learned about toilet paper disposal etiquette. Only on a United States campus can a lower class Chicano learn this! The Melting Pot works.

I might not have learned who the fuck wrote the Iliad, who is Cotton Mather, or what the fuck photosynthesis is, but hey, I learned appropriate toilet paper disposal. Thank you college.

All this from a broken toilet handle.

VINCENT COOPER

Born in Los Angeles, CA and raised in South Texas, Vincent Cooper is a writer of poetry, short stories and screenplays. His work has been featured in Austin's Haggard & Halloo, Black Heart Magazine and Aztlán Reads. Cooper has participated in several poetry readings, including Puroslam, since 1999. Cooper is currently working on a series of chapbooks titled, 'It's not Fucking Peachy', which chronicle his life in Los Angeles, Las Vegas and his tenure with the United States Marine Corps. He currently resides in San Antonio, Texas.

BREAKFAST TACOS

So I woke up Sunday morning
dragged my ass out of bed and went to take my morning piss
made some coffee with the intent of making the best cup in the world
not just for myself but for my angel who is still asleep
I remember the euphoria of waking up to the smell of coffee in the morning
and was hoping to capture that feeling for her today
and while I am in the mood I thought I'd surprise her with breakfast tacos from Piknik
I tip-toed out the front door hoping the alarm wouldn't wake her up
nor the sound of starting the car… and I'm off
I drove down a few blocks to the Piknik stand we prefer
I can already taste the carne guisada and chicharron tacos
currently steaming and an older lady that resembles my mother waiting to prepare them
When I arrived I realized that I did not comb my hair
I only put gel and ran my hand through
then I quickly dismissed my appearance arrogantly
I place my order in my best broken-up Spanglish
there's no way they can tell I'm originally from LA right?
I'm wearing shades from Van's, and rock band shirt with cargo shorts
A blue collar walks in and places his order after me
much too early to be working on a weekend, I thought

then I realized how much I had it made
and how I would be sinking into my sofa for the rest of the day in about thirty minutes
kids are lazy these days
I'm lazy
she's flipping the tortillas over
and I start to scan lottery tickets like Charlie boy in Willy Wonka
as if this lotto ticket will make dreams come true
then it happened…
… he walked in and changed the course of the morning
A teenager walked in with his shaved head
tattooed and wife-beater shirt
he was pavement tough
like the pavement of a street nearby
that can withstand stray dogs, hood rat chanclas and some of the most awful human
beings ever
broken beer bottles and mocosos chasing the ice cream van
He had the Jesus eye
You know… the eye of the Jesus that was beaten to a pulp
and is now manufactured into some sort of product that you can buy to protect your home
from evil
that eye
He walks in and grabs a lighter from the lighter display and commences to light a joint in
the middle of this convenience store
The cashier who is probably the owner begins to warn this kid and starts to yell
The kid tells him, "Hey, I just needed a light,"
And then throws the lighter directly into the
chest of our
flustered owner/cashier and he leaves
Blue collar turns over to me and tells me, "Kids don't respect shit these days."
I remember becoming instantly angry
This blue collar son of a bitch just lumped me into a status
I didn't feel quite comfortable in
I am 30 years old and I just saw Jesus Christ walk in and light a joint in front of my face,

blue collar's face, Mr. Owner and tortilla flipper.
We didn't do a fucking thing about it. We couldn't. We witnessed it and sulked.
I pay the man and leave. I walked to the car looking around for him
I should have paid for that lighter and should have asked him for a hit
to wash away my sins.

LUISA LEIJA

Drawing from the indigenous traditions of the Americas, native culture, and Mexican culture, Luisa Leija's work unifies themes of community, family, history, and ceremony. Ms. Leija holds an MFA from California College of the Arts and a B.A. in Chicano Studies from UC Berkeley. Her work has appeared in literary magazines such as Mujeres de Maiz, La Ventana, Cipactli and is forthcoming in Nauhaling-doing (a Trilingual Poetry anthology). She lives in Oakland, CA and is a writer and dedicated youth worker.

LLAMANDO EL PODER

amor

amor de la lluvia

amor de la tierra

de los cielos

del corazón del universo

del corazón de la tierra

hacia las siete direcciones

hacia el centro, el punto

del incambiable

llena nos

llena nos de amor

despierta nos hacia el amor

que esta aquí

en los ojos

que esta aquí

en las manos

escucha

aquí

en los labios

todo es

en todo esta

en todo esto esta

en todo esto esta

la respuesta siempre

el amor

GHOST DANCE

ny ny ny ny ny ny

ny ny ny ny ny ny ny ny ny ny nyyy......

sun smoke disappears

as dusk

settles into black

the moon rises

fire cracks

brrooooooooo…

four men beat a response

an ancient song wails in darkness

dancers descend a long stone staircase

movement navigated by stars

weaving

into the circle

through opposite paths

one after another

feet dance in rhythm to ancient melodies

as they approach a blazing star

offering an alchemy of medicines,

pointing tree limbs to-ward the seven directions

feeding a fire that penetrates every stone

every bone

the empress dances

her head adorned in pyramids of silver coins and moonlight

she raises her crystal staff to honor each direction

all is medicine

all has purpose

all is seized by remembrance

we awaken dead memory

and unleash upon this generation

KARINA OLIVA

Karina Oliva was born in El Salvador and raised in Los Angeles. She holds a PhD in comparative Ethnic Studies with a focus on U.S. Central American literature and cultural production. She has been published in Mujeres de Maiz Zine, Hispanic LA.com, and Poets Responding to SB1070. She is an original member of the poetry collective EndDependence, and edited an anthology, Desde el Epicentro in 2007. Her book of poems is titled, "Transverse" (2009) published by Izote Press. She is also an artist whose work was featured at MALC's 2011 summer institute, "Against Fear and Terror: Una Nueva Conciencia Sin Fronteras." Karina's consciousness of resistance was fine-tuned at UC Berkeley, where she took part of Fast4Education, where she fasted on water-only for 21 days to demand the return of funds to the California public educational system. She currently teaches in the Chicana/o Studies department at Cal State University Los Angeles.

NO LOVE TRAIN FOR IMMIGRANTS

It's not a love machine

no escapade for migrants

just metal, iron, rubber

steeling lives

calling feet that can't read

all laws written by blood

just know the spine and big toe

uphold us to walk

on an earth that cradles homes

that exist without cement and asphalt

how can hands parallel

tribal differences from the past

with the arming of a bordered empire today

and hands fall off

with the weight of inequality

on the train tracks

where a caste of untouchables is made

to evaporate

in blinding white haze

in the heat of the Arizona desert

bones are bleached to dust

that will float and coat the fruits we so greedily

consume

our heart aches

throbs with every heart beat

lost

if we came across their thirst

would we give them

a drink of our expensive water

owned hanging across our chest

or like scrawled-in blogs

condemn people for an unlawful entry?

not a law of any God

since citizenship is not of nature

or do we condone by walking away

deeming some other people's battle

willing complicit when we chant

love and light for all

love and light

is blind

duplicity

the spiral in my ear translates

the slur of hate

I never thought my neighbor could sound so ugly

even when coded

in false flattery

organically grown and swallowed healthily

my back remembers

marked tracks across my body

a privilege upheld for centuries

running down the crooked spine of America

faces change

but the know-it-more, have-it-all smile

remains the same

there's just no sharing in the land of plenty, hey hey

FOUR WAYS TO GET TO MY HOME

freeways frame

my block

where boys sip

bottles from paper bags

stumble

through eyes dilated so large

swallowing

hunger that nulls

the desire to end the need

this morning one slept

like a kitten

knocked out and coiled

next to a tarred tree

Maya Quiché snippets

Ch, and clip

men walk with men the later it gets

huddle at corners

to map out the game

as the sidewalk fills

with a mercado

even lovers shop

-he buys her a rose from the kid

with a bucket normally used

to mop

woman smiles as they stop

to order chilate and atole

on a cool

October night

Evangelicals hail

alleluia, alleluia

call in some Lord with clapping hands

as spirituals

swim through the bathroom window

the tun! tun! of rancheras

the hard crash drumbeat of laboring youth

while feet thump upstairs

the choir

of a techno salvation

enters the cacophony

Last night it occurred to me

these walls are so thin

you need the blasting tunes day in and out

to mask from your neighbor

the grunt, thump and moan of love making

Meters eat up my quarters

and I've learned to use hairpins

to make it FAIL, FAIL, FAIL

oh, I wish I had a sledgehammer

to whack the heads

off their iron poles

and when we park under trees

with broken bark peeling like shard glass

pigeons drop blizzards

poop no longer white

instead like hardened black gum

makes me laugh

to drive through a city so shit on

Zipping through 6th, Alvarado, 1st, Pico

white and yellow lines lose their rules

a dislocation

like a video game double parked vehicles

people crossing red lights

people running out of harm's way

and U-turns where they're banned

the fire truck going 24/7, the cop bird flying

across the moon

Children stroll next to ice-cream trucks

see them before and after school

wearing white and blue uniforms

like in El Salvador

daughter warns two little girls were attacked

in the building next door

as our own lock shows

the markings of a man who tried to break in

when my daughter stayed alone

and as much as folk sneer:

this place is getting gentrified

I think of protecting my children

On Burlington and Wilshire

taco truck sits

might be the very same one I ate from

on the rainy night that I arrived from the isthmus

brought to the States

a 4 year-old bundle sweetened by sugar cane

flown in by a Panam stork

first food in Pico Union USA

a carne asada taco

that burned my tongue

familiarized its heat and spice

down my throat to an ember pit in my stomach

like a familiar jalapeño ulcer

And this is where the black gangster boy

so slim and tall

asked me out

I said, "No," because my mom said so

taught me to always evade the vato

This was my elementary

steel jungle gym and falling tile ceilings

this: my high school where a tent city

flapped after the earthquake

here's where those girls who tried to befriend me

took me to buy rubber bracelets

we linked together like cat's cradle

running up our slim tanned arms

the car hit me at this intersection, a DUI

kicked me like soccer ball goal

giving me an aerial perspective

blue skies and treetops

it was the city that broke my face

Parkview is where my father still lives

at this gas station, the man opened the door

of the restroom stall and exposed

a deflated penis

as I crawled away, age 6

I get gasoline there now and remember

my mother dreaming of dining at the steakhouse

with the bronzed oxen across the street

we might have changed apartments

but the freeways still boxed in

this neighborhood

a place many call home, from

in some other place, home.

IN OUR NEIGHBORHOOD

teenagers stagger on jagged concrete

huddle beneath window sills

with loopy schemes in paper bags

clog gutters

toss furniture in alleys

with graffiti lined on walls like fences

flyers advertise curanderos

behind purple velveteen curtains

in front, sidewalk preachers use bullhorns

gray-haired women sell tamales and pupusas

with a chant from grocery carts

most own instead of cars

to get to our destination gotta walk around the block

notice clinics at each one

while a boy vomits at the cornerstone

of the Dollar Store

families buy Top Ramen dinners

wait at the bus stop at the entrance

as young mothers push strollers

visit Starbucks to buy chocolate mochas

that cost more than someone's hourly wage

her little son and daughter grasp

the metal bars of the strollers, look

at the hot paper cups she hands them

she tells them, "Drink

I didn't come here for nothing"

they exit and sit outside

"My fucken grandma. I lied to her

told her I had to stay afterschool

like it's any of her business,"

the lanky girl's voice silences

the scuffle of brief cases, books

and "free" wifi

everyone hears her

a child, I wonder when she'll feel the stab of regret

"He gave me a little teddy bear"

her voice lowers with her head

At night, children's yelps and whimpers

cannot be hidden by hedges and driveways like

in other people's neighborhoods

while laughter of get-togethers

join neighbors' apartments

for a moment sound is muffled

by the hole in the wall church

that proliferate

harmonies

rise sweet with the smooth notes of a keyboard

blankets the block with calm.

Until a man breaks like a crash of metal

with his cry "Why! Why!"

that sounds Spanglish:

Waiiee! Waiieee!

There are others, voices running

men's feet stomping

in my own place, another prayer joins

the congregation next door

for his safety and peace, simply no death

but healing for he, this faceless stranger that runs

and those who took offense.

WARNING, YOU MIGHT WANT TO DROP THIS CLASS

I pause

to look away from the documentary De Nadie on Youtube

of Undocumented

of "No Ones"

"Nobodies"

"Nowhere"

between small countries in the center of America North and América South

I pause

to look away from the movies telling the now familiar stories

of assassinated Archbishops and children with machine guns

shoved in their arms or else, to their heads

I pause

to look away from the numbers of underestimated rapes and murders

by raped and murdered gang members and authorities with the right to kill

I stop

to shove away the sensationalism piling the table

when people become a hyped sound bite

of "illegal" nibbling our humanity away

It is just another quarter and semester

another classroom of bright-eyed students with a flame in their heart

to hold us accountable for a just society

with crisp articulate voices of a future called hope for some and power for others

searching for stories murmured in the air

not yet solidified by the weight of ink on newspapers and encyclopedias

There are moments when my throat still knots and I must clear away

the tears and the boulder of this historical knowledge

when I wipe my eyes with one clean swoop of my fingers

so I may not distract

and instead discuss the topic at hand

that we still have

to raise in the air

unlike the dismembered lives

of the people we read about

in real and fictional testimonies

their voices braiding into our thoughts

changing us hopefully

from our rooms full of internet links, soft tissues and snacks

offered in glass candy plates

In this class students say such things as

"How can truth be spoken when language is already the outcome of power"

"Men were not the only ones who raped"

"Women were not the only ones who were raped"

"But if they think of their lives as fate, where is their agency?"

"It's like living in the shadows"

"My great-aunt had never talked about the war but now that she is dying, the ghosts are speaking through her"

"But the author, courts, and lawyers are speaking for her"

"So when I go back to El Salvador, I don't pretend to be rich. I tell them the truth about how hard it is to live here"

Classes on Central Americans and Central America should have some sort of warning due to the graphic nature, due to an enduring history of poverty, class and racial hierarchies, internal colonialism, the hand and foot plight of the immigrant, and geopolitical schemes, you might find yourself

in disbelief

mourning

upheaved by a hurricane

wanting good deeds of change

or yearning instead to read poems by numbers

maybe Edgar Allen Poe, or Blake

If this is a class on literature, then why not focus on the metaphor

and forget the referent

because who wants to feel the real slice of pain, in fact

why don't we finger paint instead?

Still there is laughter

their brilliance like the bright coming of a sixth sun

that will trip the script of society's shame

I wish to somehow link each person to the other like a global Xbox game

without the Xbox

or game

mentalities

but the decisive coordinated hand and eye movement of change

always the handful of students who inspire

the work-filled hours

of my single filed days.

UNTOUCHABLE REPRIEVE;

We Too Will Drink From A Shunned Hand

A tatted man with a goatee and a cane

conjured your name

made me watch from the rearview mirror

the tough stepping away

remembering the rattling knees that won't hold you

  how will I walk as an elder

was one of your questions when a knee would give

and you'd lean your tempered body on me

this Arizona heat-wave

making me long for a lilac sky

etched in gold

and white lightening

San Lazaro

leper Saint

draped in a purple sheath

with two dogs at his feet

tongues that lick his sores

and at the crown

of a balding head

a hallow disk

child hands intricately wrap a rainbow of threads

up tall rigid leaves, wide as macaw feathers

3 decades later the woman smiled he was teaching you

by showing

early offerings

reveal words as images erupt in confluence

recalling the sheen

of the lavender altar cloth

for step-father's Orisha

Babalu-Aye

I sing a makeshift hymn

in words I never learned, but with the ascending sound

of your infinite compassion

let it move like a wave risen

from the depth of our mother's

ocean

before the water enters

sweep

the softened earth with the palm

of a handmade broom

and rest the gourd gently

there is no blessing greater than the one

you give yourself

karmic memories

of opportunities revisited and rethreaded

in the parable

the rich man who denied his crumbs

to the sickened vagabond

after their death

asked the All Mighty

to have Lazarus from heaven

dip his shunned fingers

in a brook

and enter hell to relieve his thirst

and so Chango called his wife

as the ground rumbled

with four thousand hooves

of a thousand star-painted horses

descending

to answer miracles

and bring

the rain.

FRANK S. LECHUGA

Frank, a Southern California native who resides in Portland, Oregon and spends a lot of time in Los Angeles, earned a Master Degree of Education at Harvard University and is noted on Cambridge Who's Who. He is a student-founder of the Chicano Studies Department at California State University, Northridge and was arrested in 1969 at what was then San Fernando Valley State College, protesting for ethnic studies and equitable Mexican American and African American student representation His life-long passion has been writing and freed from his day job (teaching and counseling), he has embarked on his full-time writer's journey. He writes the blog, Frank Insights - Cosmos, Nations, Humanity http://www.frankslechuga.com/. He can be followed on Facebook and Twitter.

SINGEOM

"The art of a warrior is to balance the terror of being a man with the wonder of being a man."

- *Carlos Castaneda quoting don Juan Matus, <u>Journey to Ixtlan</u>*

The Order of the Exemplars of the First Harmonic; entered on this day, 5 Ehecatl 1 Tepcatl 4 Acatl, 13.10.1.7.2 in the Long Count

*

Some thirty feet in height, the e-gate controlling the Cahuenga onramp to the Hollywood freeway southbound loomed like a huge metal and concrete maw, its Response-Elicitor robot housed in the adjoining Partition wall appearing in the dim light to be a huge insect lying in wait for its prey. Ruby red laser sighters in the mobile gun pods atop the parapet throbbed with steady rhythm and faint fluorescent lights barely illuminated the two bald operators slouching behind the bubble windows of the small control room above the partially opened overhead gate. An infoboard above the entryway flashed in bright orange:

STOP - DO NOT DRIVE BEYOND YELLOW LINE

Taking on the appearance of a black sedan, the metacar rolled to a stop at the required distance from the checkpoint, about a hundred feet. Pointe relaxed his hold on the steering yoke.

Always granted Approval for Entry, he had passed through e-gates countless times his entire adult life. He had used the privilege of rank, and if the occasion deemed it, fake passes and other means of deception but throughout his youth and before he had risen from common Outer Cohort classification, he had endured the monolithic and brutal absoluteness of life under the Partition and its fortified gatehouses.

He had endured but never acquiesced, never accepted the inherent injustice of the Strategic Population Assessment System that supervised the robotized walls and checkpoints that divided the city into Green Zones and Brown Zones. And never had he forgotten what he witnessed that dark day.

The metacar's flat screen magnifier brought into focus the checkpoint's operators.

"According to my data banks," Armida XG-7 said, "they are the killers of two teenaged men from Brown Zone Sector 12. They were exonerated." Tiny reversed swastikas next to the Partition logos and identification numbers on the fore of the shaved craniums were all that the robot had needed to research the uniformed thugs' history through its special access to Metro-Kom data banks.

Typical scum recruited and cleared by the Department of Psychological-Political Surveillance, like the scum operating the e-gate that day.

--But had Morin's automated security system alerted the e-gate operators? Did Intra-City Security already know about Frag's death? Morin himself or Gail, or someone else could have made the call. MetroKom would have picked up the report and alerted all the e-gates in the area.

It did not matter...*Long-range consequences be damned, only the immediate outcome mattered. Everything would be different this time.*

He had felt it when he had first approached the Cahuenga onramp a few minutes ago - the resentment built up over the years of stomaching everything the e-gates and the Partitions represented; felt it catalyzing with the adrenaline still coursing throughout his body, the bitter remnant of the lethal bout with Frag. He had sensed the metacar's Armida XG-7 reading all his cues, his body chemistry, the intonation of his voice - priming him and priming its systems; felt it to the marrow of his bones, synchronizing with his disciplined breathing into and out of his *dan jun*.

And the memory started to come back in all its painful clarity...*He is a boy accompanying one of his Wellness-assigned fathers, a civilian without any gang ties. This man has shown him affection and made an effort to be a real father. They are at the intersection of Lanky and the Vent in the Saint Ferdinand Valley, waiting for the e-gate to let them through the Partition to the Green Zone on the other side.*

"Sir," Armida XG-7 said, interrupting Pointe's recollection, "e-gate operators are not accepting our pass signal. Their scanners have detected our electronic shielding. They demand that you park in the inspection area and shut down all power systems. Response-Elicitor will be inspecting."

Summer heat torches the day. A mangled atmosphere's torment spares no one. The War of Regulation still rages in LA and throughout South Cal. IntraCity requires all vehicles from Brown Zones to be stripped to the chassis to make it easier for egate Response-Elicitor robots to detect hidden weapons or explosives and so the boy and his father wait in that skeleton of a vehicle.

His hands still on the steering yoke Pointe inched into the inspection area, stopping between two illuminated yellow stripes imbedded into the asphalt, the hydrogen engine's transmission gearing into neutral.

Activated by inspection area's sensors, the Response-Elicitor slithered out of its niche in the Partition rampart, coolant fluids dripping from its armored cowl like some organic slime, its power cables trailing behind like gutted entrails. Scanners and sensors were already extending out - pheromone sensors; chromatographic and neural testers; dermal pigmentation gaugers; facial muscle and body language analyzers; ultrasound heart beat readers; ultraviolet sweat gland examiners; phenotype compilers; genotype indexers...

Yes, he thought looking at the monstrosity of a robot - this time the outcome would be different. Very different. He had his own robot...

He hears whirrs and buzzes, the robot's instruments are scrutinizing his assigned father. Traffic is piling up behind them and other drivers are jeering at them, blaming them for holding up traffic. His father grits his teeth, sweat pouring out from inside the cheap standard issue eco-mask he is wearing.

"Stats on the parapet mobile weapons pods," the sweet feminine voice said, "are as follows... " Pointe could feel the meld with the metacar's symbiotic C-3s weapons platform activating..."Standard R-M312 12.7mm/.50 caliber--linked...rate of fire is 260 rounds per minute, four belts with 800 rounds for each gun. E-gate weapons' systems are calibrating - our defensive counter measures are configured.

"Targets are prioritized."

And this time, the whirring Pointe heard came from the nanomotors in the metacar's gun nodules retrieving the assembly units of his heaviest weapons and munitions from their compressed dimension storage. The buzzing he heard was the decompression and reassembly of his guns' components - bolts, quick-release pins, housing covers, barrels...

Left hand on his steering yoke's handle, his right hand grasped the multi-tasking

pistol grip...

E-gate operators tell the man through the robot's voice box that violence levels are too high on the other side of the Partition. They order him to step out of the denuded vehicle. He raises his voice, pleading and cursing at the same time. Things have been hard. He protests that someone made a mistake. He will lose his job if he does not get to the other side of the Partition. But the Response-Elicitor robot is impervious to his pleas.

In his desperation, he gets off the vehicle and takes a few steps toward the e-gatehouse, his arms outstretched. There is no warning, only a rat tat tat from the parapet's robotic guns. And the man the boy had learned to call father falls onto the hard hot pavement ground bleeding, metal extensors and tentacles probing him, stealing the last of his dignity.

One of the robot's tentacles stops the boy from going to his father's side and he curls up into a little ball on the hard seat of the electro-car, terrorized and helpless.

Pointe squeezed the pistol grip triggers and a laser-guided Barret .50 caliber precision rifle in the fore nacelle fired a rapid sequence of two explosive bullets, their thunder cutting through the city's nocturnal murmur, one into each narrow barrel slot of the parapet's two armored machine gun turret pods, destroying the electronic aiming mechanisms inside.

In synchronization with this attack, automatic 25mm Bushmaster cannon fire blasted apart the clear plastonium shielding protecting the gatehouse observation bubbles, cracking them like eggshells, the sonic violence penetrating the metacar's sound-insulated cabin. Then the Bushmaster's fiery ribbon swept the gun pods, completing the Barret's work. A second later Armida XG-7 lobbed a Thermate-TH3grenade at the exposed gatehouse and fired a high explosive 75 mm rocket at the gate's overhead pneumatic mounts, its concussive force blasting the gate's jagged metal frame and panel onto the onramp surface with a screeching crash.

Immediately in the wake of that gun storm, the windshield fogged and all he could see were the fiery silhouettes of the operators, thrashing and flailing. Mercifully, the metacar's 7.62x51mm Gatling gun raked them with a quick fusillade of fiery lead, ending their futile dance of death.

Pinging against the metacar's driver side announced the Response-Elicitor counterattacking with its guns. Immediately, Armida XG-7 reversed the robot vehicle, giving it enough ground to accelerate and swerve against the arachnid-like robot, shattering it with sheer forward momentum.

Straightening out, the metacar burst through flaming debris that had been the e-gate, its sudden acceleration crushing Pointe back into the contoured seat, forcing him to hold on to the safety harness grips to steady himself. Gaining more speed, the robot vehicle raced up the long onramp and onto the Hollywood freeway, its carapace still holoflaged into that of a black sedan.

Onward it raced through the darkened Cahuenga Pass.

"Armida...XG-7," Pointe said, feeling liberated by his lethal violence, "on this night you were the instrument of my justice...after all these years." He closed his eyes, the robot vehicle's functions becoming sensate to his mind and body, its hardened radial tires grinding the freeway surface beneath, the hydrogen engine's vibrations permeating his body...*And it came upon him - the fleeting vision of a fine lady amidst the splendor of a sublime garden. Standing at her side, he bent down to pick for her the reddest, most vibrant flowers...*

A black blur in the night, the metacar raced past the great media lords' towers overlooking the north opening of the Cahuenga Pass, to turn west at 145 mph per hour onto the Vent freeway exchange. It sped on, oblivious to the UAVs that were already racing toward the Pass and would soon be swathing the nearby hillside with high intensity xenon beams.

*

A few days after that night of violence, Pointe went to a meeting at Mitsu headquarters that Mr. Song had scheduled some time back to discuss the upcoming marketing campaign for the new learning machine, the Mnemosyne Series Intelligence Enhancer. The meeting would help take his mind off the funeral for Charlie Tuna he planned to attend the next day in the Brown Zone where he grew up. It would also serve to help him quell the uneasiness he felt about his extremist actions that night - his voluntary participation in the deadly deal with Morin's retainer and the destruction of the e-gate.

He looked forward to giving Charlie his last props, but he did not look forward to going back to where he had old history. He did not look forward to seeing the poverty, misery and oppression of the regulars and civilians in his old Brown Zone.

From the onset of the drive, Pointe gave Armida XyberGuard-7 full control. Taking surface streets from his home in the Pasadena Green Zone it took about forty minutes to arrive at the front entrance to Mitsu Corporation's private entryway to its So Cal headquarters in Golden Island. Responding to the coded radio signal, the gates opened. The metacar went into the underground security garage, and parked in its special dock. He exited and made his way up several floors on the private elevator, through sumptuous hallways to an even more sumptuous executive waiting room.

An attractive secretary tall and athletic in a black leather mini-skirt and steel blue chamois blouse met and escorted him to Mr. Song's private offices.

She stopped ceremoniously at the entrance, giving Pointe a moment to admire massive bronze doors embossed with Mitsu's corporate logo of three stylized dragons entwined around a triangle - the Iron Triangle of the United States of Eternal Asia, symbolizing the three ancient nations that had embraced the teachings of the Tao, Buddha and Confucius - China, Korea and Japan. The secretary opened both doors effortlessly and ushered him in with a smile and a graceful wave of the hand.

The Mitsu marketing executive stood behind a large desk made of polished mahogany, an immensely expensive and rare material. Mr. Song looked strong and fit, his finely chiseled features and cropped gray hair completing the image of executive mastery. Song stepped around the desk and greeted Pointe. They bowed slightly to each other before shaking hands.

Pointe had known Song long before the Mitsu learning machine business.

After his mother and sister were killed on the streets, Pointe had gone to live in an Eternal boarding school and there he had met the older man whom he always called Mr. Song or Master Song. The executive had taken a liking to him and always had helped him, almost becoming a surrogate father figure. He had just returned from an extended trip to the United States of Eternal Asia and Pointe was looking forward to seeing him.

His *kwan jang nim*, his master instructor for ten years, Song had helped Pointe make the last great stride in his study and practice of *hwarang do*. Song had also helped open the doors for him at the Department of Enforcement and advocated for him to teach his first workshop at the

Griffith IntraCity Security Forces Academy. He had even met Demetria, his great and lost love through the Mitsu executive.

Song led Pointe to a private lounging area attached to his office. It had comfortable seats and a serving table adorned by a lacquered tea set and a *nageire* flower arrangement, a single long willow branch gracefully leaning out of a tall red columnar vase, shorter branches with a smattering of green foliage and two golden chrysanthemums gracing its base.

Another man, a younger man waiting in the lounge got up from his chair to acknowledge Pointe. Discipline and training had also hardened this man's face. His neutral-gray civilian suit barely disguised his martial posture and wide shoulders. He started to smile politely then the edges of his mouth slanted up in a subtle sneer, the light in his eyes hidden in a squint.

Pointe immediately disliked this man, discerning that some higher authority within the Eternal global corporation had sent him to monitor their meeting.

"Samuel," Song said, "this is Mr. Kaze. He has been assigned to assist us with the promotional campaign for the Mnemosyne Series Intelligence Enhancer."

Kaze nodded slightly. "My pleasure."

Pointe took note of a cold metallic tone in Kaze's voice. He barely nodded back. "The pleasure," he said in the same tone, "is mine."

"Please, everyone have a seat," Song said, "Some tea, Samuel? Mr. Kaze?"

"Yes, thank you," Pointe said, taking a seat.

Song went on to prepare the tea. Completing the ritualized task he poured the steaming flaxen-colored liquid with sublime technique into the three small porcelain cups resting on the black lacquered tray. He raised the tray toward Pointe, offering him the first cup. Pointe took it and thanked Song with a sleight nod, noting how Kaze took his cup without saying anything or bowing.

"I trust," Song said, "everything goes well for you, Samuel."

"Yes, Mr. Song, thank you." Pointe also noted that Song glanced over at Kaze, before asking him...

"Does the robotic vehicle serve you well?"

"Yes," Pointe said. "She...I mean...this metacar is an extraordinary machine."

Song said, "I am glad you are pleased with this prototype of a state-of-the-art robotic vehicle soon to be made available to an elite clientele. Nothing on Earth's weary roads can provide its operator with the same degree of protection and comfort."

Song smiled. "I think that if we were going to mass market it, Samuel, I would ask you to help us sell it too."

"Speaking of marketing," Kaze said, "the Mnemosyne learning machine is ready now. We have a deluxe model over in our Nortech Research Institute. It will provide the user with an advanced level of general education in the natural sciences, social sciences and the humanities...physics, chemistry, mathematics, literature, communication studies, sociology, political science, psychology...history.

Song added, "Those are just main subjects. Mnemosyne will provide users with a conceptual framework with which to specialize further, to complete what used to be called in the old educational jargon...an academic major."

"A Mnemosyne user can complete a course of study that would have taken a semester in a week. Through demonstration of a proficiency in a chosen field, Samuel, you can easily meet the requirements for Project Director Status. This will help your application for reclassification. Our marketing department is ready to work with you to start a new advertising campaign after you complete the first phase of Mnemosyne's program."

While focused on Mr. Song's words, Pointe managed to catch Kaze studying him. "When," Pointe said, looking at Song, "will Mnemosyne become available to me?"

Kaze interjected..." - Very soon. We have to make a few last minute adjustments on Mnemosyne's maximumsensorial interface unit. You will be contacted when it is ready."

There was what seemed to Pointe an awkward pause, a tension. The moment passed. Song said, "Samuel, our meeting today is providing this most opportune moment to give you a token of my appreciation for the sacrifices you have made on behalf of Mitsu - "

Kaze interjected a second time..." - Yes, your survival on the *Cherni Princ* and your willingness to allow us to use your story in our marketing. Mitsu Corporation is most grateful."

"This gift" Song said, "is also an expression of my personal gratitude, a gift I have been intending to give you for some time. I am going to present it to you now because I may be called back to the First Tetrarchy at any time and we never know when fate may surprise us."

Song turned around, walked a few steps, reached into a mahogany credenza and took out an elongated package with a wrapping of fine, patterned silk, blue and red in color. He held it horizontally with both open hands. He walked to Pointe, stopped, bowed slightly, allowing the silk wrapping to unfurl and ceremoniously extended to Pointe - a sheathed *singeom*.

"It is... " Song said in a ceremonious tone, "a copy of a great *Silla* knight's sword, made of the best steel, nano-edged and hardened with modern techniques. It can cut through plastonium alloys and the hardest steel with ease."

Surprise and gratitude overtook Pointe. Even though a copy, the gift of an honorable sword intimated hidden, portentous meaning. He took the sheathed weapon from Song with both hands and bowed. He straightened up. Holding the sheath with his left hand, he slowly and respectfully drew out the *singeon* a few inches, past the tang, to reveal the live blade glinting in the light, its wavy pattern on the sharp edge a testament to the heat treatment in its crafting and its absolute, lethal utility.

Pointe slid the blade back into the sheath. He bowed his head again to show his gratitude. "I do not have words to fully express my thankfulness for this honorable gift."

Song gestured for Pointe to sit down again. He said, "There is no need, Samuel." He paused. Then he continued..."It is very important, Samuel, that we move quickly to market Mnemosyne. It is not only good for Mitsu and the United States of Eternal Asia. It is good for everyone in this Tetrarchate because it offers a peaceful option to those who want to improve their lives.

"It is important to make our intelligence enhancing products available to the largest number of knowledge seekers possible. There may come a time soon when we will not be allowed to market this product in L.A. and South Cal."

Pointe said, "Why? Do the problems with Greater Texas and the Fatherland continue?"

" - Yes," Kaze said, once again interjecting himself into the conversation. "At the Convocation of the Tetrad we expect the Fatherland of Ameraryan States and the Republic of Greater Texas to accuse Mitsu and other legitimate Eternal Asian business interests of intervening in the psycho-political status quo of this Tetrarchy with its marketing of learning technology."

"They will accuse the League of West Coast City-States of capitulation to Eternal Asian expansionism. It is possible IntraCity's Department of Psychological-Political Surveillance will stand against Mitsu and issue an injunction against marketing Mnemosyne. This is even after we reached an agreement with their Office of Intellectual Affairs on the limitations of Mnemosyne's curriculum."

Song did not acknowledge or add to the operative's comment and the resulting silence indicated the meeting had come to its end. Pointe got up and bowed deeply. "Thank you, Master Song. I will try with all my heart to rise to the honor you have given me. If you do not have any more need of me, I will be leaving. I will be awaiting your call."

"You will hear," Song said, "from us soon. But remember, Samuel, you are always welcome to call me at any time."

Pointe gave Kaze who remained seated a token nod and turned around tucking the sheathed sword under his arm. Deep in thought, he walked out of Song's office, barely saying goodbye to the secretary. Unlike the provision of the metacar, which had been clothed with the facade of utility, this gift had the distinction of being nothing else but a weapon.

Suddenly Pointe felt that feeling of floating one gets when events are shifting so rapidly that the ground underneath seems to be moving. Perhaps a consequence, he thought of living in the light of the overworld as a minor marketing celebrity for an educational technology while at the same time living in the shadow world of a professional arbiter of lethal justice. But that was only part of it.

All the life-changing events he had experienced in the last few years had unleashed a careening momentum toward an unknown and ominous outcome. Now it all felt like a riptide dragging him down and deeper into something vast and complex.

Pointe felt a deep gratitude to *hwarang do* for instilling within him a moral code and a reverence for the Great Law. It would ground him spiritually in the face of this impending unknown. It girded him for the inevitable confrontation with the hidden force that lurked there.

Then he thought again.

His last two deeds - the duel with Frag and the killing of the skinheads at the e-gate - had taken him beyond the pale of his martial code and the Great Law. Only a profound expiation and atonement would restore his moral balance. Without doing so, he would be no better than the brutal gangsters he waged war against in the name of his Overkind clients.

*

Soldiers from a half dozen gangs streamed to Charlie Tuna's coffin. Their garish colors, emblazoned on crude eco-armor, contrasted mockingly with the solemnity and elegance of the chapel's white walls, marble altar, dark walnut benches and pulpit. The predominant colors were those of the North Valley Boyz - Charlie Tuna's old gang - a red slash of the initials, NVB, on a golden scroll embellished on the forehead of a stylized white skull. And the gangsters' faces did not reveal whether they had come to honor the dead or if they had come to give homage to Death. It did not matter. Charlie "Tuna" Mesa was receiving his last props.

Samuel Pointe waited in the chapel lobby to get seating in the pews. Without intending to do so, he could overhear the gossip..."Everyone on this side of the Valley knew Charlie had been a leader...knew he really tried to help the hood."

"He had a nice home with its own eco-dome."

"Charlie had a wife and children back then when he still had juice, before the Wellness Office pols ripped off his community improvement program."

"Yeah, before he started using."

And on and on...

Pointe mulled over what he knew about Charlie's sudden death. After someone found Charlie stabbed to death people said they saw monster hotrods like the type driven by the Iron Movement leaving the vicinity, racing away at top speed. That went along with what Maisa had told him on her killing bed. But other people said Charlie, while drunk on the streets, had gotten into an argument with a crazy regular. Some said it had been an old grudge or a drug deal gone bad that got him killed. He needed more facts.

"Sam - "

He turned to face a very attractive young woman preceded by a clean, sweet fragrance. Not too long ago Sylvia had been his lover in an affair that had been short, erotic and intense. Her eight-year old son dangled at her side. "It's terrible," she said in an easy, creamy voice..."that Charlie died that way."

Pointe said, "Yes, before his time. How are you, Sylvia?"

An artsy eco-pack hanging from her left shoulder, her full lips were still reddened heavily and her straight black hair hung down into a soft bun. A long, gray protective eco-coat opened to reveal her décolletage set off by a respectably cut blouse made of a fine, elegant lace that scintillated with a metallic blue, black and red threading - and below the short black leather skirt, black high-heeled boots and black hose encased her perfect legs. Sylvia's style had not changed much. She was the kind that did not need to renew her appeal.

"Can't complain," she said. "Are you still studying the Eternals' Book of Changes?"

"No," he said. "Are you still ambitious?"

"I'm a supervisor at a proteifac in the Eastside."

"Sylvia...Adam," Pointe said. "It's good to see you both. Adam is really big now." The brown-haired boy looked up at him somewhat sheepishly.

"Seriously...how have you been?" Her eyes swept over the length and breadth of his armor.

"I'm good."

"Samuel," Sylvia said, her red lips reshaping into an even more delicious smile..."you're always so unpretentious. Even after Mitsu advertises everywhere that you went up to Jupiter... after you've been interviewed on cable a half dozen times with replays of your tournament fights."

Wary, Pointe felt the remnant of an ember of passion flare up. He found women, always attracted to him before, now after the Mitsu marketing campaigns, gravitating toward him with a certain avaricious vehemence. He did not exactly feel this from Sylvia but he felt something. Too bad, he said to himself.

She said, "It's so sad about Charlie."

"I know," he said with all the detached courtesy he could muster..."Well, now I'm going to pay him his last respects before the service starts. It was nice seeing you again, Sylvia." He patted the boy on the head. "Goodbye, Adam."

The little boy looked up and smiled at him. Pointe smiled back and walked past the pews, up the center aisle to the casket, thinking about how Charlie had been like an older brother to so many young men in the North Valley, even like a father to some. He stood before the open casket and acknowledged Charlie, noting that his old friend had wizened but not beyond recognition. The undertakers had done their best, but a corpse rarely looked good, and a wound resulting in a heavy loss of blood always aged the face by twenty or thirty years.

When they were very young, Pointe and Charlie had often talked about improving their Brown Zone and changing things. They eventually went their separate ways. He managed to get out of the Brown Zone. Charlie had stayed in the 'hood.

Something happened to Charlie along the way. He had disappeared around the time Pointe had started the SynchroCept learning program. His old friend and mentor surfaced again after a couple of years only to go down - fast, shooting anything and everything into his veins, sucking the bottle, smoking, and popping anything and everything he could get his hands on, stealing to get money to pay for other Wellness recipients' drug allotments.

He abandoned his wife and children. Hustling on the street, Charlie became another homeless addict.

And Pointe throughout that time had gone on to become an IntraCity officer, a respected martial artist and instructor. He had gone up to space and returned to become well known through the SynchroCept marketing campaign. It had only fueled the resentment of his Outer Cohort peers. The North Valley Boyz particularly resented his ambition and aloofness from the 'hood.

One bleak day he and Charlie had met up in the old L.A. garment district. Both wore protection for the ultraviolet light and the bad air. Pointe wore a sleek eco-armored suit and a respirator, Charlie a ragged, hooded trench coat, rags around his nose and mouth.

They almost had not recognized each other. Charlie had recognized him first, openly envying him. Who could blame the older man?

Perhaps envy had been the reason Charlie had shown Pointe the golden medallion he wore underneath his filthy tunic. It gave him something to boast about - some meaning. Charlie bragged about a secret and astounding power contained within the artifact - the power to free the Outer Cohorts from the yoke the Overkind and IntraCity had imposed on them. Although intrigued, Pointe could not help but to conclude that the old homeboy's talk about the artifact's powers and secrets were nothing more than the babbling of a mentally impaired addict.

Then somebody murdered Charlie. The medallion disappeared and Pointe realized that all along he had really wanted Charlie's story about the artifact's secret power to free the Outer Cohorts - to be true.

--Why?

Having attained financial security, he lived in a Green Zone, free of most of the limitations imposed on the Cohort of his birth. He had gone farther, all to the way to Jupiter, than anybody from his Brown Zone and he had been nominated for reclassification for Emprise residency. He had recognition, status, and the power of his role of clandestine arbiter of justice for important people, for the Overkind.

--So, why had he wanted Charlie's story to be true since the first time heard it, a story that sounded like some kind of modern fairy tale?

The answer to that question existed in the same place in his mind and heart that incubated his decision to accept Frag's challenge to the deadly duel and then to go on to destroy the e-gate and its operators. The privileges he had wrenched from the society that had segregated him at birth were never enough to make him quiescent. And SPAAS and the Overkind did not have the right to deny him the truth of his origins.

Thus, inexplicably his dharma had woven into this path. Seeking justice for Charlie had become a way to find answers to the questions that he had asked Johnnie Morin, the questions that festered since his return from the ill-fated journey to Jupiter on the *Cherni Princ*.

Seeing that some seating became available Pointe put aside his pondering and walked back to the pews, sat for the service and scrutinized the thirdrate Actors hired by the owner of the chapel to play the roles of attendants. The service started with a robotized organ synthesizer, followed by a shoddy Actorchaplain whose readings of the Holy Scriptures, which were already meaningless to everybody, sounded like a halfhearted sales harangue.

When the service finally ended, Pointe left the chapel to find that it had already become dark outside. He walked past a group of regulars milling around the entrance. They wore little or no protection from the elements and the blotches on their skin from exposure to the relentless sun were unmistakable. Some were wheezing and coughing. They eyed him, their eyes bulging from anger or disease. Pointe sensed their desperation and moved on to cross the empty street.

His eco-armor sensors indicated the air was bad but before he could activate his helmet, someone called him from somewhere outside the streetlight's glare..."Whatsup?"

Pointe stopped and turned to see the caller stepping into the light. The voice, body type and posture were unmistakable, and neither were the stylized jaguar suit of eco-armor and the helmet sculpted into a streamlined, stylized jaguar's head, its yellow visage mottled with black. Garz had been the leader of a main North Valley Boyz clique for some time and one of Pointe's old opponents in the martial arts competitions, an opponent he had defeated several times, and who had never been a good loser.

Expecting to run into the gangster at the funeral service Pointe had reviewed his dossier. More than just another street thug, Garz had become a part-time Third District militia lieutenant and chair of a council of safety and order, one of the few semi-official groups in the North Valley Brown Zone providing a semblance of selfgovernance under martial law. Also an enforcer for the local Legitimate, he had arranged several executions on his boss's behalf.

The NVB leader took off his helmet, collapsed it and nestled it under his left armpit. Pointe acknowledged the gangster with a nod.

Garz said, "You haven't been around much these days, Sammy." Two NVB soldiers walked out of the shadows to give him backup. They sported black stylized jaguar helmets, black eco-conditioned, body-tight leather and nylon composite armor that did not restrain the lithe movements of their compact bodies. Appearing to move in unison, they flicked gang hand-signs at Pointe.

He responded with an impassionate, studious stare. "If we're going to talk, Garz, we should get off the street."

Garz said, "They'll drive around us. We seen your video billboard up on the Vent. You're looking good hanging onto that babe in Malibu. What's next? Making skin flicks with the pleasure babes on Cat's Island?" He laughed contemptuously, his soldier Boyz chiming in.

"You could have used," Pointe said, slowing his words for effect ..."some education yourself, Garz."

"Naaa, the educational niceties aren't for me," the NVB leader said, laughing sharply. "Neither is the reading. Don't like those screens. Hey don't think we're dissing you, Sammy boy."

"I see," Pointe said, pinning Garz's soldiers with his eyes, "you've been recruiting."

"Meet Dare and Defy," Garz said. "They're brothers. And they're down for their 'hood."

"What do you know," Pointe said, without giving the two young gangsters any more attention..."about who killed Charlie?"

"You know," the NVB leader said..."you heard it already. The Iron Movement killed him. It was all over the streets."

He looked Pointe up and down. "You got connections," he said in an accusing tone..."in high places - all the way up to IntraCity Security Enforcement.

"Your old 'hood needs your help to even things up with the Iron Movement. Those hot rod freaks have gotten away with too much. They're jackals and ghouls that don't respect the dead. What they did to Charlie has to be paid back."

Pointe said, "You know for a fact the Iron Movement Hot Rod and Motorcycle Association killed our old friend?"

Garz stared dead cold into Pointe's eyes. "I know."

"Why hasn't the local Legitimate," Pointe said, ignoring the mad dog scowl..."done anything about it and why didn't he come to Charlie's service?"

Garz said, "We're going to represent the Legitimate at Charlie's service. And we are going to do something about what happened to Charlie. That's why I'm talking to you. This isn't just socializing. "

The NVB leader stepped into Pointe's inner circle. "Sammy...I know you're good in the karate studio when everything is set up for show with teachers around and sh-t but you always managed to stay out of the real thumping on the streets. Sorry, Sammy, your teaching your karate over at IntraCity just never impressed me that much.

'I really," Pointe said harshly, "don't give a damn about what impresses you and yours, Garz.

But just for the record, I impressed you somewhat in the *dojangs* and the *dojos*. And dancing and yoga are what's studied and practiced in a studio, Garz, not martial arts.

Dare and Defy rustled nervously. They looked at their leader. He raised his arms slightly, calming them down. "Sammy boy," Garz said angrily, "you never stood up for the 'hood, but Charlie was always there to help you out. When you were a youngster, before you went to live in the Eternals' schools, he pushed you along...protected you." Garz paused, took a breath to calm himself and then continued..."You never did anything even after your mother and sister got killed in Longo. Our mothers were friends, man. You forget we were friends then, when we were squirts.

"Man, we were waiting for you to come and ask us for help but you never came around. Instead you turned your back on everybody and hid in your Eternal school."

Pointe said, "We stopped being friends the first time you disrespected my sister and now you're poking into my private family business.

"Then," Garz said, ignoring Pointe's words..."you come back and try to be a community leader. Charlie taught you everything. You need to pay Charlie back some and show some respect for your community that you were supposed to care about so much. You need to help us set things about what happened to Charlie."

Pointe chose not to respond to the insulting tone in Garz's mandate - and challenge. That Garz might know the real reason the Iron Movement had killed Charlie mattered much more. The wheel of fate had turned to give him this unexpected opportunity to obtain information about Charlie's killers and the golden medallion. He would take it, regardless of the risks.

"Do you want," Pointe said, "to keep talking on this dirty street and in this dirty air or do you want to go pay your respects to Charlie first?"

Garz said, "We have to give the homeboy his last props first. Then we talk. It's not personal or just about North Valley and Charlie. It could be important to all the Outer Cohorts in So Cal.

"Meet us over at the old adobe house off the Sep over in Missing Hells. Wait for us in the parking lot." Garz paused and then added..."Remember the adobe house, Sammy? I got the keys now."

Then the gangster turned away from Pointe and sauntered toward the chapel entrance, the crowd of wretches making way for him and his soldiers.

*

The old adobe two-story house was located in an abandoned park where Sep Boulevard veered off into Brand. Various agencies and groups had used it for different purposes since the time the population had been much larger. Not used much anymore, essential maintenance and security continued to be provided by the same faceless City agency that maintained similar sites and facilities all over L.A.

Like with many similar sites, the rumor circulated around that MetroKom, the city's mega computer system actually administered both the old house and the park.

Pointe thought about this, recalling how his application to use the facility had all been through the local area network. Not once did he have to talk to a human authority about using or maintaining it. No surprise that Garz now had access to it.

A passive air recycling membrane enshrouded the unlit parking lot and house, deepening the shadows. Pointe walked to a switch box hidden by an oleander bush and mounted the adobe house's courtyard wall. He opened the box, deactivated his glove and raised his right hand to the security scanner. The automatic switch lever clicked up and an array of light banks exploded upon the gravel driveway and parking lot, casting a harsh gleam upon the parked metacar.

Pointe looked back into the courtyard and at the adobe house's windows to make sure there was light inside. Then, he activated his helmet. Its nocturnal lenses phased in. He activated his glove and pulled the switch back down, returning the parking area to the darkness. The eucalyptus trees could be seen towering around the adobe house and silhouetting through the recycling membrane against the glow of the night overcast. He had always imagined those tall lanky trees to be adobe house park's great old guardians.

Awaiting the NVB in that darkness, Pointe ruminated on the past...*When he had been a young activist in the North East Valley Brown Zone the place had been turned into a community center. Meetings were held regularly in the adobe's courtyard. Debates and discussions about self-governance without violence bounced around the stone fountain all the time.*

Demetria Lu had first taken notice of him in this courtyard while he stood by the stone fountain, encouraging his fellows to petition IntraCity and the defunct city government for needed improvements in their Brown Zone. How naïve it had been, he realized now, to have advocated for the replacement of martial law with civil law.

"Sir, I detect two vehicles approaching," Armida XG-7 said, interrupting his recollection. "Three armed individuals in the first vehicle and four in the second vehicle. I will await your initiative."

"Thanks," he said. He blended into the oleander's shadow.

Two customized turbo-vehicles, sedans, drove onto the grounds, slowing down, their headlights on bright, their wheels crunching the gravel beneath them. Both vehicles stopped, their hydraulics sinking their sleek shapes to the ground with a soft hisses. The first sedan's back door opened and Defy stepped out, Garz behind him. Dare came around from the driver's side. The other four gangsters stayed in their vehicle without turning the engine or the headlight off. It rolled to a spot parallel to the metacar, about three car widths away.

"Sammy boy," Garz said loudly in a mocking sing-song voice..."Sammy boy...come on out wherever you are. Your homeboys have business with you."

Pointe turned on the light banks and harsh luminosity bathed the entire compound again. Defy and Dare covered their helmet visors and with their free hands reached into their armor pouches. Chuckling, Garz looked around and patted his soldiers on the paldrons of their black armor.

Pointe said nothing, stepped out from behind the oleander bush, pivoted and at a fast clip walked into the adobe house's courtyard, giving Garz no other choice but to follow him. After he passed the stone fountain, he raised his ungloved right hand. A security scanner bathed his hand with red light and the house's two large wooden doors opened automatically to a main room with a floor covered with ancient brown tiles layered with dust. Pointe walked in, Garz and his soldiers following.

Pointe deactivated his helmet and sat on one of the two wooden benches facing each other from opposite ends of the moderate-sized room. They were made out of real wood, ancient wood, not particleboard. The red velvet-covered seating had been worn smooth by decades of use.

Still helmeted, Garz said, "The goddamn security scanner still remembers you. I figured that. Wanted you to feel comfortable and at home." He sat down on the other bench.

Pointe looked around at the framed photographs and paintings. "Yeah, Garz, that's why you told me to wait for you in the parking lot. I did run this place for a time."

Garz laughed dryly. "Now I'll have to recalibrate the security system." Then he added, "That helmet of yours is damn fancy the way it just zips up like that, all automatic, but will it hold up in the action?" He chuckled. Defy and Dare, standing at the opposite ends of Garz's bench looked at each and also chuckled. Garz ripped off his helmet and laid it down on the bench in full mode, its yellow and black mottle contrasting against the seat's worn and dusty red velvet, the faux jaguar visage staring out. He sniffed the air. "Guess the air recycling membrane outside is still doing its job. Man, you wouldn't think the air is bad if you didn't see its effect on all the fools that never use protection."

Pointe said, "A lot of people can't afford the fancy gear we use."

Dare took off his helmet and made a show of inspecting the room. Then, he positioned himself by the wooden door. Defy took off his helmet and stayed by Garz.

The NVB leader smiled and stared at Pointe and Pointe stared back and waited, knowing that Garz believed he had drawn him into a trap, a deadly little game of take it all, a game of win-win for Garz. Pointe leaned back against the uneven whitewashed wall ready to play the gangster's game and risk his life to get information he might have about Charlie and the golden medallion.

No one said anything. Seconds passed. The old adobe walls seemed to absorb the tension and suspicion in the still air, distilling it somehow, making every micro movement appear smooth yet vibrant.

A few more moments passed. "You know," Garz finally said..."Charlie Tuna wasn't just another homeboy from our Brown Zone." Defy puffed up his chest and chimed in..."Charlie had respect all over the Valley." Garz got up from the bench, walked across the room and leaned toward Pointe. "Goddamn right, Sammy, you weren't the first one in this Brown Zone to try to improve and educate himself."

Pointe said, "I knew Charlie had gone to Nortech Educational Institute."

"And I'm sure," Garz said, "you know about that big chunk of gold hanging from his neck. I'm sure he showed it to you."

Pointe nodded. "He showed me his golden medallion."

Garz sat on the bench. "That's the one. It's what got him killed, but let me give some background first." He raised his hands histrionically, paused for a moment then continued..."A professor over at Nortech took a real interest in Charlie, a guy into psychoarcheology. Charlie went with him to a big dig over in a place called the Citadel of the Anazazi in Numex country.

"The Tetrad considered that dig to be of huge importance at that time 'cause the RAAC hadn't been wiped out yet. They kept everything real secret about it. The ruins were the kind of ruins the RAAC used in their ceremonies down in Mexico before they got found out down there and got wiped out. The Tetrad had first seen it from a satellite scan a while back. They got around to sending in their archeologists who found a pyramid and everything all inside a huge cave or a lost valley...something real ancient."

Pointe said, "So?" In fact, this revelation did surprise him. And it really surprised him that that even with his contacts within IntraCity and with people in high places he had never heard about this Citadel of the Anazazi discovery.

The North Valley gang leader shot up from the bench and cut an arc in the air with both arms. Garz said, "Don't bullsh-t me with that attitude, Sammy Boy. You worked for IntraCity and you know nothing like this had ever been found north of the Mother Partition, something you would've found only in old Mexico. All the powers from this region of the Fourth Tetrarchy were there, all under Tetrad big shots - the West Coast League, with the City-State of L.A. leading it; Utah and the Federation of Latter Day Patriarchs; Numex-Arizona Corporation; all the Vegas Corporations; the Rocky Mountain League; Greater Texas and Ameraryans from the Northwest.

"You know that since the big war, the Ameraryans don't have nothing to do with L.A. and the League except to participate in the election for the Tetrarch but they cooperated with L.A on this."

Pointe said, "So what did they find there besides ruins?"

"Charlie told me...what he could still talk about. They found a lot, man." The gang leader became silent. His eyes seemed to peer inward; he seemed to be contemplating something incomprehensible or too difficult to put into words.

"Go on," Pointe said calmly, almost with sympathy.

Garz took a step. "Sammy boy," he said, jutting his round head..."Charlie didn't go back to using drugs because he lost IntraCity's funding. He didn't relapse because of political bullsh-t. Charlie lost his mind because he learned something the Overkind and IntraCity have never wanted us to know about. They found something ancient...a power object Charlie called it."

Pointe said, "The golden medallion?"

"No man, listen." The NVB leader paused and touched his armored chest with his fingertips. Then he extended his arms, gesticulating..."The golden medallion they found in a crypt or something according to what Charlie told me. They found something else there. It makes you," he said slowly and with emphasis..."see and think about things they don't want *you...me... us...the Outer Cohorts* to know about or remember. They tried this thing on Charlie...experimented on him - but it didn't make him go crazy right away. He lost it afterward, slowly...after he came back from the dig.

"The site got attacked. Maybe the RAAC or what's left of them did it...or maybe just marauders. There are all kinds of cannibal tribes and biker armies out there in the mountains and deserts, could've been anybody. Anyway, whoever they were, they hit the archeological site hard but the Tetrad fought back and the fighting got real bad.

"Charlie always was good at getting out of sh-t. He took something with him in the craziness - a micro-disk like the ones used by Tetrad intelligence guys and couriers moving heavy information around." Garz paused, looked all around the room and took a breath. He exhaled and then continued..."It's a micro-disk with the report on this thing, this power object, hidden in that golden medallion. Yeah, the complete report on the thing they found and the experiments Tetrad scientists did on Charlie is in the micro-disk."

Although he had only seen it once, the artifact imaged vividly in Pointe's mind - a heavy golden chain attached with a clasp to a large, heavy golden circle, an intricate work, its details trapping and leading the eye to a sunburst around the stylized face of a god or demon.

The gang leader's gaze went inward again. After a fleeting moment, he snapped back. "Charlie showed the golden medallion to me," he said, his eyes opening widely..."more than a few times. I never seen anything like it before."

Pointe said, "You're telling me they killed Charlie not only for the medallion but because of everything he knew and probably for this micro-disk. Who ordered the Iron Movement to do it? Tetrad agents?"

Garz shook his head. "No, I don't know about that. Charlie told me the Tetrad didn't even know he was still alive. And they thought the medallion got destroyed in an explosion during the fighting. He was sure of that. He told me about a guy that he thought would come after him, a guy named Ken Leary.

"He's a technofreak - hangs out with the Iron Movement when he stays in So Cal, fixes weapons and engines, cooks special drugs. Leary got the 'Movement to do the hit. Charlie had told me it would be only a matter of time before he got whacked after Leary was onto the medallion.

More than likely, Leary wanted that golden piece 'cause it's real valuable. He can sell it to a collector for a lot of money, or maybe even back to the Tetrad."

He had to get as much information as possible. The game would be ending soon.

Pointe said, "How did this Leary find out about the medallion? Charlie told him?"

"Garz said, "Charlie was careful about who he showed that medallion to... "

Pointe could see Dare and Defy's eyes narrowing. Garz's presentation had been rehearsed and some kind of action had been planned to take place upon its ending. It would happen soon. Flashes of their plan and their intent traced through his mind's eye, the apprehension of this information made possible by his years of training in *shim sul* - his *hwarang* study of reading the human mind. *Shim sul* had given him the advantage at the onset of the encounter.

Garz shifted his stance and waved his right hand away. "Eahhh...I've told you enough, Sammy boy." Defy walked to Pointe's right side. "What you need to know, Sammy boy, is that you're going to contribute to the cause by lending us your robot on wheels."

Pointe smiled inwardly. He knew what to expect next.

"According to what I heard," the NVB leader said, "a metacar has just the speed, armor and firepower we need to get the edge on the IM. One righteous driveby and that mob of murdering hotrod freaks is history. And then you've paid your dues to your hood. Word gets out...how you contributed to the cause of getting even for Charlie and everybody in this Brown Zone loves you again. So let's start with some personal instruction on how your robot ride works."

"Yeah," Defy said, "let's see if these wheels are the real deal."

Pointe stood up. "I've seen the Iron Movement in action. I don't know if it would be that simple. Where does Leary live?" He activated his helmet. "Let's go outside," he said through the respirator. "You can tell me more about the whole business while I show you how the metacar works."

"Sammy... " Garz said, "you don't need the helmet yet. Don't worry about it, we'll find Leary."

"I got sensitive to the stale air in this room." Pointe turned abruptly and walked to the adobe's front door. Defy opened the old wooden door for him and Pointe walked into the courtyard. Garz and Dare trailing behind, he continued walking on, past the fountain to the gravel driveway.

The gangsters in the turbo vehicle exchanged looks with Garz as he caught up with Pointe.

"I told you Sammy," Garz said..."we'll find Leary. Leave the Iron Movement to us. Just show us how to operate this robot car of yours, especially the heat it's packing."

Dare walked to the front of the metacar, his hand in his armor pouch fondling something, a knife, handgun, or even a mini-machine pistol.

Silently, Pointe regulated his breathing while his eyes studied the second turbo and its occupants through the helmet's plasmatized lenses. He processed Garz's game plan once again, a simple murderous plan - get the essentials on the metacar and then steal it. Then kill him - stab him, shoot him or beat him to death. And by doing this, Garz would garner upon himself the glory of eliminating a well-known rival. Avenging Charlie had just been a pretense all along to get close to him.

"Okay... " Pointe said. "I'll show you how it works."

Garz and his soldiers started to encircle him.

"Open the door," Pointe said through the helmet transceiver. He activated his gloves.

The gull wing door failed to open. "Open the door," he repeated. Again, it failed to open.

He glanced over at Garth, shrugged and walked toward the gull wing. This diverted Dare to the passenger side's gull wing. Garz and Defy were at his back.

Pointe exploded into a back kick, striking Garz with a heel blow to the groin. He followed up with another back kick aimed at Defy. Garz dropped to his knees, instinctively reaching to his injured organ, throwing his yellow and black helmet to the ground where it bounced and rolled away. Defy blocked Pointe's back kick but chose not to hold his ground, running around Pointe instead, to the front of the metacar to stand at Dare's side. He pulled out a knife. Dare already had his blade out.

Pointe stayed by the driver's side. His machine pistol and the *singeom* were inside the vehicle. The other North Valley Boyz inside their turbo-vehicle poked their guns through opened windows shouting at Defy and Dare to get out of the line of fire. He had only a couple of seconds to get inside the metacar.

Unexpectedly the metacar's engine came to life. The robot vehicle reversed with a jerk, leaving Defy and Dare out in the open. They made a dash for their vehicle but the metacar's M134 7.62x51mm gun had emerged from its pod, its six barrels already spinning. The lead barrel spat out, puncturing eco-armor to tear and flesh and vital organs with the sound of staccato thumps. Dare and Defy went down, their lithe bodies pulped and shredded into bloody pieces.

A light machine gun opened fire from inside the other turbovec. Its ball splattered harmlessly off the metacar. There was a pop pop from a handgun. The Gatling swiveled around and stitched into the sedan, almost tearing off the roof. Turbine blades whined and the turbo accelerated out of the compound, splattering gravel and dust behind it.

Pointe's attention on the fleeing vehicle, a recovered Garz back on his feet charged him, the sound of his footfall on the gravel now amplified in the silence that had followed the barrage of battling gunfire. Garz extended his knife for a lunge. With his peripheral vision, the warrior saw the knife coming directly at his unprotected armpit. He moved aside, the blade grazing his armor.

Garz immediately retracted his knife hand and lunged again, aiming for the exposed area in Pointe's armor between the helmet and the breastplate.

The *hwarang* warrior counterattacked, transforming himself into a dark blur of speed and power in the illuminated night air; he halfstepped back and raised his arms in a cross to block with *nae dang rang*. His right hand wrapped over the top of the wrist of Garz's offending hand, his left hand scissored underneath, his right hand shifting into a circular motion, continuing the blade's deflection to supinate Garz's right wrist joint to its limit, locking his forearm to his elbow with a swift, sharp snap. Pain and pressure forced the muscles in Garz's forearm to lose tension and his hand to release the knife.

Pointe continued with the circular movement, taking Garz to the ground, forcing the gangster's right arm to extend out, twisted by the vicious hold on his wrist. Pointe's right knee descended on the humerus just above where it hinged onto the ulna. He leveraged Garz's forearm up, and forcing its ulna up against the humeroulnar joint.

Garz screamed. Another fraction of force and bone would shatter, ligaments would tear and cartilage would be shredded apart. Blinking desperately, he painfully licked the dust raised by the takedown's impact off his thick lips.

Pointe said, "When did you and your homies decide to kill me?"

"Kill ya?" Garz said. "Didn't want to kill you, just humble you!

"You're no better than us, Pointe. You think you're the only one who can move up in this f--ked-up world?" He spat dust out through gritted teeth, his round face swollen with pain and anger. "You always thought you were so much better than the rest of us. You never knew your real f--kin' father just like we didn't know ours. You're just like the rest of us. Your mother was no better than mine!"

Garz had crossed the line.

He should not have mentioned his family. A petty gangster like Garz had destroyed his family on a side street in Long Beach one afternoon. The only justice for them had been his vengeance, exacted through his secretly sanctioned war against the gangs. And one day Pointe would find out his real father's identity.

He lived by a code nothing like Garz's gangsterism and belief in crushing others. He lived by a martial code and the Great Law. *It had taught him never to take a life without cause.*

Pointe dropped his knee on Garz's elbow a micro-fraction and the NVB leader roared with pain. Garz sobbed..."Don't break me up, man! We didn't move on you, man. You attacked first."

Pointe relieved the pressure. "That's bull," he said calmly, "and you know it."

Garz said, "All right...all right. Our clique couldn't live with you, man, coming back to the hood with your big name and coins from the Eternals and your IntraCity friends. The homeboys said they couldn't stand it. We knew you'd return to the North Valley for Charlie's funeral services...there had to be a little humbling, but we weren't going to wack you"

No, he never took a life without cause...

"We got inspired when we saw your ride parked out the chapel...we thought we could use it against the Iron Movement and get some justice for Charlie. We just wanted your ride and to humble you a little bit...not kill you."

Pointe said, "So you were waiting for me - you did plan this little reception for me. There is something else I need to know. Who does Leary work for?"

"I don't know. Charlie didn't know. No one knows."

Pointe continued increasing pressure in tiny but vicious increments that induced a pathetic moan from his captive. "Where does Leary live?" he asked gently.

"I don't know," Garz said, twisting his lips. "All I know is he hides out in the old North Holly area."

"If Charlie didn't tell him, how did Leary find out about the medallion?" Pointe's knee pressed down again.

And he never looked for cause...

Garz gulped for air. "Okay! Okay!" he shouted. "Charlie made the mistake of telling a civilian he knew about going on the expedition to Numex country. After Charlie came back from the Anazazi dig, he showed the medallion to this guy. Turned out the civilian was Leary's buddy and told him about it."

"So this civilian knows where to find Leary. What's this civilian's name and address?"

"There's an association of regulars and civilians...they have a compound over on Vanny's and Sherm...they all make and fix stuff there. This guy who sold Charlie out to Leary is named Top Lopper. He makes suits of armor at the compound...sells 'em mostly to the Iron Movement."

"Come on, Sammy," Garz pleaded, "We're homeboys. Let me go and I'll never f--k with ya."

"Sure," Pointe said, "but first...what about the twin act out there in the dust? And the gunsels in the turbo...do they know about this?"

"First time Dare and Defy heard the story was back inside the adobe. The soldiers in the turbo don't know nuthin'. Come on, Sammy, the hassle between you and me is over. I swear it."

No, he never took a life without weighing the facts and circumstances, never without

cause...

Pointe reduced the pressure by one more tiny increment. "Are you sure you've told me everything?"

"There's one more thing," Garz added, "that disk hidden in the medallion...you need a special hard drive to store and process the data before you can access it. Charlie told me there's a self-contained reader with this special HDD...a Microcept R."

And he would never seek cause for taking a life unjustly...

Pointe lifted his knee off his enemy's elbow, pulling him up at the same time by the shoulder. "You should know, Garz," he said calmly..."that Ken Leary and whoever else was behind it will be held accountable for killing Charlie, not that it ever really mattered to you."

The gangster reached toward his left elbow with his right hand, attempting to regain his balance at the same time. Pointe's right forearm smashed against Garz's temple, pushing him into his embrace. With his left arm, he crushed Garz's head against his chest, exposing the neck and carotid artery. Using his left forearm, he sealed the carotid artery, stopping the flow of blood to the brain.

But Garz had come to him...

Garz stopped breathing. The warrior released him and he fell back onto the gravel with a thud, his eyes protruding from his face, staring up stupidly.

And gave him just cause.

There were no peace-keeping police, courts or real justice under IntraCity's martial law. Garz had been an enemy who had planned to kill him and steal from him, another animal without honor on the streets, a deadly rattler whose word meant nothing and who would always remain a lethal threat. Executing Garz had been a preemptive act of self-defense.

Pointe deactivated his helmet and gloves. He inhaled and exhaled repeatedly to modulate the flow of adrenalin in his blood stream. His breaths were smooth, powerful, controlled. He began calming himself, bringing himself down from the emotional spike in the wave of deadly violence over which he had become the prime mover.

Then something reared forth out of the *hwarang*, something cold, dense and shadowy, sheer negative life-force, a fury so intense it seemed to possess form and mass, a columnar form radiating out in all directions. It erupted outward, against the now-dead Garz laying on the gravel, and back in time against the mindless gangsters who had killed his family. It rampaged, in his mind's eye, this thundering anger, out of the adobe house grounds to smash against the e-gates, the Partitions, the Iron Movement, hurtling against IntraCity, SPASS, the Overkind and the Tetrad. Then in a second, inexplicably, his emotional storm recoiled and fused with the hunger for freedom and justice that he had buried in the deepest, most forbidden part of his soul.

The warrior inhaled, tightening his *dan jun* and then slowly exhaled the harsh amalgam of emotions out, back into the void. He turned away from his enemy's corpse and walked back into the courtyard to get a drink from the fountain to quench the ferocious bitterness in his mouth and throat and splash his face.

He stopped.

Weirdly illuminated by cast off light, were dead eucalyptus leaves, insect carcasses, bird feathers and other debris brimming the stone fountain's dry basin. He had once cleaned this very fountain on a regular basis and even then, when he had done so, it had been dry for as long as anybody could remember.

The *hwarang* turned and walked toward the metacar, wondering why the image of cool, clean water gurgling out of that stone fountain on this old adobe courtyard in Missing Hells had struck his mind's eye with such singular clarity.

DEADLEE

Deadlee aka Joseph Thomas Espinoza Lee, earned a position as a key player in music's latest underground movement, gay rap/hip hop. He garnered much press with his groundbreaking, genre-screwing approach, attracting cover stories in The New York Daily News, Rolling Stone, and The Los Angeles Times. Lee has been a guest on Howard Stern, The Tyra Banks Show, and was interviewed twice on CNN. He was also one of the 18 gay hip hop artists featured in the landmark documentary film on gays in hip hop called "Pick up the Mic". Lee has followed in the tradition of rappers-turned-actor and had roles in Hoochie Mamma Drama, Rampart, Meth Head, as well as roles in theater, starring in Eavesdropper and Flash Gordon. He is honored to be included in this anthology to honor his mother Margaret and his Espinoza Family who come from the Oldest Town in Colorado, San Luis.

RASPADOS DON MANUEL

Let me paint the picture - no, it's more like a mural: Just passing through the newly gentrified downtown lofts that have replaced (but not completely taken over) the cardboard digs of LA's homeless - I begin my jaunt over the 4th Street Bridge. The signs on the shoulder say 'keep your eyes on the road' but I still take one more glance back at the steel frames of downtown Los Angeles awash in an orange atomic glow as the sun sets on the City of Angels.

Down below, train tracks and the LA riverbed look like a set for a Hollywood movie. The mural comes to life as John Travolta, as Danny in the movie Grease, is "automatic, systematic, greased lightning" winning a drag race in the dry riverbed for the T-Birds.

Still heading east just pass the 5 Freeway sits Hollenbeck Park and the hustle and bustle of Quinceañeras and vendors. It is all reminiscent of the Laurel and Hardy slapstick shenanigans in the classic film, Men O' War that was filmed at this same park in 1929. The only difference is Boyle Heights, home to a large Jewish Community in the 1920's, is now home to a predominately Chicano/a and or Latino/a population.

Our mayor, Antonio Villaraigosa, golden boy Oscar de la Hoya, and Edward James Olmos are a few of the well-known residents hailing from the bluffs and the flats of Boyle

Heights. All roads lead to Boyle Heights: where Interstates 5, 101, 10 and 60 all crisscross to create the massive East Los Angeles Interchange.

The gentrification trend that has already transformed the once *vida loca* of Echo Park and Silver Lake into yuppie havens has just recently begun to trickle into Boyle Heights. All this reminiscing and reflecting and I have almost forgotten why I began this excursion into unknown territory…

It was a summer-like day and my homie had promised to fill up my gas guzzling SUV if I took him to get a Diablito at a spot he only remembered was near Roosevelt High School.

I first cleared things up to make sure a Diablito was not some code name for the drug of the moment. I was once coerced by another homie to take him to a spot where he proceeded to buy crack without my knowledge.

The homie assured me that a Diablito was the name of a raspado - a Mexican snow cone or Latino version of the 7-11 Slurpee.

So we finally arrive at a storefront near the corner of 4th St. and Mott with a modest sign displaying RASPADOS DON MANUEL in front of us. Stepping through the plastic curtains, we wait alongside school kids at a counter. Shaved ice, mangos, mango juice and chili powder make up the cold spicy sensation called a Diablito.

Instead of a helping of yogurt like at a Pinkberry Frozen Yogurt, a sliced opened bag of Flaming Hot Cheetos or Tostitos is topped with chopped mango, chopped cucumber, and cueritos (pickled pork skins) with a secret sauce of chamoy (a hot-sour-salty-sweet concoction) generously topping it all off. The toppings are different, but the concept is the same. This one of a kind snack is a perfect accompaniment to the Diablito.

Like a post orgasmic afterglow, warm and lingering, I sit back full and satisfied after devouring my snacks. The accomplishment of my feat can only be measured against my first Krispy Kreme doughnut or In-and-Out burger.

These are moments that one cannot dismiss or regard lightly in one's lifetime. 24-hours later I was feening for another Diablito. I talked a friend into taking me to the spot for my now daily fix. Two weeks in and I was a full blown Diablito junkie.

It has been three months since I was introduced to Raspados Don Manuel, and I have cut back to a visit a week. I woke up recently in a deep sweat not only having raspado withdrawal, but I dreamt my spot was replaced by a Starbucks.

Mr. Gentrification has a way of rearing his ugly head, taking over and displacing unique and local businesses. Gloria Molina, Los Angeles County Supervisor 1st District (which includes Raspados Don Manuel), was quoted about the first Starbucks in East L.A...

"The opening of Starbucks is just the latest success story in our ongoing renaissance of East L.A...." she said.

Our communities look at a business like a Starbucks as a measurement of growth but sometimes the true renaissance is right under our noses.

Entrepreneur Howard Schultz had a dream to take a local shop like Starbucks and serve coffee beyond Seattle. Maybe the true renaissance of East L.A. would be if a Raspados Don Manuel wasn't just serving Diablitos in East L.A. but also on the Westside of the city, right alongside a Starbucks, serving homegrown success.

MATT SEDILLO

Born in El Sereno California, Matt Sedillo is a two-time national slam poet, grand slam champion of the Damn Slam Los Angeles 2011 and the author of "For What I Might Do Tomorrow" published by Caza De Poesia 2010. His work has been published in anthologies alongside Luis Rodriguez and he has been featured in the Los Angeles Times. Sedillo has been a featured performer on KPFK in LA and Radio Free Atlanta. Sedillo's poetry is currently a part of the curriculum in the course Illegal: Undocumented Latinos in the US taught by Dr. Robert LeRoux Hernandez at Holy Cross University. Sedillo has appeared at numerous universities as a guest performer and panelist.

RACISM AND CAPITALISM

If you find

the confederate flag offensive

so too should you find

the nickel

If you find

the confederate flag offensive

so too should you find

the name of this nation's capital

If you find the confederate flag offensive

so too should you find the American flag

They all stand for the same fucking things...

Racism

and

Capitalism

When rich kids pass through cities

such as Watts, South Central, East Los Angeles, Compton

they are told to watch their wallets

When Mayors, Governors, city councilmen

discuss allocated funds for cities

such as Watts, South Central, East Los Angeles, Compton

we are all told to remember the budget

yet they still find ways to fund

the building of more prisons

and the ramping up of police departments

staffed by lawless men

who run wild through the streets

making the law as they go

They call this service and protection

but then again they have always had

a funny way of looking at things

like history books that teach children

to hallow hollow preambles

that include phrases such as

"We the people"

as drafted by slave drivers and land barons

invaders and treaty breakers

backstabbers and bastards

enshrined as our founding fathers

but I am told times are changing

that we are making slow but steady progress

in a uniquely American process

But to be honest

I don't feel any change

and I don't see much difference

between gentrification

and the Trail of Tears

the Chavez Ravine

or post Katrina New Orleans

cause when the hurricane struck

when the levees broke

with a few pen strokes

they set in motion

what they had already planned

It wasn't negligence

it wasn't incompetence

it was some straight up evil shit

Oh yes they plan to rebuild New Orleans

along the lines of an amusement park

a beautiful place to visit

with nowhere to live

They don't want them back

who are they?

and what do I mean by them?

Let me be clear

Let me be clear

I am not talking

About a Black, White,

Latino, Middle Eastern

Asian divide

I am talking about

the fortune five

hundred

America

incorporated

Give us your poor your tired your huddled masses

SO WE CAN WORK THEIR ASSES!!!

Send us your coffin ship Irish

we will turn their children into factory workers

Send your sickly Italians

to Ellis Island

turn them into coal miners

spread out throughout the country

have them dying of the black lung

or in Ludlow massacres

You see back then

if you wanted to form a union

the color of your eyes

the complexion of your skin

offered no protection

No

you would have to shoot it out

with Carnegie and Rockefeller's men

Jay Gould and Jim Crow

walking hand in hand

in the Robber Baron era

of white privilege

Poor whites had the right

to mob violence to terrorism

that is the privilege to lynch black men

to kill Indians

to beat Mexicans

and then starve

right along with them

because you cannot eat racism

and you cannot clothe your children in racism

and when the question

"Mom where are we going to sleep tonight"

"I don't know son but at least we are not spics"

is not a suitable answer

because racism can only ever be used

by a privileged few to divide the many

to divide us

to divide the people

We are the people

so you cannot lift a finger

for the immigrants

unless you are prepared to raise your fist

and fight for the rights of all of us

and you cannot eliminate black poverty

or brown poverty

without eliminating all poverty

because striking at racism

without attacking capitalism

is like cutting down strange fruit

and then leaving the fucking tree

GUSTAVO ARELLANO

Gustavo Arellano is the editor of OC Weekly, an alternative newspaper in Orange County, California, author of Orange County: A Personal History, Ask A Mexican and Taco USA: How Mexican Food Conquered America. He is also a lecturer with the Chicana and Chicano Studies department at California State University, Fullerton. Arellano writes "¡Ask a Mexican!," a nationally syndicated column and has been the subject of press coverage in national and international newspapers, The Today Show, Hannity, Nightline, Good Morning America, and The Colbert Report. Gustavo is the recipient of the Los Angeles Press Club's 2007 President's Award and an Impacto Award from the National Hispanic Media Coalition, and was recognized by the California Latino Legislative Caucus with a 2008 Spirit Award for his "exceptional vision, creativity, and work ethic." Gustavo is a lifelong resident of Orange County and is the proud son of two Mexican immigrants, one whom was illegal.

WHY DENVER IS HOME TO THE BEST MEXICAN DISH IN THE UNITED STATES

Originally published in Westword, a Village Voice Media publication on April 3, 2012

Tom Tancredo doesn't like Mexicans - no way, no how, no *duh*. The former Colorado congressman and one-time presidential candidate spent most of his political career railing against a supposed invasion of the United States by Mexico - and while intelligent minds can disagree about the benefits versus detriments caused by unchecked migration to this country, Tancredo flat-out feels that Mexicans and their culture are downright deficient.

"Sadly, corruption is deeply ingrained in Mexican society, from the local police to the government owned utilities," Tancredo once wrote in a column for WorldNetDaily. "It's a way of doing everyday business."

It was a direct dig at me. In November 2010, we debated in Denver about whether Mexicans ever assimilate into American culture in a standoff that made national news. (I maintained we do; Tancredo didn't accept the possibility, yet couldn't explain how I - who only spoke Spanish when enrolled in kindergarten, the child of two Mexican immigrants, one of whom came into this country in the trunk of a Chevy - did it.) The debate was held at Su Teatro, that *chingón* Chicano theater on Santa Fe Drive in the heart of what was once Denver's Mexican neighborhood, and is now Denver's Art District on Santa Fe. There's no need to get into all the details of the evening (find them in the archives of the Latest Word, *por favor*), except for one pertinent point: Before lambasting Mexicans and our supposed refusal to join American society, Tom ate a Mexican dinner with me.

We went across the street from Su Teatro to El Noa Noa, a large restaurant that advertises itself as the Mile High City's "best and most authentic Mexican restaurant." At night, art deco-style neon lights flash the restaurant's name, a reference to a legendary nightclub in Ciudad Juárez that was the subject of a famous Mexican song. A party on your plate. The atmosphere isn't obscenely ethnic: no strolling mariachis or women fluttering fans and eyelids. Eaters sit; waiters bring out baskets of chips and bowls of salsa and fetch drinks. People of all ethnicities come in to eat, though the clientele leans more American than Mexican.

Tancredo and I sat down near the middle of the restaurant; *Westword* editor Patricia Calhoun and a few staffers joined us. Patty, who's known Tom for years, was the one who had long sought to have him and me face off, and figured we should break tortillas beforehand, as she was going to moderate the Su Teatro theatrics. We traded small talk, saving our salvos for the discussion to come - but around us, tables whispered, fingers pointed. Some people came up to our table to greet Tancredo, wish him luck for the evening. A Facebook friend, a woman from Boulder who works with undocumented college students, offered me a pin that said "DREAM ACT" and her appreciation that I was confronting a person she considered a living manifestation of Satan. She wanted to make a scene, but her chile relleno supper was getting cold.

Our plates came. I drank tequila, of course; Tancredo, a dry red wine. He'd ordered the tamale dinner, hold the Spanish rice. Two tamales, slathered (or, as more accurately stated in the Denver lexicon, "smothered") with green chile, absent their corn husks, each as long as a palm, as thick as a copy of a book, sat before him. They glistened with the dabs of lard needed to make a tamale moist and more than mere cornmeal and shredded pork. I stole bites of the same plate from Calhoun: soft, spicy filling. The pork sang sweet notes on my palate; the green chile piqued toward the end. These weren't the tamales of my youth; they were smaller - familiar, yet different from anything I'd ever eaten. The chile - born of the fertile soil of southern Colorado, which Hispanics had tilled before there was a United States - seared differently from the Mexican chiles on which I grew up. It needed no extra salsa, it was so flavorful.

Tancredo thought so as well. He polished off his plate, laughing and talking between each bite, getting himself fueled for a night decrying the very culture that fed him. More than a year later, I can recall just some of the points of our philosophical fisticuffs, but the scene I can't get out of my mind is Tancredo's massive, tamale-induced smile throughout the night. Tom Tancredo may not like Mexicans, but he sure loves his Mexican food - *of course* he does. And if a *pendejo* like Tom can learn to love Denver's unique take on Mexican food, then so should the rest of the country.

Especially a *pendejo* like me.

*

I love you, Denver: You've always been beyond supportive of my work, have always sent some of my favorite questions for my ¡Ask a Mexican! column, have always provided one of my biggest fan bases outside of my Southern California home base. I've spoken at three of your universities - University of Denver, Metro State, even Johnson & Wales, for chrissakes - and at your beautiful downtown library; have done three signings at the Tattered Cover; moon-lighted as a guest judge for Geeks Who Drink; and been on many of your radio and television stations. Every time I visit, everyone is nice - except that jerk Peter Boyles, who'll never have me on his radio show, for reasons I can't comprehend. (Let's do it, Pete!)

But your Mexican food? The most bizarre in the United States - and I've had tater-tot burritos *and* Taco Bueno. The least-loved. The most unknown. The most - excuse my English - *weird*. Outside of Coloradans and expats, no one gives a shit about Denver's Mexican-food traditions, let alone wants to know about them. Your most unique culinary contribution to Mexican food, the Mexican hamburger, is unknown outside of your state, derided by every-one to whom I describe it; they're incredulous that anyone can consider *that* Mexican food and dismiss it as yet another Denver oddity à la Tim Tebow and, well, Tom Tancredo. Your most famous Mexican restaurant is Casa Bonita in Lakewood, an Oklahoman import immortalized in *South Park* and called "the world's weirdest Mexican restaurant" by this fine publication.

Your Mexican food never makes the national conversation about America's regional Mexican styles - Tex-Mex, Cal-Mex, Sonoran cuisine, Southwestern food...Den-Mex? Sounds like a cholesterol drug. If the country knows anything about Denver's Mexican grub, it's Chi-potle, the wildly successful burrito company started by Steve Ells in a former Dolly Madison shop near the University of Denver - and instead of making your indigenous burritos a na-tional obsession, he instead went with San *fucking* Francisco. Traitor. When Colorado Mexican finally reached the national spotlight, the Travel Channel's *Food Wars* decided to focus on Pueblo's Slopper. Sad. Even I, who professes to love Denver, largely ignored your cuisine in my new book, *Taco USA: How Mexican Food Conquered America*. There's a paragraph about your native food in the chapter about burritos, and that's about it; meanwhile, I devote pages to Ells. Really sad.

But after years of wrestling with the cuisine, of wondering why you wrap wontons around chiles rellenos and put hamburger patties into burritos, of marveling that your green chile is as orange as the jerseys of the Broncos, I have finally learned to love Den-Mex. Your epic Mexican hamburgers, your combo plates slathered - scratch that, *smothered* - in furious chile. Your street-corner, foil-wrapped burritos steaming with chunks of pork, the late-night runs to Chubby's. (Chubby's! The greatest Mexican restaurant in the United States! More on that in a bit.) When I first came and tasted Den-Mex, I dismissed *ustedes* as a heresy as dangerous to Mexican culture as the only Mexican thing I knew about Denver at the time: Tom Tancredo.

That's now changed: I'll devote the rest of my life to spreading your gospel, with the fervor of the converted. Let the rest of the nation snicker: Yours is a foodway deserving of love, because your cuisine is the I Corinthians 13 of the grub world - patient, kind, waiting for people to wise up to it, as I eventually did.

I first visited Denver in the summer of 2007, on the tour for the initial release of the book version of ¡Ask a Mexican! It was a whirlwind stay, one that didn't allow me to get a bite until after my book signing at the Tattered Cover - a burger at a bar. I didn't try Denver's Mexican food then, but I do remember street vendors with coolers, handing out burritos to people ranging from blue-collar workers waiting for a bus to men in suits buying them from their cars, windows cracked open just enough for a transaction to occur. It struck me as odd: I'm from California, where we think we invented the burrito, and only eat them from the fast-food drive-thru or a *lonchera,* so to see a bunch of Denverites carrying around our birthright in a container we use to store beer at the beach seemed silly.

The thought of a cooler burrito did pique my palate, though, so I vowed to buy one the next time I was in Denver - for the fall 2008 book tour for my *Orange County: A Personal History.* I returned to the Tattered Cover that September, but another whirlwind PR tour prevented me from trying the cooler burrito. Thankfully, editor Calhoun intervened. I was due to leave Denver right after appearing on Jay Marvin's old show. (Strange but true: Jay Marvin is a native of Orange County, so he always had me on his show when I was in town, for hours at a time; it's a tragedy he had to give it up for health reasons.) Right before a car was supposed to pick me up at 9 a.m., she met me in the lobby of Denver's Clear Channel operations and gave me a burrito. It initially seemed like any other burrito: wrapped in foil, in a flour tortilla, and big. Big deal. But then I took a bite. The beans were wonderful, the rice fluffy, the chorizo magnificent, the eggs silken. Then the spice hit: not the salsas I've known for so long, but something better, something fragrant, fleshy and with a kick like Jason Elam. It was spectacular, and taught me more was out there.

It was only later that I realized the importance of that particular burrito maker: Santiago's, which many of you deem the best Mexican food in Denver. Then, I just knew the brilliance of this burrito, so I happily obliged when Calhoun asked for a quote describing my experience.

"The breakfast burrito at Santiago's," I wrote," is everything I love about Denver - humble, not ostentatious, the perfect size, and resolutely Mexican at its heart, even as the whiteys that were the eggs and potato tried to supersede the green chile and chorizo for taste, with each bite provoking desires for more. In other words: *muy bueno.*"

I finally tried a cooler burrito on another 2008 trip; it was wonderful. On the trip back home, I had a chance to read *Westword*'s 2005 masterpiece on the phenomenon ("Word of Mouth," Adam Cayton-Holland, January 27, 2005) and started realizing there was something unique about your Mexican food.

Oh, was I to be proven right.

*

It was in early 2009 when I told *Westword* I was researching for a book on the history of Mexican food in the United States. "You know Colorado has its own Mexican food, right?" Calhoun told me. Why, no.

I'm sorry to say this, Denver, but I didn't even know Colorado had its own *Mexicans*. Oh, I knew about Corky Gonzalez - or thought I did. At the time, I didn't know about the proud Chicanos of this city, the long relationship with the *manito* culture of New Mexico, the unique trends, vocabulary, mores and traditions that resulted from a migration that predated Colorado's entry into the United States. Denver's Chicanos have never gotten a fair shake in Chicano Studies because, well, you're *Denver*. John Elway, Tancredo, now Peyton Manning - you have some of the most *gabacho gabachos* in the United States, and coming from a native of Orange County, California, that's saying a lot.

Denver has its own Mexican food? I needed to research, to see what abominations you could possibly create. Burritos are one thing; anything that veered from that? *¡Vendidos!*

The next time I visited, for a 2009 lecture at an art center in Boulder, the *Westword* crew took me to lunch at a restaurant called La Fiesta; the sons of the family that owns it are fans of my column. I asked which dish was most uniquely Colorado Mexican, and the answer was unanimous: La Fiesta's chiles rellenos.

Huh? What spin could Denver possibly give to chiles rellenos, a dish I had never had in any other way than a pasilla or Anaheim chile stuffed with cheese (maybe with ground beef), coated in egg batter, then fried? The answer came with my order: mini-size it with a Chinese spin. Out came something that looked like an egg roll, drowned in a sickly gravy that seemed more paste than food. The table explained it was a Colorado chile stuffed with "premium" cheese, then wrapped in a wonton wrapper and fried. Yes: a wonton wrapper. And all that yuck surrounding it? Chile. Not "chili," as in the ground-beef explosion created in San Antonio; not a salsa, but *chile*. What's chile? No one bothered to explain it; instead, they looked at me like the clueless *pendejo* I was. Oh, and the chile relleno wasn't drowned in chile, it was "smothered."

I dug in. Gooey, crunchy, spicy, but really gooey, like concentrated nachos thrown in a fryer, then covered with the most sumptuous sauce I've ever tasted: deceptive, flecked with pork, but deathly spicy. I wanted to ask for Tapatío, but none was necessary. It was bizarre, but it was delicious. I didn't find it "authentic" at all, but I figured I'd do at least a shout-out to this plate in *Taco USA*, out of my respect for Denver. I picked up another street-cooler burrito for the flight home.

It was a fruitful trip. I returned to California and told friends about Denver's strange-ass chiles   rellenos; they all laughed. I told them about the street-cooler burritos; they laughed again. And then a friend who used to live in Denver uttered the magical words: "Have you gone to Chubby's? That place is CRAZY."

*

Chubby's. When I posted on my Facebook fan page that I was thinking about a trip to Chubby's on my next visit to Denver, a war of the words broke out. One person said I *had* to eat there, then someone else chimed in to slam Chubby's. Then someone else slammed that person, and someone else said that everyone was attacking the wrong Chubby's. Finally, someone mentioned a "Mexican hamburger" - and all hell broke loose yet again, while I read on in bewilderment.

Trying to act like the all-knowing Mexican I am, I never admitted that I didn't have a clue about their conversation, not to mention their quibbles. Finally, I did my research in the *Westword* archives and discovered the amazing story of the Cordovas, starting with the late Stella Cordova, who was working at the Chubby Burger Drive-Inn in the late '60s when the owner decided to sell it. She bought it, kept the name, added her own green chile recipe to the menu, and kept working there for the next forty years. Easily another sidebar for *Taco USA*, I thought. I needed to try this Mexican hamburger, and to try Chubby's. The only problem: My book was due by the fall of 2010, and I had no scheduled trips to Denver. But like angels knowing that a wretch needs salvation, the Department of Chicano Studies at Metro State contacted me in the spring of 2010, wondering if I would accept an offer to participate in its Richard T. Castro Distinguished Lecture series, which takes place every fall. At the time, I had no idea who Castro was (now I do, of course - what an amazing man. You need to promote him on a national scale, Denver), but accepted under one condition: that my handlers take me to Chubby's.

It didn't happen. The trip was packed with everything from student lectures to public lectures to dinners and the Tancredo debate. I ate burritos, I ate hotel food, but I couldn't sneak away to Chubby's. Finally, a helpful gal took me to Bubba Chino's on Federal, part of a chain run by Leonard Cordova, one of Stella Cordova's grandsons. I finally tasted the Mexican hamburger, and enjoyed it immensely. Leonard was a gentleman, bringing me other dishes he was trying out. (Only later did I find out how loathed he is in some Denver circles; that's your fight, *cabrones*, but Leonard was nice and his food was good.) Still, it wasn't the original Chubby's.

I panicked. I thought I'd have to fly out to Denver on my own, just to visit this much-mythologized restaurant. I couldn't finish the book without a Chubby's mention - but I was already half a year late with the *Taco USA* manuscript.

Fate intervened with yet another Denver trip - this one in the spring of 2011, for a University of Denver speech. DU kindly catered the event with Chipotle burritos. By then, I was savvy enough about Den-Mex to crack a joke before the appreciative audience that I needed the burrito smothered. After the speech, I insisted that my hosts take me to Chubby's. They wondered out loud why I'd want to visit a place like that instead of a nice sit-down restaurant.

I had already learned that, according to Denver legend, the Mexican hamburger was created at Joe's Buffet, a long-gone eatery just up the street from Su Teatro. It was first advertised as a blackboard special in the late 1960s as "Linda's Mexican Hamburger," named after a waitress. From there, the Mexican hamburger spread across Denver - but only across Denver, much to the surprise of Mile High City denizens I talked to, who'd always assumed that their dish, like the local NFL squad, had a national reach. Maybe it didn't go further because it's so straightforward: Putting a hamburger patty inside a burrito? How truly revolutionary is that? More likely because you just don't get a fair shake from the rest of America, Denver. Yet that's what made the Mexican hamburger so brilliant: its simplicity, its utterly unremarkable nature, the effortless mixing of traditions. Mexican. American. Den-Mex. And at Chubby's, I finally discovered that the Mexican hamburger reaches every overblown food cliché one can imagine.

Because even Denver doesn't realize the significance of the Mexican hamburger, Chubby's is most famous for its chile, still made according to Stella Cordova's original recipe, which smothers everything there - burritos, fries, cheeseburgers. A hearty condiment for a hardy city where you need all the comfort you can get. It works best, though, smothering a Mexican hamburger, the greatest Mexican dish in the United States. This is how I describe it in *Taco USA*:

Brace yourselves, folks: underneath that Syracuse Orangeman-hued chile lies the structure of a burrito - a flour tortilla containing refried beans, your choice of meat, and a grilled hamburger patty, almost extant in shape. On top of this is the chile: flecked with pork, spicier than the competition, smothered completely over the burrito until it's little more than a beached whale over a viscous, spicy sea. The flour tortilla itself is cooked well until it becomes firm, almost crispy, so you can slice off a chunk of Mexican hamburger and it won't flop around on your fork as it enters your mouth. The patty sits in the center, well-done, its beefiness absorbing the pork fat of the chicharrones and the lard of the refried beans. When you order one, the Chubby's staff serves it on a cardboard plate, then puts another plate on top and staples them together, to ensure not a drop of the ambrosia spills and wastes.

I've had puffy tacos in San Antonio that produced visions of grandeur, glorious bowls of the green in Hatch, fabulous taco pizzas in Minnesota, and gargantuan Mission burritos in San Francisco, but the Mexican hamburger is the dish that best personifies the Mexican-American experience, a monument to mestizaje. The tortilla is wholly indigenous; its flour version, the legacy of Spain. The focus on green chile places the Mexican hamburger firmly in the Southwest; its gravy, the legacy of Tex-Mex. The hamburger patty, of course, is wholly American - but even that has a German past. This fugue is pure rascuache, the Mexican concept of creating beauty from seeming crap. And the taste? Heavy, thick, yet Chubby's Mexican hamburger at its best retains all the flavors of its distinct parts. No added salsa is necessary - amazingly, underneath all that heartiness, the chile comes through and zaps every cell of your body into attention.

Let the Baylessistas scream - this is a dish as Mexican as the Templo Mayor, as American as the Washington Monument, as Chicano as George Lopez.

I ate that Mexican hamburger sitting at a picnic table outside of Chubby's, since there's nowhere to eat inside the original Chubby Burger Drive-Inn. And I took a to-go menu, the one with a portrait of Stella and Alex Cordova, another grandson, with the blared warning at the bottom "NOT AFFILIATED WITH ANY OTHER CHUBBYS." It has a hallowed spot at my office, where it serves as reminder of everything wonderful about Denver, a reminder that I need to return again and spread your glory.

*

I'm still insulting you, Denver. The initial run of my *Taco USA* book tour takes me from San Diego to San Francisco, then across the American Southwest, from Tuscon to El Paso to Albuquerque to Santa Fe to Flagstaff to Phoenix to Tucson and a plane trip back home to Orange County...but no Denver. No drive up I-25 to *ustedes*. Couldn't convince my publisher to fly me out to the Mile High City. Again, Denver loses in the Aztlán sweepstakes.

We'll have a Denver book-signing this year, I promise - maybe at the Tattered Cover, maybe at Su Teatro (maybe at Su Teatro, sponsored by the Tattered Cover?), maybe on a street corner surrounded by burrito coolers. In the meantime, when people pick up this book, they will learn that Chubby's serves the best Mexican dish in this country. When they read about Chipotle, they will see a shout-out to your indigenous burrito tradition. When they devour the introduction, there will be El Noa Noa, the dinner with Tancredo, La Fiesta's fine, if odd, chile relleno. Den-Mex is an amazing Mexican regional tradition, one deserving of further examination - and an acolyte with a national platform, such as the one I'll soon assume in the promotion for *Taco USA.*

I am an imperfect adopted son, Denver, and I still have much to learn, and much to make up for my transgressions. But I promise to sing your gospel, to proclaim the glories of your Mexican hamburgers and smothered burritos wherever and whenever I go for the rest of my years.

Now, can someone FedEx me some Chubby's green chile in one of those freeze-dried TSA-approved bags? I'm getting homesick.

ALEJANDRO DENNIS MORALES

Alejandro Dennis Morales was born in Montebello, California. He received his Ph. D. degree from Rutgers University. He is a Professor in the Department of Chicano/Latino Studies at the University of California, Irvine. His writing focuses on chronicling the Chicano/Latino experience past, present and future in Los Angeles and the borderlands. His novels include Barrio on the Edge/Caras viejas y vino nuevo, La verdad sin voz, Reto en el paraíso, The Brick People, The Rag Doll Plagues and Waiting to Happen. The Place of the White Heron, Volume Two of the "Heterotopia Trilogy" is being considered for publication. He has also published Pequeña Nación_a collection of short stories. His latest novel The Captain of All These Men of Death – about tuberculosis and the Chicano/Latino community was published by Bilingual Review Press. Currently, he is working on several projects including a novel titled Porciúncula concerning the Los Angeles River, a love story, eugenics, and the beautiful bridges that cross into downtown Los Angeles.

*

The red stream christened by Franciscans walking with Spanish officers, mestizo soldiers, hybrid settlers come upon Pomo Indian deer hunters with their women and children singing and laughing standing knee high in the icy creek simply butchering their prey.

MATANZAS CREEK

Word tasting

in Sonoma Valley

Condor black leather

and a hint of fear

driving the narrow

ribbon red trails

tugging a past

where history deep

in roots and vines

arrow head sharp

Matanzas Creek

running red with blood

and Indians' laughter

the joy of the slaughter

the butchering of

their prey

in the icy water

while winter reaches

southward to

the native home

of a modern

tribe

ON AN ISLAND

She runs here and there

hurrying to get things done

there is so much to do

before we leave

She whirls and twirls

juggles paper and pen

organizing constantly organizing

searching for important

addresses, bills, envelopes

she had a minute ago

the duplicate house keys

she just had in her hand

"How could I have misplaced

what I just held in my hand!"

She looks at me

I quiver away

She commences the search again

never ending work

she has taken over

She has taken all the work over

It is hers to do and to worry about

She worries

getting ready

making sure

before we leave

her mental list is done

She rapidly takes a deep breath

She exhales sadness

toil and misery

as she works frantically

in the open fields

under the desert sun

in the thick jungle

in the filthy bed

in the mountain of garbage

in the suffocating sweat shop

in the over committed law offices

in the damp mine pit

in the overwhelmed emergency room

in the chaotic classroom

in the money ridden professional athletic field

on her back giving birth

in domestic attire

afraid always afraid

what might happen next

She labors unhappy

desiring to be free

In the next room she packs luggage

She did not want to leave the dog

Uncomfortable with the house sitter I got

She worries

She will finally

rest her head on the pillow

at twelve thirty

will rise at six

to toil again

She works with children

at an elementary school

She is a full time second grade teacher

She picks up after her children

She picks up after her students

She tosses shoes in the closet

She tosses balls in the recess bend

She breaths deeply

her face is tired

She worries about

each one of her students

She seldom smiles

Through traffic she drives home

a weight of finances burdens her heart

Fear of failure

adds another

deep wrinkle

to her fabulous face

"Oh Lord"

She breathes

a prayer of frustrations

She prepares the evening meal

makes sure her children

are clean and ready for dinner

She coughs and sniffles

The alarm set for six

She collapses into bed

to push my hand away

She closes her eyes and snores softly

and probably dreams

of her mother and father

of childhood

on an island

IN THE NAME OF SELF DEFENSE

1

A woman carrying a knife

slain shot thirty-five times

at seven in the mourning

while carrying a three inch knife

wandering through the streets mourning

her being raped earlier that morning

had argued with her mother

wondered why she did not listen

she ran out of the apartment

hysterical and confused

2

On that morning

the cops come

to serve and to protect

the woman

all of nineteen years

stood still

to return

a desperate gaze

at two police officers

a glimpse of help

a glimmer of hope

crosses her mind

for an instant

Drop the knife!

Drop the knife!

in unison

the officers yell

Drop the knife!

She stumbles forward

3

The first shots fired

go through

her shoulders and arms

together the cops

are terrible shots

the repeated volleys

penetrate her chest

Drop the knife!

She is still standing

the cops open fire once more

the bullets push her backward

she finally rests

on the green lawn

her body sprawled out

opened wide

crucified

in a growing

pool of blood

4

witnesses criticized the police

for using deadly force

the police countered the accusation

declaring that the two officers

were not carrying

less-lethal means

to subdue the crazed woman

the officers followed

department policy

to shoot to kill

firing into her upper torso

the department's bullets

ripped her to shreds

she was dead on site

yet escorted

to the hospital

where of course

they did all they could

5

the neighborhood

residents screamed

bring her down

a different way

jump on her

she is beyond

scared and disoriented

the knife

a little knife

it 's a small switch blade

knock it out of her hand

use a baton

a rifle

a kick

your bodies

yes sacrifice

your body

to protect and serve

6

a ninety pound

petit woman

anxious bewildered

fearful recruits

the neighborhood women

to smother the girl

in their garments with love

the knife is not a threat

to save her life

let the neighbors

overwhelm her

she poses no real

lethal danger

the two officers

can wait for

a lesser lethal means

to subdue

the woman

standing alone

on the sidewalk

before a natural green

wait for enough backup

to overpower

without obliterating

her under

the mourning sun

7

once the cops

draw their weapons

they are compelled

to repeat

department procedure

which is simply

shoot to kill

always shoot to kill

Drop the knife!

Drop the knife!

the two cops scream

once the high powered

technology

is in their hands

somebody will die

If she refuses to

Drop the knife!

they must eliminate her

from existence

8

this is a tragic case

tragic for the officers too

they found their lives

threatened

months later after

the typical investigation

the two officers are cleared

of any wrong doing

the pusillanimous grand jury

and district attorney's

office announced

the highly trained

public servants

followed established

procedures

case closed

one more

extermination

warranted

self defense

at the hands of

another police

department

justified to

serve and protect

ANNEMARIE PÉREZ

Annemarie Pérez is an Angelena living in Santa Monica, CA. She recently finished her Ph.D. in English (specializing in Chicana literature) from USC. Her interests are Chicana feminism, cooking and Chicana/o editorship. She hopes to be an English professor when she grows up.

LA CHICANA EN AZTLÁN

In the final chapter of *Border Matters: Remapping American Cultural Studies*, José David Saldívar writes of arriving at Yale and his first encounter with the other or, what he calls "Northern America" as "a secular nation living like a dream on the back of a tiger," a United States with seemingly little in common with his South Texas borderland childhood. Saldívar writes:

> *"I left South Texas to walk down the mean streets of New Haven to discover the rather different musics of America -- from Walt Whitman's "I Hear America Singing" to the Funkadelics' "One Nation Under a Groove" and Rubén Blades salsa national anthem, "Buscando America." Quickly I was immersed in the foundational myths of the Puritan ur-fathers, evident everywhere all around me at the Old Campus was something called the New England Way. To see this New England America as phantasmatics was to historicize my identifications."*

Saldívar's experience of the northeastern United States, which he renames "New England America," is part of an unknown, phantasmic, uncanny culture, while he embodies his own South Texas borderland as the historical or "real" identification is a powerful product of his own experiences. Yet it creates a dualistic vision of either one or the other having had to be more or less real, as was in fact the case for Saldívar. However, my own experience as the daughter of Angelenos, a Mexican-American father and an Anglo-American mother, both Catholic, both the grandchildren of immigrants, is that New England and the Texas border-lands are simultaneously phantasmic and familiar. While my proximity to the California/United States border makes Saldívar's Texan border culture more familiar, history classes at my Catholic grammar school and high school began and ended east of the Rocky Mountains, the occasional stray into the California missions and Father Junipero Serra excepted. There has always been something uncannily familiar about New England.

My historical real is the Santa Monica / San Bernadino Freeway linking West and East Los Angeles across the L.A. River's concrete channel. This path, which my parents' car traversed constantly, ferried us between family holidays on both sides of the city. It is the contradiction I remember in my Anglo mother's voice asking my father to speak Spanish at home with the hope my younger sister and I would grow-up bilingual (and that she perhaps would learn the language too). He agreed in words, but then silently resisted, always speaking to us English as part of his inability to see being a Spanish-speaking Latino in Los Angeles as a good thing until long after my sister and I were English-Only kids. Spanish was the language of my grandparents, great-aunts and uncles, my father the only bilingual member of his generation. It was the language of secrets, and all things unknowable. Meanwhile, my sister and I rode in the backseat on seemingly endless weekends, watching for Holy Cross Cemetery, our mid-point for the journey, which held three generations of dead from both sides of our families, reminding me that, my sister and my bodies aside, Catholicism would always be the link between them, however much their prejudices divided them.

Being my parents' first child has always been a large part of my identity. I am their mixed daughter; the result of a 1960s high school romance between an eastside Chicano boy and westside Anglo-Catholic girl. I attended Catholic school from first grade until college - Catholicism formed the bulk of my my cultural identity through out my childhood.

My parents, whose racial divide had brought them social discomfort in the 1960s and 1970s, including difficulties renting and buying homes in parts of Los Angeles, did their best to shelter my sister, brother and me from the worst of their experiences. I knew I was Chicana and identified as such, but my identification didn't mean anything more to me than my mother's distant identity of "Irish." When my teachers commented on my speaking and writing in perfect English, I didn't recognize the loaded compliment in their words. Later, when I struggled in high school Spanish (as did both my siblings and most of my cousins), I never considered why the Spanish language was so hard for me, why when my bilingual father helped me, my accent was somehow considered "wrong" and "too Mexican." It would be years before I realized my struggle with Spanish was, in part, due to an ingrained distrust of the Mexican side of myself.

Then, coming onto UCLA's campus as an undergraduate in the late 1980s, my Chicana identity became much more of an issue. Attracted to Left student politics, I first joined, or tried to join, the campus MEChA organization. It made sense to me. I was a lonely Chicana student, lost on a huge campus. Leaving Catholic education and its sense of belonging to a common religion suddenly made me feel much more of a racial outsider on the campus. Among white students it was clear, despite my middle class West Los Angeles upbringing, that I wasn't quite white enough. But the other students in MEChA saw me as not really Chicana either, not like them. As one said "maybe you're not quite white, but you're too close for me." My skin color wasn't the issue, or at least not the main issue. The leadership of MEChA looked like me or my cousins. The division came on issues of language and culture. I didn't speak Spanish, had grown up in the white part of the city, had a white mother, had attended a West Los Angeles private girls school. In short I was weighed and found wanting in nearly every way (while my abuelita's house in East Los Angeles counted in my favor it was deemed not nearly enough). In their eyes I wasn't truly a Chicana.

It would be poetic to say I railed against this redefinition of my identity, that I told them my father wasn't a sell-out for loving my mother or for having me. I wish I could claim that I argued and convinced all of them or any of them of my Chicana-ness. But the truth was, at their words, I was mostly silent and felt exposed as a fraud. There was part of me that could see their point. What did I, with my West Los Angeles upbringing, know of their Eastside experiences? East Los Angeles, apart from trips to Liliana's for tamales, was my father's and abuelita's home place, not mine. Maybe they were right that I only identified as Chicana because of affirmative action, had only experienced it as a positive without experiencing either the poverty or racism which they had collectively suffered. Worst of all though, I felt like they had been able to look inside me and see the traitorous part of myself, that secret place that wished I were whiter. The part that envied my blond-haired cousins, knew their fairness was in mine and my family's eyes, more beautiful. The same part that wished I had inherited my mother's blue eyes and willowy frame instead of my own stocky darkness. I felt like the other Chicano/a students could see there was something inside of me that found my darkness as ugly and even worse, as unclean and wished it away. Feeling stung and exposed, I slunk away from MEChA. I instead became the comfortably not-too exotic other in the white / Anglo students' anti-apartheid movement on campus. Academically I moved away from any part of Chicano/a studies and into the study of British and Celtic history and literature.

I came back to my Chicananess through reading the works of Cherríe Moraga and Gloria Anzaldúa when I was taking English literature classes at The Ohio State University. At the time I was homesick for California, for my family, constantly feeling exotic and other socially. I saw myself in the definitions of mestiza, in the notion of being torn between ways. When I read Cherríe Moraga's Loving In the War Years, it sort of all came together for me and I realized I could and should claim "Chicana" as my identity, however uncomfortable it might be.

This historical real is internally and externally a site of disjuncture, and contrast. A narrative of cultural and class privilege, uneasily coupled with socialism, prejudice and unquestioning union loyalty. For me, the phantasmic, to use Saldívar's term, is the accented "e" when I spell "Pérez" and the shadowy whiteness of its absence when my father, brother and sister opt out of its use. This may well be evident to everyone but me, but it has come as a hard-fought revelation that, as an English-speaking third generation, West Los Angles Chicana with a Chicano father and Anglo mother, I don't need to perform rituals of "Chicano-ness" any more than I need to perform my "Americanness".

If my broken Spanish or middle class Southern California childhood isn't what some-one would expect of a Chicana with my last name, this is no more a failure of my "Chicano-ness" than too-limited ideas of what a Chicana "should" or "shouldn't" be like. This is an error I can hardly blame others for making given that I can tend to fall into it myself, feeling like by identifying as "Chicana" or "mestiza" I am somehow passing for someone other than who I am.

MILO M. ALVAREZ

Milo M. Alvarez was born on Whittier Boulevard in East Los Angeles, California and raised in the West San Gabriel Valley. He holds a Bachelor's Degree in History with a Minor in Chicana/o Studies from the University of California, Los Angeles (UCLA), a Master of Arts Degree in History from the University of California, Riverside and is a Doctoral Candidate in the Department of History at UCLA, where he is working on a dissertation project entitled "The Brown Berets of Aztlan and The Long Civil Rights Era," which is a national history of the Chicano Movement through the prism of the Brown Berets Chapters active nationwide throughout the 1960s and 70s. He is also currently an Assistant Professor of American History at Bard College at Simon's Rock in Great Barrington, MA.

THE TRIAL OF QUISQUEYA

African Bodies Buried,

Deep in the rubble of time,

Now lie side by side with

Taino Souls forgotten,

Like historical epochs,

One piled on the other.

They push downward,

Until they reach the Core.

The Core where Mother Earth,

Burns with fever,

As she shivers violently,

An act of Self-Defense,

Trying to shake off,

A 520-year old virus.

Because long before there was a 7.0,

There was a 1492,

And long before there were,

Neoliberal Imperialists,

Claiming to bring aid,

Their pale-faced Colonizing Murderous Grandfathers,

Claimed to bring God.

You see, Quisqueya,

Has always been ground zero,

A special place where Mr. White and Mr. West,

Pay homage to their wargod,

Hoping to maintain their dominion,

And contain our spirits.

But to that we resist.

Because our peoples dream visions,

That run long in the generations,

And one day HIS-tories,

Will give way to OUR-stories,

And in the Court of the Taino Ancestors,

Of the Arawak Confederacy,

And in the sprit of Brother L'Ouveture,

It is we who shall preside,

To bring the warmongers,

And their god,

To Justice.

And they will be charged,

With the following crimes:

GENOCIDE, COLONIALISM,

SLAVERY, RACISM, SEXISM, HOMOPHOBIA,

IMPERIALISM and

The Abandonment OF HUMANITY.

And like brother Malcolm said,

These charges cannot be denied.

So come brothers and sisters,

Let's Sweat with our Mother,

While she quakes,

And let the lava rocks steam,

¡Ban This!

Until her fever breaks.

And you can keep your wargod,

 Mr. Missionary because it is to,

Atabey and Bondye, we pray.

In our pagan and voodoo ways.

And let's get one thing straight,

All that "help,"

All that "assistance,"

All that "charity,"

Ain't nothing but a small down payment,

On your soul.

Because you can't kill off one people,

Enslave another,

Undermine our resistance,

Make us pay for our freedom,

For One Hundred and Fifty Years,

Driving us into insurmountable debt,

Then kick us off our land (again),

To re-enslave us by,

Forcing us into your maquilas,

And all of a sudden think we're cool

Because you brought us a few bags of rice,

¡*Ban This!*

After you destroyed our rice fields,

In the first place,

When you installed,

Your puppet ass government.

Man fuck you!

And take your

Shock Doctrine and,

Your Soul snatching,

Child Stealing missionaries,

Back to the hell from which you came.

As a matter of fact,

This shit ain't even going to trial,

Because we got all the evidence we need.

So here's your double millennium plea bargain,

Mr. White and Mr. West.

I will do right by my ancestors by,

Keeping this Fire burning,

And their Knowledge sacred.

Because it is the only hope either one of us got.

And you will correct the wrongs of your people

By seeking the humanity that your grandfathers destroyed.

Starting at Ground Zero.

COLLECTING RECOLLECTIONS

Roads Traveled,

Into Hearts and Minds,

Seeking Stories,

And Tales,

Which seemingly have no end.

Memories of pain,

Deeply imbedded,

In shame,

Debasing,

Dehumanizing,

Bringing tears to the eyes,

Of the craziest Vatos.

¡Ban This!

Because even the hardcore,

Don't give a fuck,

Heat packing,

Ass kicking,

Lay it out on the line,

Toughest of Men,

Are stopped dead in their words,

When remembering Los Muertos.

Recollections halted mid-sentence,

Trying to remain stone-faced,

Lips quivering,

Offering a silent tribute,

To the unknown many,

Of any given Barrio,

At any given time,

Who gave a life,

For La Causa.

"Locos" shunned all around,

Even by La Gente,

Who paradoxically fear and revere,

Still you ride,

Like Villa's horse,

¡Ban This!

Shoes on backward,

Willing to die,

Because no amount of,

Triumphant resistance,

Can take away the pain and humiliation,

Levied when an 8 year old,

Gets slapped in the mouth,

For speaking the language,

De nuestros padres.

Fast Forward,

And one finds,

There is equally no cure,

For being laid out,

Spread Eagle,

Like a Siqueiros Mural,

By some pinchi gringo,

With a badge and a superiority complex,

In your only nice suit,

Worn especially that night,

After your sweetheart,

Finally said yes to a movie.

Because your rank in 'Nam Señor Officer,

Don't mean shit back home,

Still a dirty Mexican,

In Gringolandia.

So you resist,

Not sure how,

Nor for yourself,

Deep down feeling broken,

Because change ain't gonna come,

In this lifetime,

No matter how hard Sam Cooke tries,

To sing it into existence.

Yet remaining absolute.

With Anger to Give,

A Last Gasp of Rage,

For something "good."

Searching for an alternative,

To wasting it at the cantina,

With fists to the face of un hermano,

Who is equally fucked.

Hoping your life's work,

Will leave a legacy por La Gente.

In a collective effort to ensure,

That Las Ninas y Los Ninos,

Will never know,

The ways in which,

You suffer.

JESSICA LOPEZ LYMAN

Jessica Lopez Lyman is a spoken word artist, originally from Minnesota, who writes about Chicana/os in the Midwest. Lyman is a graduate student in the department of Chicana/o Studies at the University of California Santa Barbara.

PEDAGOGY DREAMING

When I saw them, they were almost dead.

Moving like icicle zombies, left, right, left, right, left. Each step regulated to match the first. What was the worst part was that they were too young to be dying. Chained to splintered desks, names of lovers carved in wood's flesh. Like functioning machines hand raising, line forming, docile bodies who looked up eyes open, but hollow.

And a voice on the intercom yelled, "Follow the directions for education or else face incarceration!"

The disciplining of their bodies, our bodies. Limbs no longer loosely letting go but restricted, tightened, stitched together, mechanical renditions of childhoods lost. No child left behind because drones don't raise up arms unless programmed to do so.

Crying for a new way to move their bodies I dreamt of a Fahrenheit 451 miracle but instead of burning books they were burning desks. Cages of conformity, shackles of containment. I envisioned purple clouds rising, smoke circles of SOS signals Warning! Warning! Warning! The robots are no longer functioning but dancing, swimming to the rhythms of their souls.

Brown bodies digging, fractioning apart the asbestos tile, reaching hands into the earth, connecting to roots once cemented over.

I dreamt of stages collapsing. Bells broken, time stood still only to change with the passing moon shimmering like a mirror reflecting the muscles loosening in the backs of the brown bodies who began to speak in tongues. Mother tongues, grandmother tongues, tongues of remembrance that licked clean the wounds of so many years forced to speak a standard. Fragmenting into sharp beams of light fingers began to open, knuckles cracked, heads swirled to the wind's kisses, as their body's cores fluctuated like the tide.

And ever so softly one of them put their hand on my shoulder and said, "We are a people of movement. A problem posing oppressed people. We have been exiled to the margins, pillaged to forget that we are running water, trickling knowledge holders that can no longer be contained in the rudimentary confines of western grammar. The cursor can no longer erase us. The cursor can no longer erase us. The cursor can no longer erase us. "

As she said this brown bodies began to resurrect from the dirt and fly. Wings as long as jump ropes eating each cloud as they passed by. Looking up at them starring until they turned to dots in the sky, calm came over me. My own feet began to separate from the sidewalk and I knew then that they were never dead. Just dormant-waiting, waiting for someone to notice they were dying.

DAVID CID

David Cid is a 3rd generation Xicano activist from Boyle Heights, Aztlán. As a sophomore in college, he was involved in the reformation of the Brown Berets in East Los Angeles in 1992. He has had the opportunity to work with and be mentored by some of the leading figures of the Chicano Movement. Most recently, he has been involved in the Xicana/o-Mexicana/o anti-war and immigrant rights movements in Los Angeles. He is a co-founding member of Aztlán Reads, a Xicana/o Studies literary collaborative created through Twitter. He is currently a graduate student at California State University, Los Angeles majoring in Chicana/o Studies.

YOLIHUANI

bronze skin. silk eyes.
flowery heart.
splendid touch. fragrance of desire.
alluring taste. native tongue.
sacred dance. your ceremonial
dress. a sweet caress.
moon goddess. inside the
temple of dreams. i touched your
beautiful face.

SCENES FROM AN EMPTY ROOM

scent of death
permeates
an empty room
  glow of
  fear
    or remorse
      or shame
  illuminate
  transparent walls
    of guilt
  underneath a shadow
    of blame
  lies a somber
image of
  deceit
false hopes invade
the terrain

  of despair
    a black heart
  evokes the
    nights of
longing,
    of remembrance

in your eyes
I saw
  the abyss of memory,
    of death

in your eyes
I saw
   redemption
   salvation, life

in your eyes
I saw
   our life without hope,
      in an endless
      maze

in your eyes
I saw tranquility
   beyond my reach
      within our grasp,
   without a kiss
with your love
in range

SILENT NO LONGER:

The Visual Poetic Resistance of Chicana/o Cinema in the Experimental Films of Frances Salomé España

During the formative years of the motion picture industry in the early 1900s, silent films exemplified the egregiously racist and misogynist nature of American cinema towards Mexicans. The films *Let Katie Do It* and D.W. Griffith's little known, *The Martyrs of the Alamo*, for instance, both characterized Mexicans as "greasers, bandidos, fiendish sex, and dope addicts." Film titles alone reflected Hollywood's position of hatred towards Chicanas/os: *The Greaser's Gauntlet* (1908), *Tony the Greaser* (1911), *Broncho Billy and the Greaser* (1914), *The Greaser's Revenge* (1914), *The Girl and the Greaser* (1915), and *Guns and Greasers* (1918). American cinema asserted Anglo superiority and dominion over Mexican men and women in such films as: *The Mexican's Revenge* (1909), *His Mexican Bride* (1909), *The Mexican's Jealousy* (1910), *Carmenita the Faithful* (1911), and *The Aztec Treasure* (1914).

While early films characterized Mexican men in negative terms, women were not immune to the racist images depicted in American cinema. In *The Red Girl* (1908), Chicanas were portrayed as villains. In other films, Chicanas were forced to turn against their own Mexican families such as in *His Mexican Sweetheart* (1912) and *Chiquita, the Dancer* (1912). Negative depictions of Mexicans have continued well after the silent film era ended.

Consequently, Chicana/o cinema emerged during the Chicano Movement in the late 1960s as a counter-narrative response to the racist and misogynistic cinematic renderings of Chicana/o images prevalent in American film narratives. Chicana/o cinema as an alternative metadiscursive aesthetic framed the voice of the subaltern through a methodical metamorphosis of cultural knowledge production that challenged misrepresentations of the *"Other."* In "Postmodernism and Chicano Literature," Rosaura Sánchez asserts that "The questioning and subsequent denial of the subject comes precisely at a moment in history when women and marginalized ethnic minorities are trying to assume their subject status to create a voice for themselves." Is it, however, permissible for the aesthetic of Chicana/o cinema to speak on behalf of a marginalized community? Chicana filmmaker Frances Salomé España, for instance, maintains that she does not speak *for* the Chicana/o community, but *from* the specificity of her experience as a Chicana living in Los Angeles.

The question as to what constitutes Chicana/o cinema has been a central debate in the emerging field of Chicana/o film critical studies. Rosa Linda Fregoso in *The Bronze Screen: Chicana and Chicano Film Culture*, for instance, describes Chicana/o cinema as a cultural trinity: films *by*, *about*, and *for* Chicanas/os. As the Chicano Movement struggle for self-determination diminished, however, Jesús Salvador Treviño offered a redefinition of the Chicana/o cinematic landscape when he argued that films no longer have to be *about* or *for* Chicanas/os. Rather, the new criterion Treviño established for Chicana/o cinema was based on the notion that films were based on the means of production, namely films *by* Chicanas/os.

But what does the Chicana/o cinematic cultural trinity precisely represent? The Chicana/o cinema dialectic speaks from a space where the subject(s) is given an authentic voice to signify a collective opposition to the racist cultural production inherent in American cinema. Emblematic of recent developments in Chicana/o cinema to delve beyond the paternalistic images inherent in film is the work of experimental filmmaker Frances Salomé España.

Although Frances Salomé España contends that she does not speak for the Chicana/o community, her work clearly articulates an authentic Chicana feminist voice that will no longer be silent to the heteronormative archetypes established by American cinema.

In her *testimonio* "On Filmmaking: A Personal Odyssey," España speaks of "*sobreviviendo* the *fracasos* of beauty and brutal truth." España credits the Chicano Moratorium (August 29, 1970) as a "massive purification ceremony and baptism of fire" for enabling and empowering her artistic spiritual path.

Through her experimental short films, España discards movie industry standards in favor of images that speak truth to meaning of Chicana visual aesthetics. España's short experimental films: *Espejo* (1991), *Anima* (1989), *Vivir* (1991), and *Spitfire* (1992) give visual voice to the misrepresented and ignored experiences of Chicana femininity. The inception of mainstream cinema constructed the image of the Mexican female in negative stereotypes: *The Mexican Spitfire*. This negative portrayal served to perpetuate the sexist exploitation and oppression suffered by Chicanas.

The films of España deconstruct negative images of Chicanas and, more importantly, serve to empower women through poetic verses and images that are more expressive of their lived experiences. In her personal "acts of translation," España does not treat her female characters as victims, but as resistors and cultural survivors. Indeed, this is reflected through her careful selection of film titles and content: espejo = mirror; anima = spirit/soul; and vivir = to live. Admittedly, the film title *Spitfire* would lead one to believe that it is an attempt at political satire. The film, however, is just the opposite. The film demonstrates the feminine emblems of power by reconstructing the indigenous past through images of Mexica deities. This film, then, is an angry, but empowering response to the negative portrayals of Hollywood's spitfire image.

In *Espejo*, España reflects on childhood memories that she "had to learn to embrace." As in life, the images in the film are in a constant struggle to interpret the past from the perspective of the present, and thus, España captivates the viewer through the arrangement of abstract images that only a child can comprehend. The mirror is used symbolically to reflect what Chicanas/os have either lost or set aside deep in their *corazón* for fear of what it might reveal.

As if recollecting our ancient Mexica times, España summons the spirit of the Tlamatini (wise person) whose role in our ancient civilizations was to preserve, protect and pass down the tradition of the Huehuetlahtolli (cultural legacy). As the most esteemed of all the teachers, the Tlamatini's first and most important goal was to help his students know and understand themselves. If you were the Tlamatini's student, he would start by putting a mirror in front of your face because *knowledge of self* came first.

In excavating the past, España admits: "I was always in the tree, so I was safe." España, then, suggests that there is no danger in reconstructing the past, especially when attempting to come to terms with who you are/were. Chicanas must confront their own *espejo* as difficult as it may be for it is their only way to self-liberation: it is *knowledge of self*.

Anima visualizes *El Día de los Muertos* celebration through the eyes of three women. In juxtaposing images of the cemetery with that of the women painting their faces in the form of skulls or the imagery of death, España renders Jim Morrison obsolete who, in *The Lords and the New Creatures*, echoed this sentiment: "The appeal of cinema lies in the fear of death." España suggests that we return to our indigenous roots, which celebrated life and death. España demonstrates the appeal of *El Día de los Muertos* as rendered possible through the perseverance and survival of women for they are the inculcators of culture.

In *Vivir*, España critiques the traditional heteropatriarchal patterns that consistently correlate women in the Eurocentric defined passive role of mother, wife, and daughter. Furthermore, España surreptitiously articulates a critique of the expectations of female sexuality through the image of a woman wearing a white dress inside a birdcage. It is a heteronormative prescribed condition to expect women to remain sexually pure before marriage. Hence, the white wedding dress articulates the amazing grace of the woman and the birdcage functions as the entrapment of a woman's personal development. España's visual poetics is to empower women by demystifying marriage. Women must break out of their own birdcage.

España's cinematic vision exemplifies the artistic progression of Chicana/o film. What started out as a cinema of resistance has evolved into existential images of the Chicana/o lived experience. España articulates the many voices that are often ignored and misrepresented by mainstream cinema.

España has gone beyond the formulaic styles that have perpetuated stereotypical images of the Chicana/o nation. More importantly, España has established the cinematic framework for others to contribute and aspire to.

Although the notion of Chicana/o film is only about 40 years old, the future of Chicana/o cinema provides a visual and poetic forum that will serve to empower our communities.

By enabling women to speak, think, and act for themselves in her films, España hopes that Chicanas can regain their sense of self and dignity that was violently usurped with the coming of a patriarchal system. España proposes that women continue to find alternative methods to comprehend their reality.

For España, it is through the creation of cinema, for others, as she suggests, might well be through the essence of just living life, or to "*vivir.*"

DEL ZAMORA

Born in Roswell, New Mexico, Del Zamora is a writer, director, producer, actor, singer, composer and lyricist who has appeared in numerous stage, TV and screen roles. He is most famous for his roles in Repo Man, RoboCop and Born in East LA (as the Waas Sappening guy). Zamora is also known for his work in Channel Zero Chicano Comedy at its Finest, Frida Kahlo in the Casa Azul, I'll Be Home for Christmas and the series True Blood.

WHERE ARE THE LATINOS IN FILMS, TV?

*Originally published in the Los Angeles Times, May 20 1996

There has been much dialogue recently regarding the issue of racism in Hollywood. It started with the targeting of the Academy Awards by the Rev. Jesse Jackson, which in turn was commented on by Cameron M. Turner in a Counterpunch article. Then Whoopi Goldberg and Oprah Winfrey had their say, followed by three Counterpunch writers responding to televised remarks made by Marlon Brando.

Throughout this, there was little mention of the representation and participation of Latinos, aside from an article on portrayals of Latinos in prime-time television that reported statistics from the Center for Media and Public Affairs ("Latinos on TV: Mixed Findings, Progress," Calendar, April 16). While showing a recent increase in Latino roles on prime-time television, the report also indicated that Latino participation was 2%, which is still below 1955 levels when Latinos accounted for 3% of all characters. The article also estimated Latino population in the United States as 10%.

As a Chicano actor-writer-director with more than 14 years of experience, I can provide firsthand knowledge of the dearth of Latino roles in the film and television industry. The irony of the situation is as thick as the smog that hangs over the city of Nuestra Reina la Senora de Los Angeles (named by Latinos in the 18th century). The United States has close to 30 million Latinos. Many of this population's ancestors lived in and predated the Anglo takeover of the Southwest. Just take a look around at the names of the states, cities, streets, etc. In modern times, Latino audiences have purchased enormous amounts of tickets to Hollywood movies (as shown by several studies and surveys), yet Latinos hardly ever portray lead characters in these movies. A sort of financing of their own exclusion.

Here's the rub. Though on the one hand, we are taught, subjugated, sometimes even beaten into assimilation by this society and told to lose our pride in our culture, language, heritage and history, we are also expected to accept our exclusion in the participation in the media - the same media that shape the world's images of who we, the respective Latino cultures, are.

What is the record of major U.S. studios employing Latinos to play Latino heroes or heroines? Mexican revolutionary Pancho Villa was portrayed by Wallace Beery and Yul Brynner. Argentine-born revolutionary Che Guevara was portrayed by Omar Sharif. Mexican President Benito Juarez was played by Paul Muni. Mexican revolutionary Emilio Zapata was played by Marlon Brando. Argentine First Lady Evita Peron was portrayed by Faye Dunaway and will be played by Madonna in the same feature that has Jonathan Pryce as Argentine President Juan Peron, who has also been portrayed by James Farentino. In the future, we'll have Anthony Hopkins playing Spanish painter Pablo Picasso and Laura San Giacomo at one time was considered to portray Mexican artist Frida Kahlo.

This smacks of the same racism that supposedly did not exist when African Americans were not allowed to play major league baseball. "What problem?" America protested. "They have their own leagues."

Much talk is made of qualifications and merits of the actors. Tell me, who is more qualified to portray Latinos? A Latino actor who has knowledge of the culture, language, history, etc.; or a non-Latino who has, at best, cursory knowledge of what a Latino really is? To this date, I have not seen one portrayal of a Latino by a non-Latino that was even in the ballpark. This is not a legacy for Hollywood or these non-Latino actors to be proud of.

When the feature film *Malcolm X* was first released, African Americans had heroes to look up to in Malcolm X and Betty Shabazz, as well as Denzel Washington and Angela Bassett. Heroes of the past and the future. This absence of Latino icons in a community that desperately needs its own heroes is despicable. Latinos have the highest per capita rate of Congressional Medal of Honor awards in all of America's wars. Two Latino Congressional Medal of Honor Award recipients even date back to the American Civil War. Yet, we suffer from false images of being unpatriotic foreigners who take more than we contribute to American society.

Of course, "artistic choice" is always bandied about to contradict the argument that Latinos can best play Latinos. When I or my fellow Latino actors hear that term, we know that it means we will be excluded, as artistic choice never works in our favor.

When you add the other numerous Hollywood projects that have non-Latinos portraying Latinos, you have a virtual Al Jolson-type brown-facing of the Latino. "The House of the

Spirits," "The Perez Family," "Waterdance," "The Birdcage," "Kiss of the Spider Woman," "Get Shorty," "Alive," "Aliens," "The Mission," "Carlito's Way," ad nauseam - all have non-Latinos portraying lead Latino roles.

A pretty bleak picture if you're a Latino actor - even sadder if you're a barrio Latino youth searching for decent role models. All you can do is laugh at the ridiculously oversimplified portrayals of what you are and walk away with disdain. In fact, just stay in your barrios and be relegated to a brief footnote, if that, in American history. You have your own Spanish stations, just like blacks had their own baseball leagues.

It's either that or stop purchasing tickets and renting videos of movies and television shows that do not include us. After all, as one Hollywood executive explained to me, "We don't have to put you in movies...there were no Latinos in Gotham City and you still came."

MIGUEL JIMENEZ

Miguel Jimenez was born and raised in East Los Angeles, California. At the age of 19, he enlisted in the United States Marine Corps and served nearly five years in an infantry unit, including one tour of duty in Iraq. Jimenez earned his BA and MA in Chicana/o Studies from CSU Northridge.

VETERANS EMPATHIZE:

HB2281 and the attack on Mexican American History and Culture

During an interview with Democracy Now's Amy Goodman, Arizona's Superintendent of Public Instruction John Huppenthal claimed that he did not seek to eliminate the Mexican American Studies Program because students were learning about their ethnic history and culture; instead, his alleged issue with the program was based on the notion that students were being indoctrinated with socialist ideologies. When I heard his comment, I yearned for a bold xenophobic politician who was not shy about stating the real "problem" with the program - it was teaching Mexican American students about their history and culture.

Then, suddenly, a retrieval cue allowed me to recall an instance where I heard a political figure make such a statement - as I am sure there have been others - when I watched the documentary *Precious Knowledge (2011)*. It was in the aforementioned documentary where Republican Representative (AZ) John Kavanagh stated, "If you want a different culture, go back to that culture; but this is America."

As I tried to comprehend the representative's statement, I started to reflect on my former military enlistment and what this statement meant for all Marines who were enthusiastic about embracing their ethnic and/or cultural heritage. Would Kavanagh, who is a veteran, have the courage to articulate this same comment to the many Latino and Euro American Marines who proudly embraced their Mexican, Puerto Rican, Irish, German, or Scottish ethnicity, or as was the case for White southerners, their southern culture? But then again, even in the military there was a double standard in regard to whose culture or ethnicity was accepted and whose was seen as a threat or foreign.

And this same double standard is also associated with another pervasive problem that Mexican American veterans have encountered, the lack of recognition from popular films and/or literature that has attributed to their perpetual irrelevancy in mainstream America. So as the battle wages on in Arizona, the attack on Mexican American culture and history is one that many Mexican American veterans can empathize with.

When I served in the military, I was surprised, with the exception of White southerners, at the level of pride that Euro Americans demonstrated for their ethnic or cultural heritage. As someone who was raised in East Los Angeles, I was conscious that this level of pride existed among Mexican Americans and Central Americans; so when I saw a similar characteristic evident among non-Latinos, it fascinated me.

There were Marines of German descent who were proud of their fluency in German and who vigorously studied their ancestral history. Then there were those who demonstrated pride for their Irish or Scottish heritage by hanging the respective flags of the aforementioned countries, in their barracks.

It was interesting to find that among these Marines, there was a keen interest in wanting to visit their ancestral homelands in a quest to reconnect with their roots. Their desire to reconnect with their heritage resonated with me because it was during my time in the military that I also began having a keen interest in reconnecting with mine; I wanted to visit the Mesoamerican metropolises of Teotihuacan and what remains of Tenochtitlan's Templo Mayor, in an attempt to reconnect with my indigenous ancestry.

As interesting as it was to learn about each other's heritage, there were Marines who explicitly accused Latino Marines of being un-American, while not attributing the same criticism to Euro American Marines who embraced their own heritage.

During my first year in the Marine Corps, I was transferred to a different company. So this meant that I was going to have new roommates. As I began to settle into my new room, I realized that at least one of my roommates was a southerner - there was a Confederate flag and a portrait of Civil War general posted on a wall. A few hours later, I eventually met my new roommates and I introduced myself. My transition to my new company seemed to be going smoothly, until I brought out a small Mexican flag and taped it to my wall locker.

From my peripheral vision, I was able to see that one of my roommates was not too thrilled about my flag. Within a matter of seconds, he told me, "As Americans, we should only honor one flag," a statement that I found absurd given the fact that this Marine had a Confederate flag posted above his bed.

Therefore, I pointed at his flag and asked him, "What do you call that?"

He then had the tenacity to state, "That's part of my cultural heritage," and I responded by simply stating, "Well, there you go then," in reference that I too had a right to embrace my culture.

Statements such as the aforementioned were common occurrences that were predominantly targeted at Latinos who chose to embrace their Mexican or Puerto Rican culture. The fact that Euro American Marines were not criticized for embracing their ethnic culture can probably be attributed to how whiteness, to many, is synonymous with being American. Although this is a theory that I have adhered to for quite some time, it was interesting when a Marine of Russian ancestry brought it to my attention.

He was a first generation, U.S. born, Russian American who was aware that his whiteness gave him a privilege that most Mexican Americans did not have; even though his parents were immigrants, nobody ever questioned his "Americaness." On the contrary, he commented on the experience of Mexican Americans, whom he stated have been in the U.S. for generations and are "still treated as if they just crossed the border."

Similarly, the biases that Mexican American veterans experience in the military, are also evident when taking into account that their contributions have been, for the most part, neglected. Even when we take into account that Mexican American writers have documented the experiences of Mexican American veterans with books such as: Among the Valiant: Mexican American in WWII and Korea (1963), Soldados in Viet Nam: Narratives of the Viet Nam War (1990), Vietnam Veteranos: Chicanos recall the War (2004), and several other publications, non-Latino mainstream writers and directors have failed to acknowledge the veterans' contributions.

For instance, it has been estimated that roughly between 300,000 to 500,000 Mexican Americans fought in WWII . Yet, Tom Brokaw's book, The Greatest Generation (1998) and Ken Burns' documentary, The War (2007) failed miserably in honoring the contributions of Mexican-Americans in WWII.

Brokaw's book did not include a single account of the Mexican-American experience in WWII and Burns' documentary contributed only a fraction of its time to honor Mexican-American WWII veterans. And the time that was allotted to honor these brave men was granted only because Burns was pressured into doing so. Furthermore, the film, Hell to Eternity (1960), depicted the extraordinary accomplishments and valor of Guy Galbadon, who was credited with capturing 1500 Japanese soldiers and as a result, awarded the Navy Cross Medal. However, the movie failed to indicate that Galbadon was of Mexican descent, and adding insult to injury, he was "played by a blonde, blue eyed actor".

It seems that without the contribution of Mexican American writers and scholars, the experiences of Mexican American veterans would almost be none existent.

When I conducted the interviews for my thesis, Chicano Veterans of Iraq and Afghanistan: Views on Race, Class, and War (2011), some of the veterans either thanked me for conducting the study or expressed that there should be greater documentation of the combat contributions of Mexican American veterans.

For those that were grateful for the study, they praised it not because it documented their own personnel narratives, but for making the effort to document the stories of other Mexican American veterans, whom they felt were not properly acknowledged. They felt that they deserved the same type of recognition that is awarded to veterans of other ethnic backgrounds.

The veterans were aware that there have been many other Mexican American veterans who have served before them and who also risked their life for a cause greater than themselves; something which they believed was worthy of recognition.

GINA RUIZ

Gina Ruiz is a freelance writer, poet and book reviewer. Ruiz has maintained several blogs over the years with her book reviews (AmoXcalli, Cuentecitos, The Flipbook). She now has several blogs including Doña Lupe's Kitchen, Slinkmag, and Twirling and Typos. Her poetry has been published on Poetic Diversity.org and her book reviews and articles published on La Bloga and Xispas. She is also a columnist with Blogcritics.org and has a regular section entitled Minor Considerations, a column dedicated to Children's Literature. In her spare time, she puts on feathers and does Danza Azteca. She also throws a mean chancla.

CHANCLAS & ALIENS

1

It was a night like any other in Lincoln Park. The sounds of the drums, pounding feet and chachayotes filled the small gym, but soon the tired Aztec dancers streamed out, got into their cars and left. The park was quiet except for the occasional cricket and the sound of the freight trains pushing through the tracks on Valley Boulevard. The last taco stand shut down for the night and a group of cholos from across the tracks gathered in the now still park eating chile relleno burritos, drinking some Coronas and just hanging. If you were looking, you would occasionally see the flare of a lighter or the red-tipped ash of a cigarette illuminating one of the guy's faces. Handsome young men, all of them, with the stances of Aztec warriors of old. They were fierce and dangerous looking to some, comforting and homey to others.

The aliens above watched from their strangely shaped ship wondering what manner of creature these tattooed, brown Gods were…or so they seemed to the tiny and bent luminescent creatures invading their planet with destruction in mind. To their race, only Gods were tall. Still, they thought that their Gods were more powerful than these savage-seeming ones. Didn't they have technology? Hadn't they conquered world after world, galaxy after galaxy?

These God-like creatures had to be unintelligent life forms - just in a large mass and like all lesser life forms, they would die and their planet's resources would get siphoned into pure energy to take back to their world. They never left survivors. Their very name in their language meant destroyers of all life. Not being burdened with conscience, they saw only their need for energy and the way to get it. Nothing stood in their way - not even strangely marked brown Gods.

They waited. Soon, no one was on the streets. The traffic was gone and only the small group of young men stood alone. The ship turned on its lights and made its way into the parking lot near the gym. It seemed a clear enough space to land.

Jaime saw them first. "Trucha, homies! Watcha. What the hell is that?"

"Holy shit cabrón, I think it's a spaceship!" Ruben dropped his cigarette and reached for the knife he kept hidden.

"Call the homies," he said calmly, as if a spaceship landed in Lincoln Park every day.

His heart was beating fast, every sense on alert. He knew there was going to be some shit happening tonight and everyone needed to be on the watch. He sensed it. You didn't get to come out of some of the places he'd been - not alive if you didn't have that sixth sense - instinct, whatever you want to call it. It had saved his life on more than one occasion. Something was up, and he and the homies needed to be on guard.

Little Alex was already texting, sending out the word that some crazy shit was going down at the parque. Like wildfire and chisme, it spread quickly. In houses, apartments and cars around the small barrio in Eastern Los Angeles, the vatos were arming up for a war. They didn't know what the hell was going on but it sounded like all hell was going to break loose in the park. Guns, knives, chains, you name it, were getting pulled together in a hurry and guys were running out the doors still combing their hair back or buckling belts. The women were getting ready as well. La Smiley realized far too late that she still had a can of Aquanet in her hand, so she jammed it in the back pocket of her Dickies and kept running, easily jumping the few fences between her and the park.

Back at the park, the group of seven young men knit themselves together in a tight circle, every muscle tense and waiting. Slowly, with Ruben at the lead, they crept towards the spaceship like jungle cats or the jaguar warriors of their distant ancestors. As they neared the parking lot, Shorty whispered, "Damn, yo...that thing looks like a chancla!" And sure enough, it did.

The ship was glowing purple like the neon color of strip joint signs and was oddly shaped like a sandal. It was lit from within, for they could see no outside lights and it smelled sour and rotten. One of the guys gagged and Ruben whirled to glare at him, finger on his lips. Six more steps closer to the ship and they heard a sharp cracking sound that stopped them in their tracks. They immediately hit the ground thinking it was a shot, then realized it was just the sound of the door opening as the strange purple light grew brighter and the smell of rotted meat grew thicker in the night air.

2

The cholos arose silently from their prone positions and watched the opening door. Ruben pulled his bandana out of his pocket and tied it around his face, covering his nose as the smell grew thicker. The others followed suit. The door opened wider and out from the ship came scrambling these tiny purple creatures who seemed to be made of light though they smelled horribly rotten. They were small, not more than three-feet and seemed bent and crookedly shaped to the young men who watched from the ground. They had long, gnarly teeth – fangs really, that hung in a massive overbite that left their mouths open and gaping. The stench was getting even more powerful and the quiet of the park seemed to be waiting for something to happen.

Suddenly, a screech of tires exploded into the silence followed by the sounds of running feet. The aliens stopped their descent and stood for a moment as if scanning the new threat. Ruben, peripheral vision and other senses sharp, saw and heard the homies arrival and closed his eyes for a brief second. He felt stronger now with the neighborhood there but still had no idea what these foul creatures wanted from him. By their stench and the hairs prickling up on the back of his neck, he knew nothing good would come of this visit. They weren't here to party. They were here to rumble.

From all around the park he could hear low whistles and, "Holy shit, what the fuck is that?" as the neighborhood realized they had a spaceship and aliens in Lincoln Park.

A vato named Dopey was running from the direction of the driveway on Valley holding a long, heavy chain. He almost ran right smack into the ship before he saw it. In horror, Ruben and the homies saw a purple creature turn towards Dopey and suck him right into its gaping maw, chain and all. The creature spit and all that was left of Dopey was a puddle of purple slime and two broken links of chain. From all over the park, howls of outrage, grief and horror thundered in the air.

"It's on motherfuckers!"

"Cabrones!"

"Hijos de la chingada!" were repeated over and over as the creature just slowly turned its crooked head and opened up its mouth.

Ruben could feel the gravitational pull and knew the creature would suck yet another of his homeboys into the horrible mouth. He whistled a long, sharp sound and the park fell instantly silent. He raised his hand in the air, pointing and shouted, "Run!" Everyone hauled ass in the direction he pointed - to the hill just beyond the gym.

The aliens laughed to themselves at how easily these seeming Gods could be killed. They knew then that they were no Gods, only pathetic little creatures. They were in no hurry so they watched in amusement as their food ran, all the while tracking their scent and energy as they lumbered off the ship and towards the hill.

On the hill, the homies were regrouping. Ruben, with all the strategic brilliance of a four-star general gave orders.

"We know from poor Dopey that chains are nada so probably all metal will be no good. Still, everyone with a cuete get on the roof of the gym and go sniper on those pieces of shit.

"Who's good at throwing knives? Yeah, ok all of you over there behind the trees. Mujeres to the rear over by the pool. Maybe water will kill them and si no, there are the showers and other places to hide behind in the building."

Quickly, the neighborhood grouped themselves at his direction. There were a couple of vatos with blowtorches and Ruben put them at the frontlines. The younger vatos he sent running home to gather sticks, chemicals, whatever they could find. It was a good way to get them out of danger too. This was a war he didn't know how to fight, but damn it, he was going to try everything he could. He shuddered thinking about Dopey, but shook it off. Damned if he was going to end up as a puddle of purple spit on the asphalt. He thought of his girl Smiley and their little boy at home with his mother. Then, as if he conjured her, there she was on the hill looking at him as she panted from her long run. Her long black hair blew in the wind and he looked both fierce and scared. He knew then she had seen what happened to Dopey. He pointed to the pool area where he'd sent all the other women and she slowly shook her head.

"No way, babe. We fight together, we die together," she whispered still out of breath.

Ruben shrugged and said, "Well hell, what did you bring to this party?"

She laughed. "All I have is a can of Aquanet and some mascara. I just ran when I heard stuff was going down."

"Fuck it" he said. "Pull that bitch out and spray the bastards if you need to. At the very least it might blind them and give us a little time to haul ass up out of here."

He whirled around to take a good, long look at her, kissed her fiercely, then pulled away. He nodded his head and turned back to watch the parking lot. The creatures were getting closer and the guys on the roof started shooting.

Nothing happened.

More shots, then stillness as the creatures just kept slowly moving towards the hill. One stopped long enough to pick up a bullet by inhaling it then turned. It opened its mouth and inhaled again as the air around the park seemed to shimmer with purple-scented funk.

Cholos flew off the roof screaming into the creature's mouth, guns and all. They went down fighting, kicking and beating the creatures, but down they went. The last guy on the roof turned and ran, leaping off into the swimming pool and coming up on the other end. Ruben, Smiley and the others froze in terror as their friends were consumed.

One of the creatures started after the lone guy from the roof who was sopping wet and still running in his soggy denim shorts. His chanclas made a wet, squishy sound as they slapped against the concrete. He kept running, trying to make it up the hill where the rest of them were trying to figure out what to do next. Ruben and Smiley shook themselves off and began to make their way down the right side of the hill to help him.

As they ran, the running man (Ruben remembered his name was Alex) stumbled and lost a chancla. Without thinking, he bent to pick it up only to feel the creature's hot and nasty breath starting to suck him in. He felt his body begin to lift off the ground and in terror, he pulled his left arm back as far as he could and hurled the soaking chancla at the creature. He heard a cry of agony and in surprise found himself sitting on the grass.

Alex heard cheers from the homeboys on the hill and to his utter shock, he saw the creature gasping on the ground his wet chancla sticking out of its head. It wasn't dead but it was hurt and hurt bad.

Alex jumped up and ran the few feet left to Ruben and Smiley. Together, they ran back up the hill to the rest of the group.

3

At the top of the small hill the cholos were still cheering at the fallen alien who was struggling to get up. Ruben got everyone quiet. He was thinking fast: *was it the chancla that had damaged the alien or the water from it?* He was taking no chances.

"Everyone with chanclas or huaraches take them off and put them in a pile. Joker, you grab four of the vatos and run down to the hynas at the pool. Get water in whatever you can fill from the dumpsters or whatever and start sending it up here. We're going to start throwing chanclas! A los chanclaso cabrones!"

Payaso laughed and said, "We should go get my Ma, yo. She throws a mean chancla!"

"Sabes que homie? That's not a bad idea. Send one of the dudes running to the back of the park and tell him to round up every chancla in the hood and get the abuelas and mamas over here. My mom can still whip my ass with a chancletazo al diablo," Ruben said.

Payaso looked at Ruben kind of stunned, then grinned wide, said, "Orale, ese," and ran off to round up the neighborhood's meanest chancla-throwing women.

On his way down the back end of the park he ran into the younger kids, who were coming with everything from rakes and machetes from Tio Chuy's gardening truck to bags of fertilizer. He got them headed back down with him to round up chanclas and women.

Quickly, a rather large pile of chanclas of all varieties formed and the best hurlers in the group took the frontline armed with chanclas. Buckets, old beer bottles and soda cans of water were being rushed up the hill while the aliens still lumbered forward slowly, their wounded friend at the rear.

From behind them, the cholos could hear the women of the neighborhood coming. The highest pitched voice was that of Doña Belen, a mean old viejita with the strongest throwing arm he'd ever seen outside of Dodger Stadium. Not a kid in the hood was without scars on their nalgas from her 'chanclas of doom'. He winced and tensed up his butt involuntarily, then tried to relax as he remembered that this time, she was on his side.

Doña Belen's high voice was screeching out: *Donde estan esos desgraciados que han matado a mis chavalos? Cabrones, veten de aqui pinches espacemen!*

She was marching as fast as her little old legs could carry her, chancla in hand and the pockets of her apron filled with flip flops. She looked like a cross between an avenging angel, La Llorona and a crazy homeless person.

Despite himself Ruben laughed and got a whack to the back of his head.

"Malcriado! What are you laughing at cabron? This is a war pendejo! Portate como un guerrero not a stupid kid," she shouted and hurled her beloved and very bedazzled chancla at one of the aliens.

It flew through the air with a wicked whistling sound that every Latino kid knows all too well and landed right smack in the gaping mouth of the closest alien. Fuaca! The smacking sound rang through the park and the alien fell to its knees. Cheers rang across the park and more chanclas started to fly through the air as an army of apron-clad, masa fingered grand-mothers began their assault.

As the chanclas began to wound the aliens and their horrible howls of pain resounded through the air, the cholos realized they didn't need water so they sent for more chanclas. They were wounding these cabrones like crazy but not one had died and they were speeding up, getting closer. Ruben and Smiley at the front of the group looked at each other in concern. Could they be killed?

4

The pinche aliens were getting closer. Ruben couldn't feel that pull though, they had wounded them enough to where they couldn't just suck them in from a distance, but still they kept coming. The line of purple creatures seemed endless and when they fanned out to try and block the chanclas, he could see there were hundreds of them. Smiley's eyes widened and her face paled a bit under her heavy makeup.

"Shit babe, the chanclas aren't killing them. What are we going to do?" she whispered

"I don't know mija, keep hurting them and we'll keep trying to find something else. Maybe if we hit them hard enough and fast enough they'll go down for good. Fuck, there's a ton of the bastards though."

He scratched along his jawline thinking as he paced along the front line of cholos and abuelas. Seeing a blowtorch on the ground, he picked it up and nodded to the guys who had brought the torches.

"Let's try and hit them with fire too, eses. Maybe that will kill them."

The group of cholos with the blow torches nodded and moved up as close as they dared then turned up the heat and blasted the aliens with a fiery wall.

Nothing happened.

They got closer and Smiley saw one trip and fall after it had been hit with both fire and chancla. She wanted to burn it. She hated it so much that she was beyond reason. The damned thing reminded her of one of those pinche potato bugs or niño's de la tierra that used to crawl out of the dirt in her yard as a little girl.

Suddenly, she remembered she and her brother burning those bugs with hairspray and a lighter one night. Her dad had caught them playing with fire and they'd both gotten it good with the cinto. These damned aliens reminded her of that night and of those hideous bugs that gave her nightmares. She was going to burn one if it killed her.

Sneaking away from the group, she grabbed the torch on the ground and crept down the hillside slowly. Smiley was good at keeping quiet. It had taken all her stealth to sneak around to see Ruben when they were secretly dating and she'd become an expert.

Flattening herself against the ground, she slithered like a culebra down the hill. The aliens were distracted with the chanclas that were still flying and getting in some good chingasos.

She choked and almost vomited as she neared the alien that was down on the asphalt. Its reek was intense. Steeling herself against the smell, she crept closer and at that moment the alien turned and looked her dead in the eye with pained yellow eyes full of hatred. It began to open its mouth and Smiley felt its horrible pull. Without thinking she grabbed the blowtorch and turned it on, feeling the blast of heat on her face. Snatching the can of Aquanet out of her pocket with her other hand she sprayed it, causing a huge conflagration that burnt off the few eyebrow hairs she had. She screamed and yanked herself back, dropping the blowtorch on the floor in her hurry to get away from the creature.

Aquanet in hand, she kept spraying and to her surprise saw the creature dissolve in a purple puddle. She'd killed it. Smiley wanted to scream out her victory but she kept quiet and ran as fast as she could up the hill to Ruben.

5

Smiley found Ruben on the hill hurling chanclas with the old ladies.

"Ruben!" she panted, grabbing his arm.

He turned and saw her blackened face. "What the f..."

"Shut up. I killed one! It's not fire that kills them, it's my Aquanet!" She pointed excitedly at the purple puddle below.

"You went down there? You pinche loca you could have been killed!" He was yelling, out of control.

Smiley shook him. "I. Fucking. Killed. One." She said in her most pissed off '*I'm talking to a real pendejo*' tone."

The realization hit Ruben and he sent the four vatos running to grab all the hairspray they could get their hands on. How was he to know they'd break the windows of the 99 Cent Store? They returned with an arsenal of hairspray just in time. The abuelas were tired and there were no more chanclas to be found.

The best and the bravest vatos and cholas grabbed cans and ran headlong into the fanned out group of aliens, spraying Aquanet for all they were worth. One by one the aliens dissolved into nasty purple puddles on the asphalt till the whole damned parking lot was purple. A few cholos found themselves pulled up in the air and sucked towards the mouths of the remaining aliens but as they neared those nasty bocas, they'd spray right into the face and the alien would melt. One guy slipped on the sticky purple mess but got up and sprayed just in time to kill the alien bearing down upon him.

From up on the hill the abuelas were now hurling full cans of hairspray whenever someone would pull there arm up and scream out, "empty!" It seemed like hours but then Ruben saw the last alien coming towards him and he sprayed it right in the face. It dropped and melted before his eyes.

Stunned, the neighborhood looked round the parking lot and cheered. They'd done it! Saved the world and killed a bunch of cabrón pinche alien babosos. They were sticky, dirty and smelled as foul as the creatures they'd killed so they all jumped into the pool and rinsed off.

A few of the homies went to check out the spaceship, Aquanet in hand to make sure no one was still aboard. Seeing no one, they stripped it for parts and the younger guys pulled it all away to store in garages around the hood. They'd sell that stuff somehow and raise money for the families of the guys who'd died. Grief-stricken now that the adrenalin rush was over, they mourned their fallen homies whose bodies couldn't even be buried. Struggling with grief and insane happiness they headed home to sleep and plan a pachanga in honor of the guys who'd died.

274

The next morning the LAPD rousted the homies demanding to know about the purple "graffiti" all over the park, their "sniffing" of Aquanet to "get high", littering the park with its bottles as well as the broken windows of the 99 Cent Store.

You could save the world, but some things never changed.

Pressed up against police cars in handcuffs or kneeling on the ground with their hands behind their heads were the vatos who'd saved the world. As Ruben turned his head against the hot metal of the police car hood, he saw the goddamned ICE van pull up and knew he was going to be deported yet again. He could see Smiley on the porch holding their baby boy and knew that she'd be driving down to TJ tonight with her uncles to get him. He'd be home in time for the pachanga and hoped there'd be some of his mom's great salsa negra to go with the tacos he was already craving.

Ya estuvo.

JOSÉ-ARIEL CUEVAS

José-Ariel Cuevas was born in '77 to immigrant parents (from Arteaga, Michoacán de Ocampo, México) who hung their hats in the east side of San José, California. Cuevas throws himself into vice as he does into literature and the day-to-day living that comes with being employed as the office equivalent of an itinerant worker. John Fante, Charles Bukowski, Roberto Bolaño, and Alberto Chimal are the faces of his post-modern literary Mount Rushmore. Cuevas is a lover of the word, of women, of lyric, and the world.

WE WALK ALONG THE GUTTER

We walk along the gutter,

following a floating cigarette pack.

Our feet slosh through the runoff,

wetting the soles of our shoes.

It is Thursday night,

we are going from place to place,

each locations gets hazier and hazier,

the drinks, stronger and more potent.

We hold hands and laugh,

it is the time of our lives,

even the smoke of our cigarettes

playfully mingle with one and other.

Tonight, I am all about you,

my body shudders when you run your finger

over my tattoos, over the logo

of my Love and Rockets t-shirt.

Tonight, you are all about me,

as I stare into your eyes

and play with your hair

(how it looks like Bette Davis' in "All About Eve").

Without knowing, we turn the corner,

passing the Greyhound station,

the bustle and the idleness is much like life

(stop and go; going everywhere and nowhere, all at once.)

The vintage sounds of Manchester

can be heard from behind the black curtain,

the outside of the club is teeming

with chain-smoking hipsters.

We heed the siren's call and make our way in,

and after one shot each of Jägermeister,

we make our way to the floor,

to dance our way into a singular unit.

WE RUN LIKE THIEVES

We run like thieves,

we hide in the shadows

and from one and other.

We feel guilty,

like Catholic sinners

and regretful lovers.

We rue the night we mixed,

long after the pleasure elapsed;

we proved its transient value.

We blame the alcohol,

we blame it for finding

and igniting our suppressed urges.

We blame the weather

for driving us to find shelter

within each other's arms.

It is morning now,

but I am pretty sure it's midnight somewhere,

so, we run...

THE SHAKY CONVICTIONS OF THE EASILY AMUSED

Monday morning:

the traffic lights only seem

to be going from yellow to red--

cars are bumper to bumper,

giving birth to smog and anxiety.

Everybody's destination seems to be distant,

distant like the idle gods above.

I have no place to be,

so urgency is far from what I am feeling.

Off the path, a castle of a basilica

can be seen from a distance-

tenderly woven into the tapestry

of office buildings and half-empty condo units.

Its bells dance and play with the wailing sirens

of a speeding police cruiser.

A surly priest can be heard lamenting

over former parishioners, how they

walked into the dark side that is Protestantism.

In modern times, tenets are only as firm

as the shaky convictions of the easily amused.

The faith of my Fathers is thrust onto me-

and that religion replaced religions-

by the sheer virtue of my birth.

Though baptized, it felt as if

there was no indoctrination, no rite,

just a book full of arcane prose

passed down by generations

(and through a now-fortified border)

and a sense of instilled shame:

I search for redemption,

not knowing what I did.

SOLIPSISTIC

I am a caffeine junky

that sits alone

at the patio of a café,

in a silence occasionally broken

by the writhing and spasmodic fit

of a body that wants to

¡Ban This!

jump and shout in a way

familiar with Methodists

and snake-handling Christians.

On my second cup,

I am sipping it gently,

uttering to myself,

"I like my coffee like I like my women - nerve-fraying."

(My nerves are starting to resemble

the cuffs of my well-worn blazer.)

On my third cup,

the sips are more frequent;

the hands, more jittery.

I start to think about time,

how it passes people by,

how the hours overlap the minutes,

leaving the seconds behind to eat dust.

A fourth cup beckons me,

but the mind is in overdrive,

going at a million thoughts per minute,

thoughts that are jagged, disjointed--

a stream of consciousness

barely contained by puckered lips

and self-awareness.

Fidgeting, I reach for a cigarette

with a twitchy eye staring to my left,

weary of the same scavengers

with their same refrains

("I ran out of smokes and the stores are closed.")

Today has been hobo-free,

and aside from an occasional

 misanthropic fit,

I really cannot complain.

But my mind, my mind is racing,

racing somewhere,

trying to keep a date

I did not even know I had.

FAIT ACCOMPLI

On the surface,

life seems to be a series

of random occurrences

crashing into each other

(chaos trapped in flesh and bones,

wrapped in skin that has seen better days.)

Mistakes and regrets

are cleaned up

and passed off as "learning experiences".

That is what one does

to maintain self-control -

a flimsy façade.

More than likely,

life is more like a casino,

where the house usually wins

and you hope to break even.

Yeah, a rigged parlor game

where you are fucked no matter what.

ART MEZA

Art Meza is a third generation Chicano born and raised in Los Angeles. He works for the Los Angeles Public Library, is married and a father of two. Meza is self-proclaimed bibliophile and active in his community. He is a founding member of Aztlán Reads.

MEMORIES IN HD

I saw us on TV last night

Well, at least it looked like us

You think I'm crazy, right?

That's funny but it's okay

I know they say hindsight is 20/20

Can you explain how my memories were re-running in 720p?

(As if I needed them in HD)

I didn't need to press the remote's info button

I know the original air date is in the 1980's

I remember this episode so well

I mean I should right?

I've seen it so many times

This is the one where the police had to be involved...

You were drinking again

The camera man panned over to me

I saw myself sitting there, so young and afraid

I remember at the time

wishing those nights were just bad dreams

Instead you made them memories

Not much of a difference really

I can wake up from 'em anytime I want

I can't help but shake my head & say:

Poor kid

when I do think about it

Or, really, is it poor you?

I remember the self-loathing in your eyes

And now your pain comes through in high def

All these years later

You still carry that hurt with you

I also shake my head at that

I pray for you

That you'll find a way to let it all go

I say the same prayer for myself

I just want to be at peace

MY FIRST LOVE

Almost 30 years

you and I

we go way back

So no matter who I'm with

I'll slip away to find my way back

These memories are so clear

they seem like just a day back

Like when my number used to start with a two five oh

Every time I'm up in you I feel alive...oh

Remember those times when I would sit out at night?

My mom was out doing wrong

but you made it all right

You would show me the skyline

I would feel your concern

You would keep me company 'til it was time to turn in

Or the times I would go down

so I could see the real you

Bonnie & Alvarado fighting over who could feel you

You've had plenty of lovers and I won't be the last

Like guys who knew you as Eden

we all have a past

In the blink of an eye time goes by too fast

Sometimes I wanna steal you but no I won't try to

Couldn't do it cuz so many love you just like I do.

There's no place like you

tell me I'm right sis

People who've met Echo Park know how I can write this

HECTOR A. CHAVANA JR.

Hector A. Chavana Jr. is an activist and independent business owner in Houston, Tejas. He has been active with different community organizations since high school. He is a former president of MEChA and danzante Azteca. He blogs at OurNewAnahuac.org. Both of his parents were active in La Raza Unida Party.

BIRTH OF ANAHUAC

For Our Restoration and Our Future Generations

We dream and teach our original creation

The Creator planted us as indigenous mais

Foreseeing in our future our autonomous pais

We were watered with the oil called sangre

Then man and woman were born

and for each other they had hambre

Soon they united the ome and the teotl.

Then a prince was born;

then a godly cihateotl

Then Ehecatl carried the maiz for pollination

Then Tlalli hugged them as the mother of the nation

The ground was flooded by the water we call Atl

And Tletl made the parent's passions truly hot

¡Ban This!

The whole world felt the caracol and his presencia

With his call our gente birthed our first conciencia,

Throughout the ages becoming masters of ciencia,

Math, geometry, philosophy and art

Then the hue huetl cried, and she birthed our nation's heart.

This heart protected us throughout esclavitud

and through oppression and even lack of food.

So this is how our ancestors were originally seen

The same ancestors to Tlatohani Cuahtemoctzin

The same ancestors from the constellation called Pleides

The same ancestors of Tupac E Acostzin

Chinampa to chinampa our society was formed

Milpa to Milpa our nation was so born

We organized the arts through a symphony of flutes

And we mastered botany by domesticating fruits

Our own progenitors of writing using knots

We pioneered the medicine field without the need for shots.

The seeds of Anahuac were planted with such care

Our brilliant tonal we were instructed to thus share

We planned with seven generations on our mind

The future harvest for them would be so kind

And so ended the first age of our birth,

The origins of how WE WERE HERE FIRST

Translations/Traducciones:

Ome and the Teotl: In Nahuatl, the creator is called OmeTeotl. Roughly, ome means dual and teotl means spirit.

En Náhuatl, el creador se llama OmeTeotl. Ome, se aproxima a la palabra dual y teotl se aproxima a la palabra espíritu

Cihuateotl: The literal translation is female spirit, but it has a greater significance, as it is conceptualized as a female warrior or a woman who dies in childbirth.

El significado literal es espíritu femenil, aun asi tiene un significado más grande, como el concepto espiritual se trata de una guerrillera o una señora que fallece dándo luz.

Ehecatl: (Manifestation of) wind

(Manifestación de) viento

Tlalli: Mother Earth

Madre Tierra

Atl: (Manifestation of) water

(Manifestación de) agua

Tletl: (Manifestation of) fire

(Manifestación de) fuego

Hue huetl: Drum

Tambor

Tlatohani Cuahtemoctzin: Respected Speaker Representative Cuahtemoc

Respetado Portavoz Cuahtemoc

Acostzin: Respected Acosta

Respetado Acosta

Chinampa: A rectangle of agriculture planted over water, a technology invented by indigenous peoples.

Un rectangulo de agricultura, sembrado sobre agua, una technología inventada por los

indígenas.

ADRIANNA SIMONE

Adrianna Simone received Bachelor's degrees in both English, with a creative writing emphasis, and History, with a Latin American emphasis from Dominican University of California. She also received a minor in Women and Gender Studies. Adrianna earned a Master's degree in English at Humboldt State University, with an emphasis in literature. She is currently a graduate student at the University of California, Santa Barbara in the Department of Chicana and Chicano Studies. There, she researches Chicana and Chicano literature through a poststructuralist, de/postcolonial, feminist, and cultural studies lens. Adrianna has a passion for learning, teaching, and writing. As a Teaching Associate, she will teach Chicana Writers in the summer of 2012.

FINDING A VOICE

When I read about the injustices in Arizona,

the banning of these inspirational and important

Chicana and Chicano texts,

I am overcome with frustration.

I want to scream the truth

until my body reverberates

with righteousness.

Who are you to say what

the facts are?

Have you experienced this

racism and prejudice?

Your privilege and

"colorblindness"

just perpetuates

the same raping of our culture that has been forced on us

for decades.

We cannot sit idly as we are silenced.

I, for one, will not be denied

my voice.

When I was young, I had no voice.

I tried to speak, but no one understood me.

I spent fourteen long years in speech therapy.

I knew I was different, and I was tormented for it.

I needed to learn perfect English

if I wanted to "fit in."

Over a decade of tongue exercises

assigned by teachers and undesired tongue lashings from peers.

Say "Ah."

Hold your tongue there.

Final letter - "R."

Just say clorox.

"You have no friends."

¡Ban This!

"Throw it at her! Hard!"

It was a lonely time in my life

because my inability to communicate isolated me

from potential friends and the family who loved me.

Some may understand this intense loneliness that I write about.

The pit in one's chest that makes it difficult to breathe.

One. Breathe.

Two. Breathe.

Three. Breathe.

It is easy to feel hopeless,

but I found an intense and unexpected kinship

right in front of my eyes:

Books.

I spent every waking moment reading.

I devoured whatever materials that were given to me

by my teachers

and what I discovered at the local libraries.

Librarians and teachers were mentors that kept me

voraciously seeking knowledge.

It was this drive that kept me afloat and helped me find my voice

I started with the classics

the books that European society said I had to read.

"Oh wherefore art though, dearest Shakespeare?"

I started with *their* tradition, *their* norm.

What I discovered was my culture, my history.

Always there, sitting on the bookshelves,

if a bit hidden behind other crap.

Michelle Serros.

Cherríe Morga.

Isabel Allende.

These were stories of adversity and hope

bound up in the ugliness of history

and a willingness to believe in the changing effects of love.

These women, and many others, helped develop

and refine the voice that I could not find.

Stifled by my own inadequacies and the spitefulness

of those around me,

I found truths mixed with facts and fictions,

many that hearkened to my own experiences.

The greatest gift my abuela ever gave me

was the ability to read.

Patiently sitting with me on her lap

in our black rocking chair,

the soothing motions almost lulled me to sleep.

Back and forth.

Forth and back.

But I listened.

I learned.

I read, and it saved my life.

_____. "What did you say?"

I don't know.

They told me I could never speak Spanish –

that I shouldn't try.

I try anyway.

Finding voice does not happen at just one moment in our lives.

It happens in many.

I eagerly embrace these times

no matter how frustrated I get

porque, sí, se puede.

Solamente juntas, podremos!

JONATHAN GOMEZ

Jonathan Gomez is a poet and graduate student in Sociology at University of California Santa Barbara with an emphasis in Black Studies. He also facilitates a poetry workshop with high school students in the barrio of Santa Barbara.

PIÑATA (PART 1)

For the El Puente Poetry Workshop in Santa Barbara, CA. May you all continue moving toward the Marvelous. In memory of Josefa Loraiza also known as Juanita of Downieville, Emmitt Till, Trayvon Martin, Javier Quezada and all of those whose fate on earth ended by state sanctioned violence. And in remembrance of all those who took flight in the 1992 Los Angeles Rebellion, and the many grassroots civil rights organizations that work toward the abolition of institutions that produce exploitation and hierarchy, Adelante!

Swing!

And the crowd of onlookers circles round the body

It waves backwards and forwards

Together with side-to-side motions-

As the ancient winds recognized an awful contemporary,

but failed in their attempts to blow the body away

from the reach of a systemic beat down

Piñata!

And polished wooden clubs strike the body

suspended away from the earth by a lasso around the neck

Pulled higher and higher by seasoned hands

Over a thick branch with no choice,

but to take part in the misery that accompanies every tug and pull-

scars etched into its elderly coffee brown skin with all the ups and downs

Blood drops out

like red confetti in an attempt to cover up its roots

But the gurgling sound the child makes

will forever echo in the company of bird chirps in springtime

Swing!

And legs are now broken,

but still reach with every bit of tippy toe strength

for the ground beneath dangling feet

Fingernails unsuccessfully pull at the rope

While the moans become louder and louder

Swing, Piñata!

The ceremony if far from over

As body is not yet dead

Even though the contact has busted open

the side of a rib cage...

And what is left of comrade and kin?

Just meager leftovers of meat that begins to fill

the people's hearts and eyes with a rage

and an all too familiar memory

Clubs are still swung in batter up-style swings

that have many times made a piñata out of sister and brother

And as the rope rips from the terrible force

The bruised face now slams to the dirt ground

Cameras on to capture the savagery

But the truth will be transformed

Black and Brown body begging for life

in communion pose

into the historic beast of burden asking for it

So, no mercy!

Just pain

As slow but constant rage fills the eyes of the people

Now wide open

Awakened from an imposed gaze

While backbones have begun to lose their curled form and stand
tall

With mighty fists taking shape of hands

that once held nothing but trembling fingers

No more

The time has come to enter the people

onto the main stage for a performance of tomorrow

all their own

with a rage undammed…

Piñata!

Santa Barbara, 2012

THE RAIN WASHES EAST LOS

East L.A., sitting on Herbert Circle thinking of mama, Big Dad and Big Mom, and injustices Early Spring 2009

The rain washes East Los
Filthy, Stinky, Lovely, Beautiful East Los
Born again to the sun
A baptismal ritual offering a painted mural to the masses through the eyes of Botello
Public masterpiece of gente taking up space put together by the hands of Ramirez
Laughs and ruthless critiques of everything existed by D. Gamboa
The rain washes East Los A new beginning and the answer of prayers to the barrio
Goddess
It's what washes abandoned gutters and streets where El David once did the Marijuano
Pachuco Boogie to El Hoyo
A labor of love washing stains from sidewalks that send Malo's blood first to the sewer
then to the sea
A gentrifying force that displaces alleyway syringe and holly Cobra tall can burial
grounds to make room for the kids
The water from above opens valves of rooster song awakenings that birth marvelous
poems of the old days and child hood memories of City Terrace kids playing kickball in
the streets before the impacts of C.R.A.S.H. and Hammer were consolidated
The rain comes down hard, but it's what cooled Chico's skin as he lay on the corner of

Brannick and Folsom having heroin dreams

It's the custodial artist of the neighborhood that comes by just before cardboard houses are erected from market cart dwellings

Sacred beads of life that cleanse the pathway where Lucy walks her kids home from school

It's the rain that washes East Los

Not nightmarish politico/a dreams, I.C.E. raids with "best" intentions, nor other capital beat downs, naw…

It's the rain that washes East Los

Filthy, Stinky, Lovely, Beautiful, Powerful East Los

MASSACRE OF THE KISSES

For Danny "Troubles" Trejo, for the Routina! Gracias, a ti!
East Los, Cleaning up Twin Towers, 2009

The witness stares at the executioner

Legs shackled and sitting quietly in County Jail Blues

gazing at the massacre of the kisses

Thick plated visiting glass separates them

as it's wiped clean of red lipstick

and greasy palmed presses of:

I LOVE YOU'S!

What gets him through

Hope in the days

while stuck in the dungeon

as the kisses try their best to survive

like colorful moths resting on a tree,

a dull shade

An invitation for a feast

So the bluebird picks them off

one by one

devouring each with a spray of Turbo Kill

and swipe of the county bleached-white towel in hand

The inmate witnesses humanity's death

For I am the executioner

And WINDOW LOVE does not stand a chance,

Wax on wax off.

THERE ARE NO CRIMINALS HERE

For my God Son Adam, cousin Lily, and all the youth who have been touched, or are in reach of the Prison Industrial Complex. This piece is in response to the blame placed on "two bald headed Latinos" of the City Terrace barrio for the self-inflicted gunshot wound of LAPD officer Anthony Razo. He was later found "guilty" of insurance fraud. A formal apology has yet to be made to the community for the police-mob invasion on that sunny Saturday morning, or for the legacy of racism, institutionalized harassment and hyper-surveillance that pours down violently on ELA and other racialized and working class communities. They continue to "police the crises" and shoot before we speak.

East LA, City Terrace hills, 2009

We have been blamed before and we're sure it won't be the last time

Officer down at 4:15 a.m. on a Saturday morning

The comal is just getting hot

and the barrio near Folsom St. and Hazard is already under siege

A search and destroy mission

for two bald headed Latinos

in a community of bald headed Latino youth

But we know the lie was constructed over a century ago

We have been blamed before

Prosecuted and punished to the fullest extent of the law

The Book has been thrown at us with impunity,

and it's not filled with poetry

Gun pointed at the back of our heads

Hands on the hood as we assume the position

Spotlight checked

Helicopter surveillance

'Stop before I shoot' called out too

But there are no criminals here

Just people surviving against all odds

Multi and never ending circumstances of racial repression

Class war accompanied with post-traumatic stress syndrome-like symptoms

Marshal law-like conditions

Magic trick tactics transforming Brown and Black pearls

into perils with K-9's searching the perimeter

Face filled with hate abracadabra'd to cop

smiles with a gun and a badge

The bullet is faster than the eye

Judges able to devour justice with a single courtroom motion

¡Ban This!

not missing a crumb

Now you have your freedom now you don't

But there are no criminals here

For we are the people marching in the streets

with cardboard house sleepers from

Gente wrapped in the news of the world

to hatch to the early morning cold

to be everywhere forgotten,

but we of the righteous will never disregard you

We're the street corner people

hanging to Billie Holiday's "Don't Explain"

told to get lost with no place to go

Gente trying to survive in the shadows

of a racist capitalist eclipse

waiting for the sweat that drips

from paletero chins between concrete cracks

to sprout organic revolutionaries that rise

from wretched living conditions

The graffiti artist throwing up the crew on the wall

with a roll call of brothers and sisters from the clika

Yet the writing on the wall that screams,

"we need social justice"

is not read with a progressive lens

For they see,

put your hands on top of your head,

kill, incarcerate,

deport, gay bash, good for nothing,

violate every single one of their rights,

divide and rule,

divide and rule,

and send the dogs

But my people,

We already know,

There Are No Criminals Here!

ODILIA GALVÁN RODRÍGUEZ

Odilia Galván Rodríguez is an Chicana/Apache community artist and activist. She has worked as a Human Resources professional, community and labor organizer, teacher and cultural worker, writer/editor and translator. Rodríguez has published two chapbooks of poetry and her latest book of poetry is titled Migratory Birds New and Noted Poems.

¡BAN THIS!

disgust

lurks in corners

of your mouths when you look

at our children who you don't want

to grow

to grow

into people

strong in their soul's searching ~

for those truths you twist into lies

our strength

our strength

is in knowing

that we were not born yours

to do with us as you will, no

we're free

we're free

we, descendants

of Teotihuacán ~

of Toltecs, of Chichén Itzá,

Aztlán

Aztlán

the place you fear

we might want to reclaim ~

our ancestral home, occupied

by you

by you

who erase truths

that can not be silenced

by boxing up or burning books ~

words live

words live

we remember

them, our love, our stories ~

history, cannot be erased

not banned

not banned

because their life,

their truths and beauty beat

brightly in our yoyolo, hearts

always

always ~

we a people

of hope and of struggle

we never give up, being us

living

living.

So ban our books

put out a gag order ~

yes, they charred our codices in

fire

fire

burned our tongues mute

¡Ban This!

but never our minds ~ to

envision the future, your fall

from grace

MARIA TERESA CESEÑA

Maria Teresa Ceseña is a lecturer in the departments of Ethnic Studies at the University of California, San Diego as well as the University of San Diego. She received her Ph.D. in Ethnic Studies from the University of California, San Diego. Her research examines U.S. and Mexican indigeneity, and represents a critical movement among ethnic studies scholars from diverse backgrounds to form a common analytical lens from which to scrutinize the perpetuation of false dichotomies, such as the one commonly understood as the Immigrant-Native divide.

THE TURTLE CAUGHT IN THE FIRE

As women of diverse backgrounds, we experience education often very differently. Some of our experiences have not always been pleasant. For many of us, it was and continues to be a struggle, just to exist, let alone thrive in institutions of higher learning; myself, no exception. But along the way, it's these struggles that can potentially teach us the most.

Chela Sandoval, who wrote a book called the *Methodology of the Oppressed*, introduced me and many others I'm sure, to a concept called "Oppositional Consciousness." When I read this influential work during my first year of graduate school some ten years ago, I took it to mean that basically, we need to be able to assess our circumstances of existence, and the positions we occupy, especially when we are in positions that leave us disempowered or made to feel that who we are is somehow wrong or not quite suitable to the groups we're trying to enter. It's during these times and within these situations that we learn how to navigate through contested terrains. When what we're doing doesn't seem to be working, or the conditions have changed from when

We began, we need to be willing to change course and try a different approach.

In this sense, we can use the ways that we have been and continue to be oppressed, as tools for empowerment. Additionally, if we don't fit in the spaces we're attempting to enter, we need to rethink and re-shape those spaces. In my experience, I've never fit any sort of mold. Probably most of us don't. I've often had to carve out a space for myself, where a space did not previously exist. And what has been important in this process has been being able to take away a new understanding from every situation I've experienced, especially the times when I was not successful and/or had to change course.

I wanted to share one such experience with you. Though I weave in and out of various memories, hopefully you will be able to follow this portion of the journey as I remember it.

I'd like to begin it with a poem.

PIECING IT TOGETHER

A pile of shards

A chip of paint here

A line cuts my face

Glue conjures fear

Clean off the dirt

And you wash away me

I don't know how to act

I don't know who to be

Why not myself?

It worked for those who see

My eyes are shut

These looks, they aren't free

I rode my bike without a helmet

Before they made that law

Sound was much more amplified

Emotion much more raw

Crickets and Sprinklers, and Trains along the track

¡Ban This!

A sense of knowing what I was

And never looking back

A woman, slash child of God

Without a golden ticket

A student slash teacher

Both Saintly and Wicked

Grasping at straws

When a spoon's what I needed

To eat of the sopa

De arroz y green chile

Soup for my soul

For strength, for warmth, for flavor

Ingredients for life

To do what I was made for

To offer up my gifts

To those who come before me

The wisdom you share

Your energy surrounds me

I praise you with laughter

This gift is my song

This earth did not belong to us

To this earth we belonged

I wrote the first version of this poem on Friday, October 26th 2007, while sitting at a picnic table, outside the commons, on the campus of the University California, at Davis. I was there for their annual California Indian Conference which took place from October 26-27th. I flew up the night before. I had just listened to a panel chaired by Inés Hernandez-Avila that discussed among other things, the dual spirit woman. Roughly 500 miles south of the table where I was sitting, San Diego was on fire. And it was a wild one.

Feeling an uneasy combination of relief, helplessness, and survivor/escapee's guilt, I checked the news constantly for updates and hoped for a report that people were safe, that people's homes were safe, and that the fires were dying down. Unfortunately, communities in fact had already been completely destroyed, and people had already in fact, died - burned to death in the flames.

Of the seven lives lost, four were Mexicans attempting to cross the border, described in an article posted on MSNBC.com as "4 more bodies found after So. California fires." The sub-heading read, "President tours hard-hit region; most mandatory evacuation orders lifted." The article went on to report:

> *"SAN DIEGO - As firefighters gained the upper hand in their five-day battle against the Southern California blazes on Thursday, Border Patrol agents discovered four charred bodies in the rugged mountains near the Mexican border…If fire was responsible for the four deaths - which authorities said was not immediately certain - the discovery would raise the death toll to seven, more than doubling earlier estimates."*

In just a few words, the story bombarded me with real and symbolic arms of state "pro-tection": firefighters, Border Patrol agents, random "authorities" who could not determine with certainty whether the deaths of the "charred bodies" were the result of the fires.

Was I dreaming? What was up for debate? Then I thought to myself, fire was *not* the sole cause of death. While the fires may have "charred" the "bodies", fire alone was not what killed them. It was the fact that their bodies, and their lives, did not matter. They were invisible, the only evidence of their existence, their charred remains. They became quantifiable casualties to add to the body count. A spokesman for the San Diego County medical examiner's office was quoted as saying," "They could have been out there a while."

All of this was going on down south, and it occupied my mind as I listened to a woman present her research project which involved collecting a series of oral testimonies from mem-bers of her family. She called this methodology a venture in "piecing together the shards."

In piecing together her family's history out of fragments of memories, she reflected on how difficult it was to speak to her father. As a researcher, she had to dig deep and get him to share details of traumatic events, events that a father would not feel comfortable sharing with his daughter, events that would break a daughter's heart. But they were things she felt she needed to know, and she sought this knowledge in a way that privileged her father's and her family's voice, and did so in *their* native tongue. The project required her to experience a certain amount of pain in a way that only she could.

When she spoke, I couldn't help but think of my own family history. I related to the shards that she spoke of and to the pain, and to the sense of loss that can never fully be articulated sometimes. But her shards offered me hope and somehow lifted the load of trying to uncover, or rather, recover pieces that sometimes seem to be gone for good.

When asked, why did you go to grad school? I always say that I wanted to re-write the history books. But honestly, I wanted to learn about my people, and myself, and to combat the invisibility I felt in the American history books I was required to read and memorize throughout my K-12 education. I learned the counter-narratives at home.

Then I thought of my trip to Quintana Roo, México, about an hour into the jungle, and an hour outside of ultra-touristy Cancún the summer I turned 20. I was there to participate in an archaeological field school. As an undergraduate scrub, my job was the most tedious - collecting and mapping pottery shards onto graph paper. As the youngest of five kids, I was no stranger to tedious tasks; tasks that to me had no meaning yet somehow took FOREVER! Collecting and sorting random screws, nuts, and bolts scattered around the garage floor of our Riverside home, left over from some project not my own. My parents were (are) always building. Planting trees, growing gardens, painting fences, arranging chicken wire, digging small ditches, mixing cement, building walls, tiling floors, fixing cars, and the list goes on and on and on toward infinity. So many projects of such great variety, the Great Wall of China, my brothers and sister would call IT. Rather than separate tasks, they envisioned IT as one large home improvement endeavor that simply took on many forms, and that simply refused to stop. But they were building something.

Back to Mexico, Quintana Roo, that summer of 2000, which turned out to be the summer I decided I no longer wanted to be an archaeologist. I had always loved getting dirty, and digging things up, but this was not the way for me. On one of the days out in the field, a particularly hot one, the sun burned my skin and the ground burned much hotter, the heat leftover from a recent fire. The fire had been deliberate; a technique called slash and burn, employed by indigenous groups throughout the Americas and globally for centuries as a way of clearing out dry brush that if left out of hand, could eventually cause a more severe and potentially devastating fire - a controlled type of burn. And the residual ash made for good fertilizer, a way for new growth to take place.

However, as our workday went on the intense summer sun intensified the stink of decay. An eerie feeling came over me as I noticed three buzzards circling overhead. They too smelled the rotting flesh. But from where and what was it coming? What in the hell was stinking up the place so badly? I was surprised when we found that the overwhelming stench, that stench that made me nauseous, was coming from a tiny tortoise that hadn't been quick enough to escape the flames. That little thing was too slow to survive, yet so powerful to leave its mark, literally for miles and days after its death. No matter how hard we tried, it would not go unnoticed.

For me, this was such a powerful experience that still gives me chills all these years later. No, this wasn't the start of my career in archaeology. Actually, I ended it right then and there. But had I not done all that studying, which inspired me to travel to the depths of the Mexican jungle, I would not have ever encountered that little turtle. In a way, that turtle caught in the fire gave me hope, and reminded me to consider the potential for empowerment in every situation, no matter how small. My formal education has definitely empowered me to travel, to explore my interests, to teach. But it's the informal education I've received along the way in really unexpected places that I tend to remember best.

JEHUNIKO

Jehuniko is an internationally known hip-hop artist and activist. His albums include "La Pura Vida", "Spiritual Warfare 1, 2 and 3", "Almas Intocables" and "Cold in the Hot Sun". Jehuniko's video, "el animal humano" from his debut solo album, La Pura Vida, began airing on MTV Spring 2008. Jehuniko has opened for Ghostface Killah, KRS One, De La Soul, Black Sheep, Raekwon, Sen Dog of Cypress Hill, Mellow Man Ace, Mack 10, H.R. of Bad Brains, Lupe Fiasco, Kemo the Blaxican, the Coup, played benefits for prolific Community Organizers such as Sub. Marcos of the Zapatista EZLN.

WARRIOR SPIRIT

A culture and people so rich

vibrant with color

with flavor

with charisma

A community so preyed upon

for their hard earned

dollar

because Corporate Amerikkka knows

that Raza works

in more ways than one

Too many gate keepers solely

want to eat our food

and exploit our culture

while our community deals

with these vultures and vampires

From overcoming the times of Cortez

to the modern day NDAA

Raza

has been at the forefront of the battle

since day one

Because we have birth right

to this land

and beyond

so why then do we fight each other?

within our communities

over and over

I witness

this internal conflict

between mis carnales y carnalas

Abuelitas y Abuelitos sacrificed much

to fight for our people

I imagine the endless possibilities

if we were only unified

yet we are but a fraction of our former selves

We come from a long line

of gente

with tangible roots in these lands!

For Ernesto Bustillos

Cesar Chavez

Comondante Ramona

Dolores Huerta

Leonard Peltier

and so many more

We owe it to them

to fully engage one another

con todo respeto

and tap into the warrior spirit!

LAURO VASQUEZ

Lauro Vazquez is a MFA candidate in poetry at the University of Notre Dame's creative writing program. He is assistant editor and contributor at Letras Latinas - the literary program at Notre Dame's institute for Latino Studies and maintains a regular blog at granmaforpoetry.blogspot.com. He lives in South Bend, Indiana where he teaches a poetry workshop at South Bend Juvenile Correctional Facility.

AUGUST 22: MORNING

the dial on the kitchen radio is clicked to a Mexican station/

on plastic trays

the kitchen takes to the air/

    like a cannibal time-clock/

/it eats away the day

the radio leaps/ like a tiger over the flames/

  becomes a tiger that roars/ sing sing

there is no other way to describe this/

our tiger/ moonbullet/ moonsong

it shoots/

/it eats away the sun

AUGUST 25: MORNING

voices race through the air like fiery greyhounds:

HELLO! HELLO! HELLO! NEWS.... FROM THE NEWS WIRE:

...every 3.6 seconds....
.... one ▊ dies of starvation....
usually it is a child under the age of 5....
the total number...the total number today
...the total number.... of children
younger than five...
living in France, Germany, Greece and Italy:
10.6 million....
....the total number of children ▊ *who died from* ~~preventable~~ ▊ *in 2003 before they*
were five:
~~*10.6 million....*~~
....investigators in Arizona have released a tape of the 9-1-1 call made during the deadly
home invasion robbery that claimed the life of nine-year-old ~~Brisenia Flores~~*...*

... you probably have never heard his ▊ *..but you likely know something...*
...about how nine-year-old ~~Ali Mohammed Hafedh Kinani~~ *died....* ~~he was the youngest per-~~
~~son killed by Blackwater forces at Nisoor Square...~~
these and ~~other Auschwitzs~~ *...other exclusives... are brought to you...endowed to you*
by the TV guides... the Wall St. journals.... the academic journals of the "poetic I"

5.56MM NATO/ ~~BULLET WOUNDS~~

nine-year-old Ali Kinani died from a bullet
bite to the head
in the Nisour Square Massacre
meanwhile the sun went red/
and the mercenaries
unfurled their fists with tenderness
or drew/ sweet/ three-legged cows/ for their children
or a little gasp or bird/ flew from Ali's little mouth like a bullet
fired at death/ that lovely lady
oh little bird that flew and ate and gouged little Ali!
oh little bird that drank/ flew away/ little Ali!
and this happens every day
it happens like that
the blood of children falls
like blood of children

nine year old Brisenia Flores died
from a vigilante's kiss to the forehead
and her smile went red/
blood smiles from Brisenia's bullet wounds
and this happens every day
the sun goes red
the warmth of children smiles/ spills/ evaporates Brisenia
your bullet wounds or little suns glow red red red
in your tender skull Ali

blood of children glows/ red
little Brisenia goes red/ dissolves/ falls
or is swept away/ by brooms or sand
and this happens every day
this happens every day

it happens like that

the bullet bites/ kisses the skull
splinters the children's sleep/ and nothing will come from there
no/no / nothing/ no little bird
no poetry or three legged cows
and this happens every day
it happens like that

SEPTEMBER 16: MORNING

this morning
in the dish-room sink
i found a chicken bone wrapped like an onion in a paper napkin
i peeled off the napkin/
    the bone spoke/ horses fell from its mouth/ Brisenia fell
        ali fell *good morning death lovely lady*
        said the bone *widen your gates* Brisenia rides on Brisenia
    enters death as if into a house/ and is naming her little bones
    under the earth/ her bones without bread or milk/ her bones are rising
    right now/ and are filling their little mouths with stars
    /and are beating against the world's forgetting
    and are little fires/ they set out/ to dry the bones of the world's forgetting
and are a bone/ that writes in the womb of the earth/
womb that never forgets a name or face
and gives off bread or milk/ womb that writes letters to the sun
telling him to start a new/ the bone spoke/
i love you / it said
i vomited fire

MARIO BARRERA

Mario Barrera is professor emeritus in the Department of Comparative Ethnic Studies, University of California, Berkeley. During his academic career he has taught at five UC campuses, most recently at UC Santa Barbara. His best known publication is "Race and Class in the Southwest" (Notre Dame, 1979) An article on neofascism has just been published in the international journal "Race and Class." His film work includes the documentaries "Chicano Park" and "Latino Stories of World War II," and the short comedy "The Party Line." He is currently at work on a novel and his memoirs. He was born and raised in Mission, a South Texas bordertown.

SCIENCE AND RELIGION IN A BORDER TOWN

Some alleged thinkers have speculated that human beings may have a "God gene," a biological predisposition to believe in a Supreme Being. I don't know about that, but I think I may have been born with a "skepticism gene."

The best way I can put it is that even as a kid I was obsessed with truth and its hand-maiden, logic. Maybe it was encouraged by my parents never saying "because I said so," but always explaining why it wasn't a good idea to, say, light matches next to my mother's hairy cactus, may it rest in peace. Or put chili squeezings on my brothers' lips under the pretext of brushing off crumbs. Especially with those tiny red peppers that grew on a bush in our back yard.

As one might suspect, my penchant for pursuing the truth wherever it might lead has not always endeared me to people.

Some of the things you're told as a kid are pretty easy to see through. The tooth fairy? Give me a break. Not even fairies want dead teeth. As to Santa Claus, most of the houses in Mission, Texas didn't even have chimneys. Granted a lot of people left their doors unlocked, but still….The way I saw it, even if Santa had been able to land on our sloped roof, the sleigh bells would've woken me up.

Anyway, those sorts of fairy tales were never told with much conviction, so they were easy to discount. Just put the quarters under the pillow and the presents under the tree, thank you, and go ahead and tell me anything you want.

On the other hand, people have a lot of investment in the whole God thing, and when everybody's nodding their heads up and down it's not easy to shake your head from side to side and think it's all some sort of collective delusion. And the Lower Rio Grande Valley was a pretty conservative place in the fifties, theologically and politically. The local newspaper, the McAllen Monitor, routinely carried editorials denouncing public schools as a socialist plot. You would've thought the teachers started each day with "Comrades! Please come to order." Instead of, "Please stand for the Pledge of Allegiance."

My high school science teacher, Mr. B., was an interesting example of the intersection of religion and science. In the interest of giving you a sense of his style, I've taken the liberty of putting a few words in his mouth.

***

(Mr. B., Mission High School biology, chemistry and physics teacher, and square dance aficionado)

It's true that I died several years ago, but fortunately I believe in an afterlife so I can still give you my impression of Mario what's-his-name. Bandera...Barbarian...I know it starts with a B.

Worst little whippersnapper I ever tried to teach biology to. I don't know where he got all those ideas about evolution. Maybe his parents subscribed to National Geographic with all that fossil non-sense. [they did] He and his pal Fausto just wouldn't take my word for anything, And as far as what the Good Book said, forget it. They irritated me so much I had to tell them if they really thought they were descended from monkeys they should go swing from the trees by their tails.

Inconsiderate little wretches, on top of it. Insisted on coming into my study while I was relaxing with a low-tar Lucky Strike or two. They didn't say anything but even with all the smoke I could sort of see it in their eyes: "How dare you lecture us about the evils of smoking, you hypocrite." Not to mention the smirks when I gave the class my "this is your brain on alcohol" demonstration. Probably sneaked across the border to Reynosa every chance they got, where there was no age limit on drinking. [we did]

***

The Fausto that Mr. B. alludes to was my best friend through high school. Mr. B. is correct that we loved to get his goat, beard him in his den, prick his little hypocritical word balloons. Served him right, too, worst excuse for a science teacher I've ever heard of. They probably have a lot like him in Alabama or South Carolina.

Fausto I thought of as Theory Man. That's because every now and then (*de vez en cuando*, as Mexicans would say - certain things I first heard in Spanish have stayed with me even after English became my dominant language) Fausto would spring one of his theories on me, about religion or whatever.

"Mario," he would say - "Mario, I have a theory…" It was an incantation, like "once upon a time"---a formal rhetorical device indicating a forthcoming verbal performance.

"Oh, aha, what a surprise."

"It's about the afterlife."

Fausto needed encouragement like a bowling ball needs a handle, but I encouraged him anyway, since it was expected of me. On these occasions I was the straight man: Abbott to his Costello, Margaret Dumont to his Groucho.

"The afterlife. That's what you've been thinking about?" It seemed an odd preoccupation for a seventeen year old.

"Yeah, man. I started thinking about it after that sermon last Sunday."

Fausto and I both went to El Mesias Methodist Church, the Methodist church for Mexicans in Mission. So whatever you've heard about all Mexicans being Catholic, forget it. Not that we were exactly devout Methodists.

"You know," he went on. "Streets paved with gold and all that stuff. Didn't sound too interesting, sit around playing harps. Accordions, maybe."

"Yeah, guy, accordions. So what's your theory?"

"Well, I've been thinking about my *abuelito.* You know."

Sure, Fausto's grandpa lived a couple of blocks over. Nice old guy, widower. What about him?"

Fausto knew what he was going to say, but he liked to play Plato, pretend we were having a dialogue when it was more of a monologue. Since the Spanish word for monkey is *mono*, monologue" about sized it up.

"Thing is, he wasn't always an abuelito, hanging out at home listening to the radio. He was like everybody else, had kids, a job, liked to play *beisbol* with his buddies on Sunday. Maybe had a girlfriend over in Reynosa."

"He did?"

"No, man, I'm just saying. Maybe he did, we don't know. The point is he had a *life*. But then my abuelita died, the kids moved to Houston or got all wrapped up in their own families."

"So what he has now is…"

"Yeah, an afterlife. You know how those guys in the bible: Moses, Abraham - they always show them as old guys with beards. So what I'm thinking is maybe that's how the idea of an afterlife started, all these old guys sitting around thinking about how things used to be, and now here they are, *nada*."

"Kinda like being in hell." Shoot, I could follow a train of thought as good as the next guy.

"That's it! Simon que yes! They started out in the Garden of Eden, they fell from grace like the minister says, and now they're in hell, seems like it'll go on forever. So what do you think?"

"Maybe that's it, vato. You should go talk to Brother Gomez about your theory."

"Oh yeah, sure. Like your talk with Brother Martinez."

"Maybe I caught him on a bad day. Everybody has bad days."

"Bad day my nalgas. All those guys know is what they learned in divinity school. They're like parrots, just repeat what they're told."

That sounded like an overly harsh judgment to me. Our present pastor seemed like a thoughtful kind of person. But his predecessor, Martinez - not a bad guy, I suppose, but maybe three wafers short of a sacrament.

***

The occasion that Fausto alluded to - that was an early expression of the personality trait I mentioned before. About seeking the truth come hell or high water. In this case, hell.

What I didn't realize then is that people believe what they believe for a lot of different reasons, and you have to make allowances for that. In those days, if somebody described something they believed, I dealt with it one-dimensionally, you might say, in terms of its "truth value." And I applied this attitude to Brother Martinez's sermons, comparing them to what I read in the San Antonio Light or the Reader's Digest my folks subscribed to.

I must have been junior high age when I requested a private session with Brother Martinez to explore some of my thoughts. My father asked to sit in, which was a little surprising given that he only attended church on Christmas and Easter, and then probably because my mother insisted. Maybe I inherited the skepticism gene from him.

We met in the main church sanctuary; me faced off with the minister, Dad off to the side where he could more easily maintain his interested observer stance.

My opening gambit went like this: "Brother Martinez, you say that God is just and merciful. But there was a story in the San Antonio Light about a minister and some choir members in a van that got hit by a truck, and they were all killed. And they were on their way to a church conference. Why would God punish them for that?"

Brother Martinez appeared to give the matter serious consideration. Then: "Perhaps he wasn't punishing them. Maybe he just wanted them to be with him in heaven."

I looked over at Dad. But his face was expressionless.

"But didn't you say that God was everywhere? So he was already with them.....and what about their kids? They're orphans now."

Father Martinez looked at me pensively. I don't think he had been expecting this kind of third degree - probably thought I would ask his advice about some problem at school.

"You know, Mario, those are very good questions. Wise men have been thinking about questions like those for centuries. But we don't know all the answers. We're just human beings, with limited understanding. We can't necessarily know God's motives. Our minds are finite, and God is infinite. So we're trying to understand the infinite with the finite."

I learned years later that ministers take whole courses of study called Apologetics where they learn how to parry these types of questions.

"But then how do we know anything about God? How do we know he's just and merciful? How do we know He really wants us to do unto others, and love our neighbors, or turn the other cheek?"

"Because those things are written in the Bible."

I knew that settled the matter for Brother Martinez, so I didn't press it. And I thought about what my biology teacher, Mr. B., had said when I brought up dinosaur fossils. He'd said that God had put them there to test our faith. But if God could play games with our heads like that, then how could we trust that the Bible was really the word of God?

What I said to Brother Martinez was: "So you're saying God doesn't have to be logical?"

"No, I'm saying he must have a higher logic that we can't fully comprehend."

Afterward I reported the conversation to Fausto, who said "You know - it would've been better if he'd just started out saying he didn't know the answers, and let it go at that."

"Yeah, but if he doesn't know the answers, who does?"

Looking back at it now, I'm glad that Theory Man hadn't developed his theory about the afterlife yet. If he'd laid that on Brother Martinez he might have given the poor man a heart attack.

***

So that was pretty much the story for science and religion in the Lower Rio Grande Valley. Religion 2, science and logic, 0. But, now and then, I tend to listen to my own inner logician who tells me that if there is indeed an afterlife, I'm living it now rather than later.

¡Ban This!

CPSIA information can be obtained
at www.ICGtesting.com
Printed in the USA
LVOW05s0050290916

506655LV00003B/17/P